With A Good Eye

A novel

Gila Green

AOS Publishing, 2024

Copyright © 2024

Gila Green

ISBN: 978-1-990496-41-7

Cover Design: Chanelle Poupart

Visit AOS Publishing's website:
www.aospublishing.com

There's a payphone that's been ringing
        since 1984. The snaky metal cord
            you can't quite wrap around

your wrist as you talk. Keep feeding it
        flimsy dimes. Keep pressing in
            each squat square numeral you've memorized.

Chapter 1

Nineteen-year-old Luna Levi struggles to hold her family together. She was hoping to get a break from it this month, but her mother's latest play has a revised schedule. The announcement hit Luna like one of the new OC Transpo accordion busses in Canada-red-and-white with the maple leaf design around the front wheels.

For a few weeks in August, while Luna relaxed in the velvety sand at Ottawa's Mooney's Bay after long, boring shifts at the motel where she works, she could forget about her crazy family. She spread suntan oil on the dark brown back of her best friend Aiden Betel and rubbed it in up to her friend's long neck, careful not to get oil in her thick wavy hair, so different from Luna's own tight curls that kink and coil.

"You'll block the pores on my scalp with that stuff," Aiden scolds.

Aiden poured equal amounts of oil on Luna's similarly brown legs and back and the two women baked to a golden brown. They ate Aiden's Moroccan cinnamon cookies and drank small cups of nonalcoholic *Mahia*, a Moroccan Jewish brandy distilled from figs, dates, grapes and jujubes, flavored with anise and mixed with pomegranate or mango juice.

Their number-one beach entertainment was watching brides and grooms take photos by the Bay's arched wooden bridges and weeping willows. At these times, Luna fantasized about finally getting a boyfriend this year, so she could double date with Aiden and her boyfriend-since-forever, Isaac Biton.

But as September approached, Luna's mom announced her opening night was pushed up and she'd be on the road in September, instead of after Halloween as originally planned.

"These are charity events," Judith explains, as she does a last-minute check of her dresser drawers, yanking them open without closing them. "That nursing home wouldn't survive without us. We got them a whole new floor last year."

"I'm sure they're grateful," Luna says. She eyes her mother's bedroom, the dirty laundry kicked into the corner, the unmade bed, the empty coffee cups and crumpled napkins. The room permanently smells of baby powder-scented deodorant and stagnant air.

"But the rent has to be paid and the water and electricity. Someone has to buy food, clean, do the laundry, deal with the cable and phone bills, and the front lawn looks like the place is abandoned. How can I do all that with shift work?"

"Who told you to get stuck behind the front desk of a motel? Besides, you're a worrywart like your father," Judith says. She fans herself with the new playbill with her rolled-up photo on the front cover. "I get that it's your way of saying you'll miss me. I'll miss you, too."

Judith throws her arms around her daughter and Luna hugs her back. This will be a disaster. She can feel it as surely as she feels her mother's fake eyelashes against her cheek. Already Luna has a headache behind her left eye. There's no point in explaining to her mom how she has the only boss in the world who keeps taking her back every time she quits to help her family out with their crazy business ideas, how much she prefers solo shifts where no one can ask her questions about her family to any job where she'd actually have to reveal herself to people.

On top of the heap of daily cleaning and cooking for her and her older brother Ronen, there are bill collectors who come knocking on the front door, waving big white envelopes or oversized documents like dirty bedsheets Luna's sure the entire street can see. They don't appear when her mother's home or even in town.

This is her mother's karma, the way the car never breaks down when she's driving it, she gets the lead in every play she auditions for, and why everyone else's light dims around hers.

Judith Levi is one of those people who naturally casts herself as the damsel in distress and a royal knight comes to save her each time in one form or another. She ends up the heroine of her own tales, indispensable to others with an aura of invaluableness.

Judith has never asked her daughter about the times Luna's had to flick off the lights and hold her breath until collectors give up knocking and screaming at the front door and stomp down the front steps. Judith has never had to avoid the windows until the sound of a car screeching off plunges her into relief or crawl on all fours if the blinds are up.

Then there's Luna's father to worry about. But the only message she's ever received from her mother about Nir Levi is that he's nothing more than a mystery Luna's not clever enough to understand. Judith downplays his unpredictable comings and goings with "other people have much worse problems" or "what's waiting around for him going to do?"

Now Luna's mother makes her way down the stairs carrying four heavy suitcases. Each case is crammed with costumes, wigs, shoes, and stage makeup. Judith gives off the impression that she's disappearing for months—it wouldn't be the first time.

"Help me to the car with all of this stuff, will you?" Judith calls to Luna in the kitchen.

Luna forces herself to put one foot in front of the other. She feels sick wondering who will show up first: a debt collector representing Avon or Tupperware or some other sell-from-home company her mother fell in love with for just long enough to order boxes of products she forgot to pay for; or her father who will wander in, give his winter coat a huge shake (no matter what the weather) and expect her to help him gather the Clover Leaf salmon tins, Colgate toothpaste, and Nescafe coffee jars he's shoplifted from a grocery store and reassembled in piles for poor people he finds on the streets.

Luna breathes deeply. She must take charge, hold the family together. They would be the ones on the streets without her. She needs a roof over her head and some sort of functioning home, at least until she can save up enough money to leave, find somewhere to study art far away from here.

Luna helps her mother pile her four suitcases into the back of her car. Her mother mumbles lines from her script. Luna leans in closer to her and listens.

"I remember a time when a cabbage could sell itself by being a cabbage," her mother says. Luna recognizes the line from the "Madwoman of Chaillot." The role of the madwoman is one of her mother's favorites. No wonder she's excited.

Finally, her mom gets in, starts the engine. Luna steps back. She forces herself to smile. She read somewhere that if she smiles, she'll actually feel happier.

"The stage calls," Judith says to Luna, but before Luna can respond, she rolls up her second-hand Oldsmobile window and wobbles down the driveway, onto the road.

"You'll be great," Luna calls from the curb. She shivers in the evening breeze. There's no point sharing her real thoughts with her mother, who is already on stage.

"I'll be unforgettable," Judith responds. She smiles as though she's addressing an audience. "Now, my chubby chicken, I've left a few credit cards in the kitchen drawer. Keep going until you find one that works and don't forget about your promise to go with Ronen down to our new goldmine." Judith wags her finger at her daughter with one hand, the other fixes her lipstick in the side-mirror. "And I'm looking past my missing eyeliner, but my makeup's for blondes. Go get yourself a real black, and remember, you can only grow up to be whatever you want without a man around."

Judith winks at Luna who swallows. She is wearing her mother's brown eyeliner, slipping her hand this morning into one of half a dozen cosmetic bags in the bathroom cupboard and leaving with a jumbo-sized pencil in her front pocket. But it's her mother's mention of her promise to Ronen that roots her to the spot.

"You'll be back way before I have to go with him anywhere," Luna says.

"No telling what big ideas he'll get on his own." Judith puts the car in drive. "You'll keep his feet on the ground, eh?"

Her mother's promise to return on time was more meaningless motherly talk, probably pulled from an outdated play, where the mother is a saint who longs for a child or a witch who eats them. Luna can no more prevent her older brother from engineering whatever he wants than she can compel her mother to keep her promises. Still, there are a couple of days left until September and the lease on this new corner store, her mother's new goldmine, only starts in October. Plenty of time. Maybe her mother will be back and leave Luna out of her latest business idea.

Luna waves instead of responding. She watches her mother drive around the potholes on the road until the car rounds the corner. She swallows hard and shuffles back inside the empty house. She may as well get right to the grocery store. Finding a credit card that works in her mother's pile can take some time.

Chapter 2

Luna can't sleep, of course. She hasn't seen her mother in three weeks and Aiden's father is on the warpath, threatening to send her to a university in Montreal if he catches Aiden staying at Luna's house one more time. The thought disturbs Luna so much, she has to trick her brain into pretending it's merely a scare tactic, something that could never happen, like reading with her eyes closed. Aiden hates her father controlling her life but can't give up the perks.

They should have predicted he would figure out Aiden was lying about the essays that forced her to sleep at her study partner's house night after night. Mr. Betel was likely already outside while the moon still had a pale glow. It was only at dawn that violet and blue appeared in the Ottawa sky. They should have looked closer at the shadows passing over the windows.

It wouldn't have surprised Luna to discover Mr. Betel didn't need to sleep at all and leaned back comfortably in his plush car, a Tim Horton's extra-large coffee in one hand, a Benson & Hedges cigarette in the other. Even before the mourning doves were awake, his eyes were glued to the front and back doors at the same time and they didn't have a hope of fooling him. From a young age, Luna attributed supernatural powers to Aiden's father and she still can't shake them.

Aiden taught Luna long ago that backtalk only prolongs the inevitable or makes it worse, so they bit their tongues when he caught them at the corner store, realizing he'd been following them all along, as though they were still high schoolers.

Mr. Betel made it clear in front of the other half a dozen people waiting in line to pay for their milk and cigarettes that he's completed all the phone interviews, filled out the forms, and even bought a new set of luggage. All it would take is a bank transfer, the final signature at the bottom of a white page and Aiden will be living two hours away in a Jewish Montreal suburb somewhere. There were a couple of perfectly good universities there and no reason to stay in this one-horse town.

It's rare for Luna to invite anyone to her home, even Aiden, but she's lonely and when her best friend's around, she feels normal. They cook dinners with paprika and oregano, dicing purple onions and green chives, not by turning a can opener and slipping a finger under the tab of a box.

Ronen spends most of his time with his girlfriend, Stephanie, and when he is home, he can shut himself in his room for hours, devoted to his free weights and bodybuilding obsession. Tonight is a Stephanie night.

Now Luna ambles down the stairs in her sweatpants and Mickey Mouse sweatshirt and flicks on all of the lights. The living room is spotless. Excessive cleaning is something Luna does to fill the emptiness. It's less vacant with a bucket, washcloths, Windex, and sponges occupying the space.

Still, there's nothing left to scour, the vacuum and dusting rags are put away and Luna feels disoriented alone in the middle of the night. She senses her father was here. She can't say what it is, but there's a new sound denting the usual hum of the refrigerator and occasional car passing by. Whenever she's overtired or extremely lonely, this feeling comes to her, a presence or a dip in the usual background noise, when no one else sleeps under the roof with her, or perhaps, she's haunted by her own insecurity, ghosting herself.

Instead of ignoring it, Luna lets it in and follows her instinct to the front entrance. She unlocks the knob, absorbs the coldness of the metal in her palm, flips back the safety lock at the top, and opens the door. A cool breeze chills her bare feet and she blinks in the darkness. She stretches her hand into the rusty mailbox attached to the side of the house. It creaks and there it is between her fingers. A letter but for Luna it's a hug.

Luna smiles and relocks the door. She pads back to the living room, sits cross-legged on the couch with the envelope already torn open.

Dear Luna,

I have started seeing someone. Maybe you know. He says if I cannot be with you all the time, if I worry I'll scare you, then I must write to you. He says it can help, like anyone's ever tried to shoot him. He laughed when I told him this. Better to make people laugh.

I am no writer, but I will answer a question I remember you asked me once. I will tell you how I met your mother. Start at the beginning, the doctor said.

We met eight years after your mother had already been alone until the age of forty. Parents dead, no siblings, nothing. I was sick of wars, Lunaleh. I wanted to stay in Canada. Honor thy father and mother. I was taught to do what God tells us. I didn't listen. Maybe that's why I was punished. Who understands God? Not me, that's for sure.

I became a paratrooper after my father fell from a ladder at work. Who cares about one more dead Yemenite immigrant on a construction site? Nobody needs more black Jews. To them, the elite, we were Arabs.

There was a war going on. I abandoned my mother and fought with my friends. One friend, I can still see his face, David. Did I ever tell you about David HaLevi? Yes, we almost had the same last name. Brothers.

David pulled a string on his parachute and it didn't open. Simple as that. He chose the broken one and I didn't.

He plummeted to the ground, while I fell through a cloud.

Clouds are soaking wet, don't let anyone tell you anything different. On the ground I was wet and cold, but David was dead. Twenty years old. Gone. Mine opened. His didn't. *Chik chak.* Parachutes in a pile. We each made a choice. He died for what? Can someone tell me?

Some of the new Canadian habits made no sense. People took off their shoes at the door and roamed around other people's houses in their socks (!) or in the summer, barefoot. Disgusting, really. People's toes, toenails. The sweat, smell and the dirt.

But it was calm and quiet. Nothing to worry about from morning until night, except the weather. I asked your mother out for coffee after I saw her fill up a stage. She took up so much space, while I felt like half a person, she was so alive. Later she introduced me to Chinese food (so much sugar, no way real Chinese eat like that) and I was in Jerusalem, too, studying at the Bezalel Academy of Art and Design.

But I didn't want to be there anymore. Everywhere faces of my dead friends who weren't coming back and the army said: the war is over, go back to your life. So long and don't worry, we've got your number for next time!

The wedding was fast and you two came along even faster. Who knew then she would run back to her plays? She was used to a stage and with two babies, she became a shadow, that's what she said.

"I meet people and they ask me about the children, like I don't exist, like I'm a shadow."

Your English is so much better than mine. You might understand this.

Now, I am tired from my security guard shift, protecting people I don't know, like anyone is coming for them. But the boss lets me sleep here for free.

Remember, feed the ends of the bread to the birds. It is a sin to throw out food.

Love Abba

Luna reads the letter a second time. Her father is seeing a doctor. She can't think who is paying for that. The Canadian government? Her father's employer? Her father is so careful with money, never wasting a penny. He worries that he scares her.

His friend David died in the war. She's never heard of any of her father's friends. She didn't know he had friends. Her mother turned into a shadow when she was born. The words link and spin in her head. She's sure her mother doesn't know about her father and any doctor. Or is she?

The clock on the wall marks 2:20. The room is a little too cold, the lights a little too bright. The side tables shine from her endless wiping of them. The letter in her hand is too heavy. Her father's friend and his faulty parachute. She runs her finger down the paper to the end, gasps when she sees she's smudged a word, but it was nothing. A shadow. Like her mother.

This will make more sense in daylight. She must warm up in her bed. She's turning into an icicle down here. She can't be late for work tomorrow. Luna double checks that the door is locked, returns to her bedroom, slides the letter under a drawer of her own drawings. The whole time she moves, her feet ache as much as her heart.

Tomorrow, she'll begin the search for her mother.

Chapter 3

Blobs of Laura Secord strawberry jam are smeared on the kitchen table. The Blue Bonnet margarine-covered knife clatters to the floor and hits Luna's toe in a way that hurts so much, she kicks it under the chair and leaves it there. She yanks out a new knife from the drawer and spreads the Blue Bonnet all over again. Luna polishes off her second English muffin quickly; she doesn't even taste it. She double checks the calendar with sticky fingers. This is it.

Luna must speak to her mother, insist she admit she's not a professional actress, but a very inconsistent door-to-door sales lady, who has enough of what her mother calls "good months" to keep the roof over their heads, gas in the car, and the lights on, but not much else.

It's the name Judith Levi written on a lease on a decaying corner store and grill her mother knows nothing about running, not Luna Levi. Judith must act like an adult and a mother and go with Ronen herself, not Luna. To hell with the ridiculous promise her mother extracted from her.

Luna came downstairs early this morning to do just that before work. There's a stack of marked-up phone books on the table in front of her: Ottawa, Montreal, Toronto and a smaller pile of Jewish community directories for each city on top of the larger one. Next to the phone books are scrap pieces of paper with various names and numbers of community centers and small theaters written in blue and red ink.

Sometimes traffic-light green.

Luna's notes regarding her mother's potential whereabouts grow a little more each day since she began her search two weeks ago. They're Turkish coffee or Israeli chocolate stained, which remind her she's been out of chocolate powder for a week. She scribbles that on her grocery list, which she keeps under a Future-Oscar-Winner magnet on the fridge.

Luna leans against the kitchen wall and picks up the phone. She dials the first number, a community theater in Kingston, a small town, a two-hour drive away. After a dozen rings, a recording chirps: *Thank you for calling Kingston Community Theater. Our offices are closed. Our opening hours are 6 p.m. to 11 p.m. seven days a week.* Click.

Luna hangs up. The same thing happens with the next five numbers. It takes two more calls for Luna to listen to another recording to the end and realize that no community theaters are open at 7 o'clock in the morning and you cannot leave messages on their answering machines. Luna shoves the phone books onto the floor.

She sighs, picks them up and stacks them neatly on a kitchen shelf.

Two weeks ago, just as Luna began her search, Judith phoned (there were unexpected, too-hard-to-explain delays) to say "The Mad Woman of Chaillot" was a sell-out and they'd been asked to tack on another week of shows, she'd raised so much money for charity they could now offer grants at the nursing home, they loved her, and she received not one, but two standing ovations.

Luna tuned out the rest. Her mother's reviews are all the same. Destined for the stage. Luna's never actually read one of these reviews, though her mother leaves them in-view all over the house, the way other people might leave tissues or air freshener. She doesn't need the reminder and stuffs them into a drawer in her mother's room—out of her sight.

She rocks in her new second-hand chair at the kitchen table that tips when she leans on it. It's one of the last pieces of furniture her father, Nir, dragged in from the garbage dump halfway down the street a month ago when he noticed the leg on the kitchen chair was broken. He was gone before she had a chance to ask him where he's sleeping now that autumn has hit and the nights are cooler. Since then there had only been that one letter from him. At least now she knows he sleeps at work, wherever that is.

Her father's appearances often coincide with the winter months when more homeless people need blankets and used coats, which her father keeps in a fridge-sized cardboard box until he has enough to distribute.

Luna still has childhood memories of scrounging through garbage bins, especially after garage sales and looting the overflow from lost and founds from libraries, malls and bus depots with her father on a one-man-one-daughter mission to eliminate waste and poverty.

Luna refused to go with him one Sunday in third grade and he never asked her again. She'd grown old enough to feel ashamed instead of adventurous. She realized the other fathers in her class took their daughters skating, skiing or sledding on Sundays, not garbage picking. Does her father remember? Has he told his therapist about their Sunday outings? A heat comes into her cheeks at the thought of it.

This doctor must think she's nasty.

Sometimes Luna finds Israeli coffee, chocolate drink powders and sweets in the cupboards. Where Nir gets them is anybody's guess. If there's foreign chocolate in the house it's a signal to Luna that her father's homesick for Jerusalem and if she digs at the back of the fridge, she'll find small glass jars of green and red *zhug*, the crown prince of spicy spreads in Nir's eyes.

To Luna they're jars of blended fire and garlic. Occasionally, in a hyper bout of nostalgia, Nir takes the *zhug* and adds fenugreek powder, salt, water and lemon juice to produce *hilbe*, another Yemenite paste he smears on pita.

In a fit of longing, Luna checks the fridge for a trace of her father. Someone shoved the chocolate powder in its purple plastic bucket with the bright yellow lid and the Turkish coffee in the shiny red and dark brown packaging next to her mom's orange cheese slices, Granny Smith apples, and opened canned Del Monte peaches.

Luna puts the coffee and hot chocolate back in the cupboard, as though they were precious heirlooms. She feels a lump in her throat. Then she does what she always does when she's about to let her yearning for her father take over. She opens the freezer and sticks her head in as far as it can go, blinking in the ice cold, guaranteed to dry her eyes and snap her out of anything.

"Did you hear the one about the ice cube's great escape?" Ronen says.

Luna hits her head on the roof of the freezer. "Ouch!" She hadn't heard her brother come in.

"You could say it was a well thawed-out plan." Ronen chuckles and slaps his thigh. "Read that the other day."

Luna rubs her forehead.

Blond, blue-eyed Ronen couldn't look more different from his younger sister.

People call Luna olive-skinned or worse, "exotic." Her eyes are the identical color to her skin and her hair is black.

"You ready?" Ronen says.

Luna shakes her head and looks at her brother in a way that says I'll never be ready, so forget it.

"I'll tell Mom."

"Good luck finding her," Luna says. She leans against the fridge and feels the cold on her back through her sweater. "Break a leg."

Ronen pretends to thumb through the Toronto Jewish phone book and Luna doesn't bother to tell him their mom probably left Kingston— the only town she mentioned—and is now as far as Thunder Bay, where cancer researcher and activist Terry Fox was forced to make his last stop not long ago. The whole country was talking about the Canadian hero with the amputated leg, who embarked on the Marathon of Hope. She doubts her brother or her mother had ever heard of someone the entire population was tuned into.

"Let's just go," Ronen says. He replaces the phone book on the shelf. "I've been putting the guy off for two weeks."

"Remind me what you need me for?" Luna asks.

"You can't avoid the new business. Tell that stupid motel goodbye forever. It's mind blowing you don't want to see it."

"This family's blown my mind enough," Luna says. She finishes her black coffee and washes the miniature mug at the sink. "And I like that motel."

"It'll be dead there until Christmas and I'm about to make your day," Ronen says. "Promise."

Luna shivers, though Ronen's cranked up the central heat in October. He does that the minute her mom pulls onto the street, so he can strut around in butt-length shorts and tight t-shirts that saran wrap his biceps for fake courage. Ronen picks up a hand-weight, one of many he has lying around the house, and does a few bicep curls.

There's a knock at the door. Luna freezes.

"Visitors this early?" Ronen asks.

"Bill collectors," whispers Luna. She creeps over to the front door and looks through the eyehole. She tiptoes back to the kitchen. "He's brought doughnuts in a bag," she says in a low voice. "This one's determined."

Ronen groans and Luna holds a finger to her lips. The coffee in her stomach sloshes around and threatens to go in reverse up her throat. There's a bitter taste in her mouth.

"Mrs. Levi!" A male voice shouts through the door. There are three more bangs. Five.

The years pass but the bangs and their effect on Luna never change. She hears the pounding at the door and, in her mind, she travels back a decade. After her father lost his job designing and fixing jewelry when she was ten, the Levis had few friends over but more of what her parents called visitors, usually somehow when her mother was out. It didn't take long for Luna to learn what to do with them. She must run upstairs and hide under the bed. She chokes on dust bunnies, while some man bangs and yells on the front door.

An incident Luna can't forget: her father is home. He makes her answer the door.

"Tell him your mother ran off with an Egyptian camel driver," he whispers to her in his heavy Israeli accent.

Luna's so scared, she almost pees in her red checkered stretch pants.

"Go on," her father nudges. She can smell his hand lotion. Her father's obsessive about having smooth hands that don't smell like anything but aloe vera.

Luna inches toward the door. With her hand on the doorknob, she holds her breath and flings it open, while her dad darts behind the fridge.

"Mrs. Judith Levi?" a strange man says. He wears a suit and tie and a trench coat over that. His shoes shine. He's ordinary looking, not like the monster Luna imagined.

Still, his face is flushed pink from yelling and there's sweat on his forehead. The dull yellow envelope in his hand is huge and thick, but Luna's certain it can slide under any locked door.

"My mom ran off with an Egyptian camel driver," Luna blurts. Only it comes out as one breathless word: mymomranoffwithanEgyptiancameldriver. She slams the door in the man's face and runs upstairs, where her father has moved from the kitchen.

"That's my girl," her father says. Nir Levi gives his daughter a big thumbs-up and laughs, showing off his one gold tooth. "Let him think she's gone to Egypt. They're *her* bills."

Luna hasn't seen her mother in a while now. Could she be in Egypt riding on the back of a camel? The thought increases her panic. Luna stuffs as much of herself as she can under the bed and stays there in the dark and the dust until her limbs go numb.

But Luna's not ten years old anymore. Finding herself in front of the door again, the same pounding that buzzes through her body, the same smell of sweat breaking out under her armpits, she knows not to look to Ronen as a shield any more than she could look to her father. Her brother avoids confrontation the way some people avoid elevators.

She wishes he'd stop clanging his breakfast dishes around. It only makes it harder to think. She stomps back into the kitchen and glares at him until he gets it and stops eating his Shredded Wheat mid-spoon.

"Mrs. Levi, I know someone's in there. Who else do you owe? Open up. I don't mind sitting here all morning. I will put this summons in your hand."

There's a side door one floor down, out the spare room that leads into an empty parking lot. It's hard to see from the outside. Luna looks toward it. She hates that her hands shake every time this happens.

Luna notices Ronen's followed her gaze.

"Let's go," he mouths. Already his breakfast dishes are in the sink, the drowned cereal clogging the drain.

Luna ignores her brother. How dare he take this opportunity to manipulate her into going to see that dumb store.

"Mrs. Levi, do you understand I'll get this envelope to you in person one way or the other?" the bill collector yells.

Luna's sure the whole street can hear him. She needs the bathroom but flushing the toilet will only give him hope. When they have hope, they stay longer. She flicks off the kitchen light, even though that makes no sense. Ding dong. The man discovered the doorbell works. The last time he came it was broken. The dinging and donging echoes in her ears. They're prisoners. Those guys are paid to hold out for hours.

"Had enough?" Ronen whispers.

"Boots," Luna answers. She crawls on all floors to the front hall closet and takes out her short black boots. She slips them on.

"Okay," she whispers. "But this doesn't mean I agree."

"That's my girl," Ronen says.

Luna wants to vomit. "Shut up," Luna says.

Chapter 4

Ronen and Luna get in the car Ronen calls Warp after his favorite TV show *Star Trek*. They can still hear the bill collector calling their mother's name on the other side of the house. He's shrieking. Good. The neighbors will complain about the noise to the police. He's woken half of them. Collectors come early in the morning or late in the evening, when they figure people must be home.

Luna tries to ignore the toothbrush, bent spoon and fork at her feet. A stranger couldn't be faulted for believing Ronen's homeless. She squints through the bird poop on the windshield.

"By the way, love your style with those visitors," Ronen says. He rolls down his window and steps on the gas.

"They're bill collectors, Ronen," Luna says.

It's taken Luna a long time to realize her parents have taught their kids to speak in code words that pad anything distasteful. Bill collectors are visitors, shoplifting is taking, stealing is a forbidden word the way some people might not want to say cancer or curse words. Debt is right up there with stealing.

Ronen sings along with the AM radio. He sways to Billy Joel's "You May Be Right" as he drives. If he senses her frustration with his coded language, he doesn't show it. Luna wishes she could catch her brother's good mood instead of brooding about her mother's crazy decision to take over the lease of a corner store.

Luna will have to hear about it day and night, continue to manage work and bussing anywhere she needs to be on her own, not to mention the house, a bottomless pit. The inevitable collapse will be nothing like an incoming tide, rather the slow bob up and down of a raft in the ocean once it gets past the breakers.

All Luna gets for speaking up is another lecture about how the show must go on. In addition to her need for some sort of functioning home, Luna's so filled with pity for her mother's impulsivity that she falls down the well of trying to help her out of the scrapes she gets herself into every time.

"So where is this goldmine?" she asks.

"In Britannia, stupid Sabra. Hey, that rhymes."

"You know, I hate that nickname."

"I may be crazy," Ronen sings with Billy Joel.

Luna glares at her brother. He pretends not to notice. Sabra is a nickname she received at summer camp when she was nine that stuck and she hates it. It means born in Israel and prickly pear at the same time. Luna's never been to Israel and to her it means outsider, not from here, you're not white. She doesn't know which nickname she hates more: her mom's Chubby Chicken or her brother's Sabra.

"Relax," Ronen says. "Enjoy the view."

Luna searches for a view but can't find one. The only thing she associates with the Britannia neighborhood is the drive-in where her father used to take them on Saturday nights when they were little and he was around more often and his kleptomania was more under control.

They coast down to Carling Avenue, pass Lincoln Fields shopping center, and turn right on Britannia Road. They reach the corner of Howe Street and Ronen turns and parks in the front lot.

There's a three-way road: one leads to the yacht club, one leads to Britannia Park, and one ends in a row of rundown houses. There's a 'closed' sign on the front window, even though most corner stores open early.

The man, who must be the previous owner, sits in the front. It's obvious he's been waiting for them. The keys to the shop dangle in his hand. He wears baggy jeans and an oversized faded sweater. He has a brown beard and sideburns and when he smiles at them, Luna notices a front tooth is missing.

Ronen gets out of the car and Luna exits on her side; her stomach already sunk into her shoes. Coming face to face with her mom's actual plan for making a living is always traumatic and it gets worse every year as her mother gets older and more desperate.

Luna reads the large sign hanging over the front window: After Hours. There's an apartment over the store and dogs bark in the backyard behind it.

"Good afternoon, sir," the previous owner says to Ronen. They shake hands.

Ronen wipes his on his pants. "Who is this pretty lady?"

"My sister, Luna." Ronen puts his large hand on Luna's head and messes her black hair. "She'll be working here with me."

"You sure this is your sister? I wonder what the milkman looks like."

Luna and Ronen exchange familiar glances.

"Oh, her dark color's not permanent. I only went blond last year." Ronen flutters his light eyelashes. He turns so his blue eyes sparkle in the autumn sun.

Tyler looks back and forth between Ronen and Luna and bursts out laughing.

"Good one, buddy." He puts out his arm and shakes Luna's hand. "Tyler Beach."

"Those dogs barking, are they yours?" Luna asks Tyler. Luna loves dogs.

"Heck no. They belong to the renter upstairs. You don't want to go too near them Dobermans, they're not too friendly."

Luna shuffles around to the side of the store and sees a fenced entrance in the rear with a separate gate. There's a large cage and two dogs on their hind feet up on the fence barking. Her heart skips a beat. No. She doesn't want to go near those dogs.

"Come, see," Ronen calls as Tyler opens the front door.

"Well, she's all yours. I cleaned her up as best I could," Tyler says.

Tyler leads them into the store. Inside the place is worse than Luna imagined. To the left of the entrance is an old cash register on a counter. Beside the counter is a snack bar with a big black grill and a deep fryer for French fries. The place smells of burnt bacon. Across the counter are six fixed bar seats and three booths that could seat two or three people each. There's a fridge for soft drinks and juices and the rest of the store's lined with shelves, some partly filled with canned goods.

They walk to the back and there are freezers and fridges for dairy products, cold-cuts, and whatever else needs refrigeration. There's a rack for chips and other bagged snack foods. This tour takes them ninety seconds.

Tyler picks up the odd tuna or tomato sauce can here and there and Luna's busy trying to imagine her mom running this place. The customers, the orders, the accounts, the clean-up and maintenance, the bills. It needs so much work.

"Come to the back," Tyler says.

Luna follows them to the storage room that's unexpectedly big, at least half the size of the store itself. There's a big metal freezer and a metal walk-in fridge to keep produce.

"I reckon that's about it then," he says, handing Ronen over a ring with keys. "Just one word of advice, and I ain't one to go poking my nose into anybody's business but," he pauses for a second, looks at Ronen. "How old are you?"

"Twenty-three," Ronen answers.

Luna clears her throat, but she won't bother saying Ronen won't be twenty-one until January. They're only one year apart. He passes as older because he's six foot three. Inside she burns as though someone's slapped her. She cannot believe how bad this is.

"Well, just be careful. This is one tough neighborhood and—" he turns to Luna and says, "Yessiree it's a, well, let me put it this way, there's good folk living here. And you can do a good bit of business in the summer time when the boat season is at high peak, but you got to keep the darn teenagers out of the place. They'll scare off the clientele and nobody'll, I say nobody'll come in and do any business if the damn kids scare everyone off."

Luna has no idea what Tyler's talking about. Her brother will scare off the clientele just fine on his own as soon as a customer complains about an expired cottage cheese or someone refuses to pay for something they broke and he blanks out.

Throw in her always-on-stage mom and the place is a sinkhole.

"They mostly come from the projects," he adds.

"The projects?" Luna repeats.

Ronen shoots her a scorching look.

"Ritchie Street projects, on the other side of the park. Not good people. There are also a few runaways, homeless in the park that ya gotta be aware of. They're almost as bad, not as violent but they'll steal ya blind if ya ain't careful."

As they go outside Luna looks at the greasy grill, this time with sharper eyes.

There's a menu on the wall and she stops to read it: *hamburgers, hotdogs, French fries, club sandwich, bacon sandwich, milkshake, grilled cheese sandwich.* There's a breakfast menu of fried eggs and cheese omelets.

Luna glances at the coffee pots and runs her finger on the side of the grill. It's soon a greasy black. Her mom can't cook. She feeds them cheap fast food when she can't talk them into her expired meals from a box or frozen bag. Now she'll whip up fresh breakfasts and lunches.

Ronen takes the keys, locks the front door, and thanks Tyler for giving his mom such a good deal on the building. The two of them shake hands and Luna and Ronen watch Tyler drive off, leaving them alone in front of one of their mom's long line of fantasies.

"I bet you're super excited now," Ronen says. "How cool is this?"

Before Luna can respond, the Dobermans in the back begin to howl.

Chapter 5

"Putz," Ronen says as they get into the car. "Know nothing."

They're on their way to one of Ronen's friends. Luna keeps her eyes on his hands, both on the dull steering wheel that lost its luster two owners ago. He still has the scar on his forefinger from when he got into a fight in grade five. Another kid in his class called their father an Arab and their mother an Arab-lover in art class and waved the teacher's box cutter around at recess, a little too close to Ronen's hand.

"Tyler gave us honest advice," Luna says. "We should back out now while there's still a chance. Mom could claim something about the lease—undue stress or sudden lack of funds."

"Where's your family loyalty?"

"That is so bogus. Have you even tried to find Abba? If mom's not here, at least he should be—not us."

"Your definition of loyalty is what's bogus. I'm not wasting my time looking for someone who doesn't want to be found."

"You're embarrassed of him."

"And mom embarrasses you."

"Mom embarrasses herself."

"So does Abba."

Neither of them says anything. Luna shakes with adrenalin. She's never breathed a word about Abba's letter to Ronen and this proves she's right. She can't put her finger on it, but it would be some kind of betrayal. If he wanted to write to his son, he'd have put his name on the envelope next to her own. Every time they've ever gone down this road, it always ends the same way. Mutual shutdown.

Ronen presses on the accelerator.

"Glad that's settled. We're here," he says.

He parks the car and disappears into a house Luna's never seen. Where Ronen finds these friends is anyone's guess, but they're not the types of people Luna wants to associate with. A few minutes later, Ronen and Luna leave Warp at the friend's house and get into a van. A trade has transpired in the time it took for Ronen to leave his sister alone in the car and return.

They still aren't speaking when they arrive at an old warehouse in who-knows-where and pull up to the back. Inside the warehouse, another man appears and opens a big metal sliding door to reveal three pinball machines.

Ronen brags about the great deal he's getting on them and his genius plan to put them at the back of *his* new grocery store. It's on the tip of Luna's tongue: Tyler's warning to keep teenagers out of the place.

"Dummy," Ronen repeats, deriding Tyler, the stupid old man who only half an hour ago warned him not to scare off customers. But Ronen knows much better; rather than banning kids, he would make money off them. He'd rake in twenty-five cents at a time.

"I don't want you badmouthing my plan to Mom," Ronen says on the drive home.

"When she shows up, you mean," Luna says.

"I'm asking," Ronen says.

Luna can't help it. Her brother's ridiculous excitement makes her smile. She looks at him and remembers how after that box cutter incident he was suspended for two weeks; the first in a long line of school punishments. She feels a twinge of sympathy and admiration. When the cutest boy in the class asked her what her mother was doing with that Arab once in grade six, she ran and cried in the bathroom until the school bell announced the end of the day.

"I'm telling her what a great idea you came up with all by yourself," Luna answers.

"Thanks," Ronen says.

His smile of gratitude makes her heart sink. Ronen's hair is still a shade blonder from the summer sun and will stay that way until December. The new freckles over his nose and cheeks will fade by then, too. Luna's skin is smooth as wet sand, not a mark or a mole on it.

Luna turns up the radio as loud as she can stand it. Maybe this time Ronen will get lucky and turn out to be right. She snorts. There's about as much chance of that happening as there is of her dad living with them permanently after solving his identity issues with a therapist and accepting that in Canada anyway, unlike the Middle East, the wars are over.

Chapter 6

Luna admires her mother's devotion to her grandparents, her fearlessness as the only white Jewish woman she knows in the whole city married to a dark brown Jewish man, but it doesn't make it easier to deal with her frustration.

It stretches her patience to see her mom in a Peter Pan costume at the breakfast table, even if underneath her anger she's relieved. She's not alone in the house anymore and someone else is running it.

It's her mom's first morning back home and she's already in rehearsal for her next gig, a Christmas-Hanukkah fundraiser. Judith didn't take off her makeup from the night before and gobs of bright red and powder blue mixed with black run down her face. Good thing Luna showered early. Her mom fills the tub to the rim and uses up all the hot water when she's around.

"He did what?" Judith says. She piles the morning newspaper to one side on top of a week's worth of flyers and papers.

"I told you everything," Luna says.

"Tell me again." Judith puts each of her palms open behind her already pointed Peter Pan ears to show she wants to catch every word.

"Ronen brought in these ridiculous pinball machines when that Tyler guy warned him not to attract teenagers to the place," Luna says. She stands over her mother. "Did you know you bought a business in the projects?"

"Ottawa doesn't have projects," Judith answers. She stands and puts on the kettle.

But Luna's on a roll now and her pent-up frustration overrides her usual restraint with her mother. "And don't ask me where Ronen got them." Luna's voice rises with the whistle of the kettle. "You told me to go with him. No, you made me promise to go with him, and that's what I did."

Judith runs her hands over her face, making her appear even more clownish. She peers at Luna, but as usual, her daughter can't read her eyes. Luna wiggles her toes in her boots. They're already pointed at the front door. Judith reaches for the last blueberry Danish on the plate dead center on the kitchen table—there's never a crumb left of fresh pastries when she's around either.

"*You'll* be running that food counter then?" Luna asks.

"In the daytime," Judith says. "Nights are for rehearsals."

"Ronen's your nightman?" Luna says. "Unless you think *Abba* might pitch."

"Your father? I'm sure he'll make a grand entrance sometime," her mother says. "But there's no counting on his cameo appearances."

"I'm getting a lot of shifts this month, you know for my job, which is not running this house."

Luna grabs her purse and slings it over her shoulder. She must get out of here before she says something she shouldn't. It's clear her mother doesn't know about her father's therapy or his letter. Worse, her mother won't do anything about the pinball machines because she needs Ronen to help her run this.

"You're a big girl," Judith says. "I can't force you to put your family first." She slides a copy of her newest script, *Peter Pan* out from under the stack of newspapers. She already told Luna that her rendition of the play will bring in enough money to renovate the games room at the nursing home's new branch in Hamilton, five hours away.

"Though it would be a huge help," Judith adds. She snaps her script in the air and polishes off the Danish.

Luna hesitates. Should she tell her mother she'd be better off reading a book or two about business management? She shifts from one foot to the other.

"But you're like your father when your mind's made up," Judith continues. "A little appreciation from both of you would be nice." She turns her face from her daughter.

Luna wants to spit out something about the bill collector, but she already knows her mother's response in advance. She'll put on her singsong voice, throw her shoulders back and let her know there are dozens of Judith Levis, no doubt he was confused, end of plotline.

"Well," Judith says to Luna. "Still here? If you miss your bus, I'll take you. We can swing by the new business."

"See you after work, Mom," Luna says.

Luna hurries out and almost slips down the front step. She forces herself to relax and walk normally to the bus stop.

"Luna," someone calls.

Luna looks up and it's her best friend, Aiden Betel. *Please*, she prays. *Please let this be an optical illusion*. She blinks and Aiden's still there. Her gorgeous black curls shine in the fall morning sun.

"What are you doing here?" Luna asks.

"Surprise! My car's getting a new paint job," Aiden says. "Abba noticed a scratch and you know how he is about his babies." She uses the Hebrew term for father.

"So, you came all the way over here?"

"Did my morning run to your bus stop. If you'd picked up the phone last night, you'd have been expecting me."

It's a half hour run to Aiden's neighborhood from here, nothing for the champion of the university track team, who isn't even sweating. Aiden hasn't bussed since she received wrapped car keys in a bow on her seventeenth birthday from her dad, and she never will, especially if she keeps hiding her friendship with Luna Levi.

"Sorry," Luna says. "The ringer must be off." She doesn't add that the ringer is off, so she doesn't have to answer bill collectors.

"You look like you've had a rough morning already."

"Something may have happened," Luna says.

"Something like what?" Aiden says.

She forces herself to smile. Aiden is her sporty friend who doesn't mind Luna's crazy parents. Maybe because she lost her own mom when she was too young to remember and considers Luna lucky to have one. Aiden's father takes the opposite view. If he could, he'd separate the two forever. His threat to move Aiden to a private Jewish dormitory school in Montreal two hours away started in high school and still hangs over them like a satellite tracking their movements.

Luna's told Aiden more than she's ever told anyone about her family, but Aiden has never seen any of her mom's bankrupt businesses up close or met anyone from one of Judith's casts, some of whom brag about living in converted busses.

"You there?" Aiden says. She speaks in a low voice. Aiden's always been sensitive to people around her listening in. She doesn't have to worry. There are only two men at the stop and both have their heads stuck in their newspapers. The wind's picked up and there's the sound of thunder in the distance.

Luna clears her throat. "Your sports bag's open. Let me close it for you in case it starts to rain."

The sun that was out only a moment ago is already covered by dark clouds. Luna buries her face in her friend's sports bag and rebuckles it. This gives her the extra minute she needs to compose herself, make sure no trace of the conversation she just had with her mother remains.

"Wasn't your mom away for ages?" Aiden says. "She's back now, right?"

"Bar mitzvah," Luna says, looking everywhere but at Aiden. "Toronto."

"I thought you said wedding in Montreal," Aiden says.

Luna shrugs. "You know how she is; the world is full of actor friends."

The bus pulls up before Aiden can respond. Luna can't board fast enough. She'll do anything to get out of this conversation and she's the first one on. She pats the seat beside her as Aiden approaches and makes a big deal out of being hungry.

Aiden always has some out-of-this-world treat in her bag.

They sit, shoulders touching and Aiden takes out a bag of homemade chocolate chip, cranberry and almond granola bars. They share the snack and Luna pretends to listen as Aiden goes on about her boyfriend Isaac and his upcoming family roots trip to Morocco.

In her mind Luna pours her heart out to Aiden. She tells her how she took a bus back to After Hours the same day Ronen brought her there. She didn't want to arouse his suspicions by driving. With her door closed and the car in its spot, Ronen thought she was sleeping-in.

Luna noticed an identical store across the street called True Convenience and had a little chat with the owner, who told her how True Convenience is a longstanding family run store. The few customers she noticed entering After Hours were smoking, long-haired teenagers. Regular adults occupied the aisles at True Convenience. By the end of her visit, it was clear to Luna what True Convenience would mean for her mom's success. Offering to help her mother by working the nightshift would only prolong the inevitable.

"You think I should go to Morocco with Isaac?" Aiden is saying when Luna tunes in.

"The family really invited you?"

"Yes. Haven't you been listening? Pretty eye makeup today, by the way. I guess that's one advantage of an actress mom."

Luna swallows. "Thanks. Yes, and yes," Luna says, though she feels ridiculous making up her face for her motel job. Aiden's father wouldn't let her go to Morocco with her boyfriend's family in a million years. Isaac has a Moroccan Jewish background and there's still a small Moroccan Jewish community in Casablanca.

"You really believe my father will let me?"

Luna doesn't have the heart to say no. It's bad enough she's down in the dumps, Aiden might as well enjoy her optimism. She shrugs instead of speaking and stuffs another cookie in her mouth. This time she pulls out a Moroccan chocolate chip cookie Aiden calls *chebakia* with white chocolate chunks. Aiden's grandmother sends them in overnight mail from Vancouver.

The bus is crowded, noisy and it's raining. Luna's grateful for the drumming of the downpour on the roof. It's easier to eat than talk. She stares out the window. There's nothing to see but wet roads and a parade of umbrellas as her cheap motel approaches.

Soon her friend will offer to give her the umbrella because Aiden always comes prepared and has a big heart. Luna will spend the next eight hours squeezed into a space between the cash register and the wall. Besides the shelves stocked with chocolate bars: Snickers, Mars, Aero and cigarettes: du Maurier, Player's Light, Export, there was one swivel chair and a large registration book, pencils, pens, erasers, liquid paper, a roll of tape, and a telephone.

After work, when Luna gets home, her mom and her new business will be waiting, like a bad dream. But Luna has at least eight hours before she has to deal with that. A whole day's break from her family is in front of her. She throws back her shoulders and straightens as the rain lightens.

The motel office was built on the road, the thirty rooms stood behind it. The parking lot was large and faced an isolated bus station. The door creaks when it opens and, in spite of the light rain, Luna does so slowly in case Billy's waiting for her. He doesn't startle well.

Billy's a glue addict who hands over his welfare check at the beginning of every month and stays in the backroom no one else will rent because it's next to the laundry room. When he's there, the smell of glue permeates the place and Luna spends more time than she likes with an ice pick, scraping the glue that drips from his nose onto the countertop after he's bought a Snickers or a pack of du Maurier Lights.

Today Billy's not there. Instead Nir sits on the dirty brown couch, folding a tissue on his knee into increasingly smaller squares.

"Abba?" Luna says.

For a second, she freezes while her father slips the tissue into his pocket. She can't believe it. Her father not only found out where she works, but came to see her. She puts her bag behind the counter and hides her surprise as best as she can by avoiding eye contact while she opens and closes the cash register, as if that's part of her morning routine.

"The other girl," Nir begins.

"Kira?"

"Kira, yeah. I told her I'll watch the place. She could see you coming from the bus stop, wanted to beat the rain."

"That was nice of you," Luna says. She pats her own hair and feels its slight rainy dampness, smells her own peach conditioner. She wipes her hands together. Her eyes dart from the front door to the phone and back to her father. All she wants is for no one to show up while he's here.

Nir wears thick-rimmed eye glasses she's never seen before and a thin mustard colored corduroy jacket, a typical choice to wear in the rain instead of an actual raincoat, something he never got used to. Like her, he has no umbrella. The laces on his brown loafers are far too long to be the original pair. He stands straight as a soldier and holds out his arms and Luna goes to him. He smells like black coffee and toothpaste.

"How are you?" Luna asks. She glances out the window but there's no sign of her boss, Roberto. He rarely comes around unless it's the first of the month to hand out paychecks. Another thing she likes about working here.

"I don't want to bother you," Nir says. He releases her and sits on the edge of the couch. "Work is good, stops you from thinking too much."

"You're not bothering me. Would you like some coffee? It's free all the time."

"No, no," Nir says. He holds up his hand as if to say stop. He clears his throat and pats the seat beside him. "The doctor, you know, the One." He lowers his voice. "He told me to come. I mean, he said it a bunch of times, but today I thought, okay. I'll try it. Get him off my back."

Luna smiles with her lips stuck together and sits beside her father. She rubs her palms on her thighs. The foam coming out of the couch arm embarrasses her as if she dragged it in from a garbage heap outside. She takes off her coat and covers it.

Her father clears his throat again. Luna can feel him staring. No one says anything for a few minutes and Luna can hear the conversation with his therapist. My daughter wants to be her mother all over again. What a disappointment! The sound of the rain isn't loud enough. She can still hear herself think.

"Your eyes look like your mother's today."

Her father's voice is too low and flat.

Luna fake laughs, as though he's told a private joke. Her body tenses. The tissue reappears and Nir's folding it into squares on his knee and Luna resists smearing off the liquid eyeliner she laid on thick this morning. What was a bit of fun an hour ago is now a trigger all over her face.

Why today of all days? She couldn't help herself. It wasn't the first time. The oversized cosmetic bag was open on the bathroom counter, eyeshadows and concealers spilling out the side. An invitation. Digging around in it, she found the darkest brown she could, and couldn't resist the liquid eyeliner her mother puts on the moment her teeth are brushed. Her father's right, she doesn't usually look like this with little graphic wings at the ends of her eyes, but her mother always does.

"How's work?" Luna says. Her throat feels parched. She feels as though someone's squeezing her heart. This soaring from zero to ten never fails to rattle her.

She jumps up and puts the coarse coffee in the filter paper, smoothing it down with a spoon. She adds the water and watches it turn to mush. She forgot to boil the water first. She picks up the pot and puts it down again. It lands with a small clunk.

"You like it?" Nir continues. "The eyes."

He ignores Luna's question about work. She doesn't want to answer. There's a cause and effect to every word. Her second wish and it's only 10 a.m.

"I draw, remember?" She fights with herself. She wants to return to swimming in a calm sea. Best to take the eyeliner off. It would only take a minute.

"Yes, you're my drawer." Nir's voice is full again.

Luna sees his facial muscles relax. His normal tone of voice is a piece of wood to hold onto. She finds the plastic measuring cup and opens the door to the bathroom, fills the cup at the tap, pours it into the machine, repeats the action.

All the while Luna's traveled back eight years. She lied about never attending one of her mother's plays. She did once when she was twelve years old. Judith had the lead role in "Alice in Wonderland" and there she was in a childish blue Victorian dress, shoulder-length blonde hair in long curls, a wig she still has, and mesmerizing cat eyes.

But somewhere between falling through the rabbit hole and growing as tall as a house, somebody whistled and then another somebody. It was a private fundraising dinner with a bottle of red and white on each round table, shiny cloth napkins, forks and spoons Luna didn't know what to do with. If others shared their table, Luna can't say who they were. She only had eyes for her mother.

Luna has no idea how many catcalls it took. One? Five? But Nir leaped onto the table, rocking it with his weight. The thin vase with the plastic rose smashed to the floor, chicken gravy splattered, two full bottles of wine stained the wall to wall carpeting.

"Stop looking at my goddamn wife!"

"Get down or I'll take you down, all right!"

"Shut your mouths!"

There's a jumble of Judith's responses in Luna's head.

"I'll get down when I'm good and ready," stands out as real. Luna might have invented the others.

In the end, it was Nir who was dragged outside the large hall. The kicking and rough screaming like someone in pain still controlling him. Nir could easily have snapped the guards in two. Perhaps he did outside.

After that she sat still as a guardrail with tears running down her cheeks watching the rest of the play with an empty seat beside her and Ronen two chairs away. At some point he filled her father's place and his hand briefly touched hers. She recalls the long stares, the taste of shame, her heart beating dully inside her chest, and running for the bus home by herself with money she stole from her mother's wallet during intermission.

That was the last play of her mother's she ever attended. Today it all seems like a dream, but Luna knows it wasn't. She isn't Alice and doesn't live in Wonderland.

Now Luna can hear the maids, their Caribbean accents overpowering the rain, crowding in the backdoor that opens into the laundry area. Their chatter is soon drowned out by pop music on the radio and the rumble of five washing machines at once. The smells of filtered coffee, cigarette smoke, and dryer sheets take over the room. The coffee. Luna's forgotten hers again.

"I got to get to work."

It upsets Luna that she wants him to go. She's failed the session.

"God made you beautiful," Nir says. He kisses her on the forehead with cold lips or maybe she's cold. "He doesn't need your help."

Nir squeezes Luna's hand and then he's gone. The door doesn't catch and it bangs in the wind. When Luna opens her hand a $100 bill is folded up into tiny squares in her palm inside of a tissue.

Through the window, she spots Billy, head down against the rain, wiping the glue dripping from his nose with his fingers. A crack of thunder makes her jump and she opens the door wide for him.

"You can always take a little detour." Billy inclines his head in the direction of his backroom while Luna slams the door shut against the wind. "It's never locked."

Luna doesn't even look up. She's never tried the backroom door before. A third wish. She should have accepted Aiden's umbrella. Then her father would have left with something.

Chapter 7

Luna returns from work and finds her mother in the family room. The lights are off, but she can tell Judith's busy stuffing whatever letter she was reading in her purse. Luna recognizes a bank logo on the envelope. She can't be sure in the semidarkness. It's typical of her mother to leave the lights off if she thinks someone's on their way home, that and to play the damsel in distress. Luna flicks on the light switch.

"There you are," Judith says. "I don't know what I did to deserve this." Her mother looks even older than she is in the shadows cast by the gloomy clouds outside.

"Deserve what?" Luna asks. She crosses her arms at her chest and taps her foot.

"Wait until you try to run a family," Judith says, slipping a cardigan over her shoulders.

"Isn't that what I'm doing now?"

"You're not running a family. You do chores." Judith folds the blankets on the couch. "Chores help teach life skills. You'll thank me when you're not dependent on some man. You'll have way more opportunities than women had in my day."

"Guess so," Luna says.

Luna drags the vacuum into the family room instead of continuing the conversation. She needs to think about applying for a student loan and getting out of here, not get caught up in one of her mother's dramas or using one of her father's visits to fall into a funk.

Soon she's attacking the rug. The rhythmic noise calms her and she cleans for longer than she has to. It's hard for Luna not to respond to her mother. Whenever she tries to speak honestly, she gets tuned out. She has to stop sticking out her neck only to have it cut off. She unplugs the vacuum. At least the carpet is spotless.

"I'll have to give up this show if I can't find someone to do the nightshift. We were going to raise a lot for the new wing for those old people," Judith says. Folding blankets exhausted Judith's house cleaning list for the day. She puts her hands on her hips. "I'm making coffee."

"I thought it was the games room." Luna raises her voice, so her mother can hear her from the kitchen.

"That too."

Luna waits for her mother in the family room. The coffee table's littered with chipped, mismatched mugs, all of them half consumed with rings of Coffee Rich creamer floating to the top. Side plates bookend the table, each with one piece of white bread toast, cut in half and thickly buttered. There are several bites taken out of both. Luna can see the pink lipstick stains blended with the yellow butter.

Bites of buttered white toast and sips of coffee with non-dairy creamer and two sweeteners is about all Luna's mother ever eats, except pastries. She rounds out her diet with orange cheese slices on Melba toast, Del Monte canned peaches in heavy syrup and an occasional sour green apple. Remnants of these meals are all over the house, on the bathroom counter, her bedroom side table, and at the top of the stairs.

Star Trek is on television but neither of them watches. Ronen must have been enjoying it, but Luna doesn't have the energy to ask where he is. Luna notices the beautiful women on the show while her mother sets a snack on the table, orange cheese slices, Melba toast and two instant coffees.

Luna watches TV and dreams of being a blue-eyed blonde like her mother and brother, like all the popular girls were in school, in synagogue, and everywhere else she's ever been or anyone she's ever seen on TV or at the movies.

"It's such a shame," Judith says. She warms her hands around her coffee mug.

"What?" Luna asks. She frowns.

"It's not as though the government will step in and make their lives better, all these lonely old people."

Luna notices her mother has her monologue-face on. As soon as Judith begins to pat her hair under her ear and loosen her shoulders, Luna prepares herself for a speech. Maybe this is the real reason why Luna's never felt another need to see one of her mother's plays, not that she's ever been invited. They are always too far away or sold out. But she's had a front row seat to rehearsals since she can remember.

"There was a time before my parents were ill. I had dreams," Judith begins. She looks into the distance as if there's an actual audience. She's so convincing Luna glances around, then rubs her forehead and shakes her head for buying into her mother's fantasy. She learned in science class that human evolution rewards lying and deception. Those who could lie and deceive had better chances to reproduce. She's not sure what it says about actors.

"You're fake listening," Judith says.

"What?"

"It's an epidemic with you."

"Not true." Luna tries to arrange her face, so her mother will believe her.

"See? You did it again. You're smiling too brightly."

Luna searches the table for a tissue and hides her face in it by blowing her nose.

Judith clears her throat. "Where was I? Oh yes. 'Come on, Judy, tell me. Is the romantic interest in the play an interest when you're *not* on stage?' That's what your grandmother used to ask. Always pushing a husband.

"There's no romance in *Rumpelstiltskin,* I told her. She couldn't even get my new name right. It's Judith now I said and I'm not giving up my Broadway dream for anything. I'm *this close.*"

Judith holds her thumb and forefinger together in front of her nose to show her daughter how close she had been to stardom. Luna has no doubt this is the identical gesture Judith made to her grandmother decades ago.

Judith flips back to her own mother's high voice with just a trace of a Yiddish accent. Then she lifts her hands to the ceiling and sighs.

"'You're twenty-two. You won't look like that forever.' Shows you what she knew, eh? I still look amazing. Now I use my talent to help the local seniors. My own grandfather, he had to be left in Montreal because Ottawa didn't have a Jewish nursing home in my day. The trips gave me nightmares, though I was dragged there every Sunday."

If this were a play, now's the moment Luna's mother would sing something downtrodden, like a character in *Little Orphan Annie* or *Fiddler on the Roof.*

"Don't you want to know why the bad dreams? It was the glass eye."

"How did your grandfather lose his eye again?" Luna says. She'd forgotten about her mother's bad dreams.

"In the Russian pogroms," Judith continues. Her mother raises her hands again. "We cleaned his eye each time. Who else would do it? But people don't care about the elderly like they used to, they barely care about their own parents and their sacrifices."

"I do care if that's what you mean. And there will be other plays." Luna gathers all of the used dishes.

"How do you know?"

"Because there are always other plays." Luna's talking to her mother from the kitchen where she's brought the dishes to the sink. "You chose a business with long hours that clash with rehearsals. Remember?"

"It's not like I can rely on your father," Judith continues as though Luna hadn't spoken. "Or do you think I could?"

"You already know the answer to that," Luna says. Her heart softens toward her mother, whose voice blooms with hope, but she can't pretend help is on the way. Her mother is steering this ship alone. "Reliability might as well be a super power around here."

Luna dries her hands on a towel and returns to the living room, but already she's weaker. She wishes she could short-circuit her knee-jerk pity for her mother. It's never done either of them any good.

"It's a shame," Judith continues. She rubs her chin. "Because it's only for a couple of months to get the place going."

Luna's weakness grows with her mother's conviction. She fills with dread. She fights it, but already her mother's words are more like a spell than a request. She must resist falling into this pattern–again. Maybe this is why her father was home less and less until he was barely here at all. There's no middle ground with her mother and she doesn't give up her battles on anyone else's terms but her own.

"Then I'll have plenty to pay someone. Just to get me started, you know?"

"They need me at work and –"

Her mother puts her arm around her. She smooths Luna's hair behind her ear. "It doesn't even have to be every night. Five nights a week say, then I could skip a rehearsal or two. I'm such a quick learner. I learn lines like that." Judith snaps her fingers.

Luna's grateful her mother has put on a normal pair of blue slacks and a matching turtleneck under her cream cardigan this evening. At least she's not being made to feel like crap by a sixty-two-year-old dressed like Peter Pan.

"Mom," Luna runs out of words. She steps out of her mother's embrace. Under no circumstances would she give in.

"I was going to be famous. I was almost there. The whole town talked about me, the small-town girl who made the big time."

"I know."

"Then you two came along and I gave it all up to take care of you and I have, haven't I? It's not like I beat you black and blue, locked you in the cupboards at night."

"Then your parents got sick, mom. You stayed to care for them. I admire that and you didn't beat us black and blue or lock us in the cupboards at night, but the answer is still no."

"You were always the smartest girl as a kid, sharp as a tack."

"Thanks, but no."

A car backfires outside. Luna stands and signals to her mother that she has to go. When Ronen returns it will be two against one. She'd rather do the laundry and make a new shopping list. While she empties the dirty clothes into the washing machine, she blocks out her father's words, the ones where he tells her Judith Levi felt like a shadow when her kids were born. She hums a Hebrew children's song her father taught her when she was young. The poem is about a little boy who finds the door of his kindergarten locked and instead of going home decides to wait, hoping someone will let him in. While he waits, he sews.

Luna always asked her father the same questions: what did the boy sew and wasn't he scared to sit alone at the door of a locked kindergarten?

But her father only had one answer, "What sort of questions you ask. It's just a song."

This made young Luna more anxious. When her father left, instead of having been soothed by his lullaby, she would lie awake imagining a dark brown five-year-old boy alone in front of the locked door of a nursery school, pricking himself with a needle he wanted to thread to create something, anything, to keep his fears away. Perhaps, a doll or a new *kippah*. She used to wonder if he was waiting for his mother or father or for the kindergarten teacher herself. And the questions that haunted her were her last ones: Did anyone ever come for him? As night fell, was he still there, waiting in the cold and the dark?

In her version, Luna rewrites the song. The boy isn't a boy at all, but a girl, a daughter. She waits for only one person at that locked door: her father. Luna knows all about waiting for fathers, who always seem out of reach, the amount of patience it requires, the resignation that it might take forever to fill the absence inside. As long as there's even the smallest chance, it's impossible to give up. She's comforted by thinking a girl in a famous lullaby, passed down through generations and over continents feels just like her. She's not the only one for once.

Luna hums louder. She feels the warmth of her father's hand and hears his voice as he sings about the abandoned boy. He used to tangle his fingers together in such as way as to make a rhythmic noise with his thumbs to accompany the song. Sometimes he even took a harmonica out of his shirt pocket and added a *wah wah* effect at the end, fluttering one hand back and forth and holding the instrument with the other.

Judith isn't the only one who is good at bluffing. While she cleans, Luna pretends she's just another sad daughter among millions who sing old Hebrew lullabies, while they gather all the dirt of the house into washing machines or dishwashers or dust pans in the shadows of their fathers' memories.

Chapter 8

Britannia neighborhood is a hilly area with duplexes and triplexes on tree-lined streets. The Levis' new convenience store, After Hours, is right on the corner at the bottom of the hill. It's no more than 700 square feet with racks of shelving carrying food and sundries found in most convenience stores.

It has a picturesque frontal view of the large local park and the Ottawa River, the chief tributary of the Saint Lawrence River, which connects the North River and Cabot Straight into the Atlantic Ocean in Canada's extreme east.

The cash register is immediately on the left as you enter. To the left of that is a small luncheon bar that offers hamburgers, fries and shakes. There are red stools that swivel back and forth for diners.

Slinging food is Ronen's new job since he quit A&W. He's supposed to make change for the few people who pop in to buy cigarettes, milk, bread, and candies.

"These new curly fries are the coolest," Ronen says to Luna as he takes off his apron. He's done for the day and she's picking him up—a rare event. Warp hasn't been cooperating and Ronen's dropped it off to be fixed at another one of his contacts who is giving him a great deal. That's another one of Ronen's code words: contacts.

"These girls come in around noon and blow smoke rings." Ronen kisses his fingers and waves the imaginary kiss in the air.

"The coolest, too?" Luna asks. She leans on her elbows on the lunch counter and rests her chin in her palm.

"Cooler than coolest," Ronen says.

"You don't smoke," Luna says. "And you have a girlfriend."

"Is it my fault I have fans who want to follow me around?" Ronen asks.

"Does Stephanie know about your fan club?"

Ronen's girlfriend Stephanie is what Luna thinks of as alternatively a bulldozer and a glutton for punishment. She's white, blonde, and Ashkenazi like Luna's mom. She wears a giant gold Star of David around her neck, and smells of hawaj spice and fenugreek from mixing authentic Yemenite Jewish recipes for her ungrateful half Ashkenazi, half Yemenite Jewish boyfriend, and she's always late.

"Very funny. I can't help it if girls like me." He flexes his muscles. He keeps a few small barbells under the cash register for a mini-workout when it's quiet, which is most of the time, so they're getting a lot of use.

"Girls like the discounts you give them on cigarettes and the free cola," Luna says.

Luna sniffs the air. Greasy burgers and fries stink 24/7. Throw in the sweat from Ronen's workouts and the place is an oily locker room.

"That's called good business, something you know nothing about. I told mom I sold two lunches yesterday," Ronen says. "You need to tell her the positive, too. I told you this is the money."

"Two lunches?" Luna cha-chas around the cash register in a clear imitation of their mother whenever Ronen tells her they sold a burger. She snaps her fingers and hums a Spanish tune like a Cuban dancer. "Yeah, we're on easy street. We probably won't have to find another rental for at least a month."

"You're on a roll," Ronen says.

"Where is Mom, anyway?" Luna asks. She jingles the car keys. "How can we leave if she's not here?"

"Mom's not coming," Ronen says. He busies himself rearranging packs of gum on the counter.

"Now you're being funny," Luna says.

"I'm serious," Ronen answers with his back to her.

Luna takes a deep breath. These two had better not have come up with a plan to force her into taking an evening shift. It won't work.

"Explain," she says. She steadies herself against the counter.

"Mom has rehearsal tonight," Ronen says. "She deserves to go." He sings to himself as he reorganizes the cigarette packs, then reaches for his jacket.

"Quit stalling," Luna says. She eyes the front door, willing her mother to appear. If her mom is at rehearsals, then who is working the evening shift? Have they declared bankruptcy already? Images of packing come to her. Luna's so used to moving apartments, she keeps her own possessions to a minimum. Trinkets and tchotchkes are for people with actual homes. Her heart speeds up at the thought of collecting boxes again, while she tries to get one step ahead of Ronen in her head, but clarity doesn't come.

Another minute of silence passes while Ronen changes from his running shoes to his boots, winds his scarf around his neck. Luna can't figure it out. Is he planning to grab the car keys, race for the door, and lock her in here?

"Last time," Luna says.

Ronen clears his throat. "Well, this was supposed to be a surprise," he says.

"I don't like surprises." All at once Luna realizes how hot it is. Ronen cranks up the heat wherever he goes to show off more of his body through his thin t-shirts. "We've expanded," he says.

"Well, that is a surprise," Luna says. She crosses her arms at her chest. "It's such a shock that I don't know what the heck you're talking about, so quit playing games and tell me already."

A man knocks on the front door and Ronen motions him in. Then he burps so loudly they can hear him through the door and he walks away instead.

"I don't know how you stand it," Luna says. "You were saying?"

"I mean, you're off the radar, she's found a new partner. Here," he throws a Coffee Crisp at her. "Celebrate."

Luna lets the chocolate bar fall to the floor. "Partner?"

"Well, not yet. Tonight's a trial run."

"What sort of partner?" Luna asks. She puts the chocolate bar back in place. Her voice is low now. Every one of her mother's past joint ventures were failures that left them in worse shape than before.

The bell above the entrance door chimes. Luna whirls around.

"Saved by the bell," Ronen says. "Good to see you, Flynn. I was just talking about you."

"Isn't everybody talking about me?" Flynn says. "Or at least dreaming?"

Luna looks from Ronen to this new guy he calls Flynn. Only now she recalls Ronen's wearing two gold necklaces and a bracelet under his jacket. He digs out his jewelry when he wants to make a rich impression. A bad sign. Luna runs a hand over her face.

"Toasty in here," Flynn says. He drapes his coat over a chair and rubs his hands together. "The new manager has arrived."

"Well, hopefully by next week," Ronen says.

They both laugh. Luna nearly chokes on her own saliva.

Flynn's tall, blond, and lanky with a red moustache but it's impossible for Luna to tell if he dyes his moustache or his hair. Under his coat, he wears a pinstriped suit and, like all Hollywood ex-cons, he's smooth and well-dressed. Luna can't get over how he's dressed for an evening shift in a corner store.

"Don't you just love the jewelry?" Ronen says. He slides up his sleeve and holds out his own gold-linked bracelet.

"Who wouldn't?" Luna says.

"She's got the family sense of humor," Ronen says. "Have to make a private call. Back in five."

Luna hears Ronen dialing at the payphone at the back of the store. She isn't happy about being left alone with Flynn. His presence makes her feel as though she needs to shower.

"You must be the knockout daughter I've heard so much about," Flynn says.

Luna cannot manage a response.

"I'm talking to you," Flynn repeats. "Didn't your mom tell you about me?" Flynn extends his hand, but Luna ignores it

Anger rises from Luna's stomach. She's not bothering to acknowledge. Her mother's outdone herself.

"Take a look at this, my little lady," he says, removing a cellophane bag from his jacket pocket. "Boss Columbian, only fifty a lid. But for you, *gratis*." He joins his thumb and fingers together on one hand and kisses them.

Luna inches backward.

"On the house. Best fucking spliff in the city," he continues. "I've got some rolled if you want to come out back with me."

"Are you kidding?" Luna asks.

"How about it?" Flynn asks. He doesn't even glance toward Ronen at the back of the store. "We don't have to tell your mom everything, or your brother."

Luna raises one eyebrow as Flynn pulls out a couple of rolled joints from the same pocket.

"No, thanks."

Luna wants to slap him. She can hear Ronen hang up and then he's by her side.

"Thanks, man," Ronen says. "We gotta go. Call if you need anything."

Ronen grabs Luna's hand and pulls her toward the door.

"Will see you real soon," Flynn says, looking only at Luna. He blows a kiss at her and parks himself behind the cash register, like he already owns the place.

Chapter 9

Luna's stomach rumbles. Hunger isn't helping her think straight. There was nothing to bring from home for lunch today and she had no money to order takeaway at work. When Aiden came by to say hello between her running practices, she pretended she'd already eaten. She can't ask her for another loan, not that her best friend ever lets her pay her back. Then she barely had time to give instructions to Anya, who takes most of the overnight shifts, about the day's quickies (rooms rented for only an hour that need to have their sheets changed at night when the maids are off) before she raced to pick up Ronen.

Luna should ask Ronen to take her to Aiden's on the way home. Her father's never around on Monday nights. Aiden will feed her something delicious and help her clear her head.

"Thanks for the ride," Ronen says.

"No problem," Luna says. She cannot believe what just happened.

"This Flynn guy saved mom's butt. She hates giving up her play group," Ronen says.

"Her theater company, you mean?"

"Of course, the grand theater," Ronen says. He speeds up and Luna remembers to buckle in. Ronen never notices that sort of thing.

"You sure he's a savior?" Luna asks.

"You think me and mom don't know what you'll say?" Ronen says. "You're so pessimistic. Lighten up. Things *can* work out, you know."

Luna concentrates on her breathing. She has to think. Already her brain's in disaster mode.

"Feel like dropping me at Aiden's?" Luna asks.

"Close call," Ronen says. He makes a U-turn. "It's not like anyone was expecting you to make dinner," Ronen says.

"That's ridiculous," she says.

"Like I said," Ronen says. "No expectations."

Luna's facial expression reveals her disagreement, but Ronen doesn't notice or pretends to be absorbed in driving. Her brother and her mom have been shooting these digs at her ever since After Hours opened. She can take it. It's the new night manager she struggles to stomach.

Ronen pulls to the side and allows an ambulance to pass. The red flashing light reminds her of Flynn's red moustache and his disgusting offer to get stoned with him.

She shifts in her seat. Her mother couldn't have chosen someone more wrong.

She pretends to listen to Ronen, who is going on about some new movie he plans to see with Stephanie.

"I wish you guys would ask my opinion before you get involved with other people," Luna says.

"Pardon?" he answers. "You made it clear you want nothing to do with the family business. You got what you wanted and you still complain."

"So, you brought in a criminal. Problem solved."

"You don't even know the guy," Ronen says.

"He asked me to get stoned with him," Luna says.

"For some people that's called being friendly," he says.

Luna looks at him with her mouth open. She feels empty. She runs her hands through her hair. They're already at Aiden's house. Ronen screeches into Aiden's driveway and looks away from his sister. Luna opens the door and gets out. She hugs her jacket closer in the wind and bends down to say goodbye. Ronen doesn't ask her how she'll get home. He leans over, closes her door from the inside, and drives off.

If Luna's mother disappears on one of her theater tours again, she might have to live with this new partner on her own—even Ronen has hung out with Stephanie for days at a time. Stephanie will eventually convince him to live with her, forget about his crazy family. It's on the horizon. She envisions Flynn dropping by when she's been deserted by the two of them. A shiver runs through her. She can't let that happen.

Luna marches to Aiden's front door to get her blood moving and to get herself together. She scans the street for Mr. Betel's BMW. Nothing. She throws her shoulders back in case she missed it and Aiden's father is home. She knocks on the front door.

"This is a surprise," Aiden says, swinging the door wide.

"The simplest thing would be to give me a key."

"You've got my dad's schedule down. I bet you're starved."

"I passed starved two hours ago." Luna steps into Aiden's warm home.

Aiden takes Luna's jacket and offers her a wool cardigan. Luna wraps it around her and inhales the comforting smell of dryer sheets. She accepts the matching slippers Aiden points to in the hall closet.

The black and white marble countertops are the first things Luna always notices in Aiden's kitchen, mostly because they're spotless. The second thing is the chandelier with its dangling crystal pendants and strings of acrylic beads over the kitchen's enormous table. She doesn't know anyone else with a chandelier in their kitchen and to her, it's the height of sophistication. She rubs her hands together until they're warm.

The Betels have a live-in housekeeper, who stays in the basement. Luna calls down to say hello to her and returns to the kitchen, where the steam pouring out of the kettle reminds her of the heat in After Hours and Flynn's offer to get stoned. She collapses on a chair, rests her head on the kitchen table and covers it with her hands.

She moans.

"It's that bad," Aiden says. She places salt and pepper shakers on the table. "Why don't you hang out in the family room for a few minutes and I'll let you know when this is ready? You know I hate any hovering around me in the kitchen."

Luna settles herself in front of the library in Aiden's living room. She scans the bookshelves that are crammed with books on precious stones, jewelry design, Moroccan Jewish history, Middle Eastern cook books and Jewish holiday baking books, but she can't focus on reading.

Luna flips through a cookbook without seeing the words, feels herself falling into the haze that can overtake her when she thinks too long about her family.

"Ready," Aiden calls.

Luna returns to the kitchen where her friend's dishing out hot soup and making giant cups of mango tea. "I've been at this vegetable soup for my father, who will saunter in and say he ate. If I don't make anything, he'll say I don't think of him, so it's fate you're here."

"Ah fate, my best friend," Luna says. She sips her tea. The mango smell relaxes her shoulders.

"It's good to remind yourself you don't control everything."

"Reminded every day," Luna says.

For a couple of minutes, the friends eat and drink. Luna fights off the mood that threatens to swallow her. Aiden looks at Luna and Luna gives her the thumbs up.

She refills her friend's bowl.

"Now that you look human again," Aiden says. She rests her hand on Luna's arm. "What is it?"

Luna puts down her spoon and closes her eyes.

"It's that stupid corner store," Luna says. "Did I tell you?"

"The one you made me promise never to visit?" Aiden says.

"That one," Luna answers. She watches as Aiden gets up and returns with a giant cookie jar. She piles a dozen peanut butter cookies on a plate.

"My mom signed a lease on it," Luna says, her mouth full of sweet peanut butter. "Did you mix this with halva?"

"Vanilla *and* chocolate halva," Aiden says. "About the store?"

"Ugh," Luna answers.

"Give me a second," Aiden says. "I can interpret that."

One of Aiden's favorite pastimes is guessing what's on Luna's mind. It started when they had to shorten their conversations, meeting in secret when they were in grade five after their fathers had a fight, an argument that only made the girls feel closer and more protective of one another. The girls learned to read each other's body language and facial expressions.

Aiden's been Luna's best friend since kindergarten when they were drawn together as the only non-white Jewish kids in the class. It was Aiden who taught Luna to be proud of her North African and Middle Eastern background instead of embarrassed by it.

Luna would watch with her mouth open from the last row as Aiden spoke to the class about Mimouna, the Moroccan Jewish holiday that marks the end of Passover and hand around fresh *moufletas* (Moroccan crepes).

Aiden didn't think twice about coming to school on the Purim holiday in a traditional brightly colored Moroccan kaftan, standing out among all of the king and queen outfits her classmates wore.

Luna would die before she'd come to school in traditional Yemenite dress, even if Aiden thought Yemenite brides had the most majestic beaded headdresses (called a *gargush)* and begged her to wear one.

Aiden's a fan of Luna's drawings, entering them into contests even without Luna's permission just as Luna was the number one cheerleader whenever Aiden raced for the school track team.

Now Aiden rubs her imaginary beard and taps her chin.

"Your mom guilt-tripped you about working the nightshift," Aiden says. "If not, she'll find some creep and you'll worry yourself to sleep every night."

"Ten points," Luna answers. She twists in her chair and wipes the cookie crumbs off of Aiden's cardigan.

"Okay wait," Aiden says. She studies Luna's face, mutters store, store, store, and paces. "Your brother's up for it."

Luna wants to laugh and cry at the same time. Hearing her own life come out of someone else's mouth makes her squirm.

"Hot?" Aiden asks.

"Boiling," Luna says. She claps.

Aiden bows and clears away the cookies. Her words hang in the air. They echo in Luna's ears over the sounds of Aiden opening and closing cupboards. Luna's face falls. The game isn't a game, it's her life.

There's the hum of the dishwasher. The phone rings. Luna can hear the housekeeper bang the washer or dryer closed in the basement. Aiden lets the phone go to voice message. The sound of Aiden's father's deep voice on the recording startles Luna, but Aiden continues to add to the soup. Her father likes to see a full pot whether or not he plans to eat.

"Did I miss anything?" Aiden asks. She touches her toes and does some side stretches. "No more cookies for me. Running in the morning."

Luna lets herself cry.

"Oh, Luna," Aiden says. "Come here." Luna stands and Aiden hugs her friend. She hands her a tissue.

"I'll have to step in, won't I?" Luna asks, drying her eyes. She pulls away from Aiden.

"I'll help you look for an art school for next year."

"What am I saying?" Luna asks.

"You tell me," Aiden says.

"You can't let a slimeball become your mom's partner, can you?"

Aiden squeezes Luna's arm. They clear their plates and wash them at the sink under windows that let the light from the streetlamps outside stream in. In the living room, Aiden puts on her favorite Blondie record and turns it up, so they can hear it in the kitchen.

"I'll put a time limit on it," Luna says over the music when the kitchen is clean. "Tell my mom she has three months to figure out something else."

"You're doing the right thing," Aiden says.

Luna smiles at Aiden the way adults smile at children. Aiden won't see After Hours or Flynn.

"I'd better go before your dad shows up," Luna says. Luna holds up her hand in a stop motion. "Don't apologize. It's late. You can't risk driving me home and him giving you the third degree. I'll bus."

Twenty minutes later, Luna waits alone at the bus stop in the cold Ottawa night. She's warm because Aiden insisted she take her wool cardigan and she wears it under her old ski jacket.

Luna can see the ghost of her own breath each time she exhales. Tomorrow night she'll replace Flynn on the evening shift. That guy has to get as far away from her family as possible and if she's the only one to do it, then so be it.

A bus rumbles toward her, blinding her in its headlights, but it's the wrong one. Luna hugs herself in the cold. She wants to know why doing the right thing feels like walking into a trap, but as usual, she has no one to ask.

A little girl
Went to school
The doors are locked
The girl sews

Chapter 10

When Luna arrives home, there's an unfamiliar car in the street and there are lights on in the kitchen and upstairs, when she anticipated darkness. This worries her. Her family's not the type to leave rooms lit. The usual look of any of their rentals after 8 p.m. is dark and empty. Ronen and her mother watch TV in their bedrooms.

Luna's palm hurts where her house key dug into it when she dozed off on the bus, but the real pain is the trapped feeling engulfing her as she tries to anticipate what's waiting for her behind the door—or who. The slow sense of suffocation makes her want to scream.

Luna shivers in the cold. It's 10:30 p.m. and all she wants to do is fall into bed, but there's someone waiting for her arrival, something her mother never does, unless she has news, which is never good for Luna. It dawns on her that she might be too late, that her mother dashed out of her rehearsal early, eager to sign Flynn on as her official partner, while Luna wasted time pouring her heart out to Aiden. Panic fills her throat and she must squash it or she will scream.

The driver of the car got the wrong address. There is no visitor. And if there is a surprise person waiting for her, it's her father delivering more secondhand goods he's collected from the streets, a backyard pool or a bicycle, items Canadians have no use for in winter and can no longer fit in the garage among the toboggans and skis.

Abba. Her heart leaps with joy for the first time today. Her father will talk her mother out of this corner store idea. Her body lightens and she breathes normally. It will be over soon and better than all right. The car is a gift. For a moment, she wishes she'd held back with Aiden. Her friend needn't have known about this madness. She could have spared herself this latest dose of shame. She's so excited at the idea of her father helping her out of this mess that she needs two hands to get the front door open instead of one.

Luna enters, neck down, trying to blow the cold off her fingers, and the sweet, garlicy smell of Chinese takeout greets her, dissolving her illusion about her father in one breath. In two beats, she knows. There's nothing and no one good waiting for her. A restaurant meal is a luxury her father would never permit. He'd be certain he was about to be poisoned by the stale food they had planned to throw out if they couldn't get some sucker to buy before closing.

In five steps, for she cannot resist the kitchen, Luna comes face to face with Flynn grinning at her across the kitchen table in a room more disorderly than usual. The blazer of his pinstriped suit is slung over the back of his chair, revealing a white button-down with a giant collar underneath, a style that makes Luna think of the men who stalk women in movies.

The open garbage is pushed up against the wall, so that the overflow stains the paint, and the yellow light makes both the paint and the wall stains even shabbier. It's impossible to see anything outside of the rectangular window over the sink. The tower of dishes is too high.

There's an ashtray in front of Flynn, an object she's never seen in her kitchen, with a nub of something already burnt in the middle. She can't tell if it's a cigarette filter or something else. This strengthens Luna's initial resolve to push back against this creep and brings a layer of relief over her disappointment. She was not dramatic with Aiden. It's all she can do not to shove this man out the door.

"Luna," her mother calls to her from somewhere.

Her mother's an expert at projecting her voice. Where the hell is she? She hears movement upstairs, but it's slower than usual. For once her mother's pacing herself as people think women in their sixties do, not racing between the bathroom and the bedrooms, when what Luna wants is for her to hurry up.

Luna longs to take off her old ski jacket, but she's not making herself comfortable in front of Flynn. Still, she's tracking slush all over a floor it will be her job to clean in the morning. She slides her boots off right there in the kitchen and leaves them under the table, streaks of slushy snow on her hands that she rinses in hot water and green dish soap at the kitchen sink, while she considers how to get through this.

She cannot believe her mother has opened the door to their lives to this man so intimately and brought him to their house. She can imagine Judith meeting him at closing time, her smile wide as he locks up and takes her arm. Or perhaps he called her from a payphone, already in line at the cheap Chinese restaurant, urged her not to go to bed before they reviewed the details of his first day, ended his trial period that very hour.

Dread takes over her and Judith's favorite words partner in her head: hunches, intuitions. Her mother's mantras. The water has run cold. There's no clean towel for her hands. She wipes them on the back of her pants.

"Just so you know," Judith raises her voice from the stairs. "Our problems are solved."

Judith enters the kitchen in a flaming red dress and everything fast forwards. Her hair is freshly hair sprayed, her eyes are on her hands, her hands set the table with plastic bowls and the plastic cutlery from the take-out bag, with the concentration of a card dealer.

"Times have changed, eh Flynn?"

Flynn twirls one gold ring around and then another.

"I remember when good girls didn't go out except on Saturday nights." Judith's ecstatic, elated, she's practically on her tiptoes.

"How about those good girls?" Luna says.

Her mother refuses to look at Luna and flops across from Flynn, her eyes on the thin cardboard boxes of food she won't bother reheating.

"Good is overrated," Flynn says.

Luna feels sick. The last thing she wants to do is ally with him. Heat spreads though her. She spent the evening crying to Aiden about her mother's poor choices, while her mother was entertaining that very choice at their sticky kitchen table. Her hands shake and she doesn't know what to do with them, so she shoves them in her jean pockets under her jacket.

"Join us," Flynn says, as if reading her confusion. He pats the chair beside him.

"Flynn was kind enough to bring over Chinese after his long shift, which went very well because he's a natural. I can always spot them."

Luna blanks. She can hardly stand to be in the same room with the two of them.

"Where's Ronen?" she asks. His car was outside, too.

As if he'd been waiting for her to call him, Ronen appears in the kitchen doorway and in a minute, he's seated beside Flynn, close enough to rub shoulders with him, loading his plate with egg rolls, wontons from the soup, garlic spare ribs, and sticky rice. Judith and Ronen dig in. Ronen nudges Luna into the chair beside him. Flynn and Luna watch the others eat. Luna runs her hands up and down her own arms.

"I feel so at sea without Douglas," Flynn says, waving his fork in the air. "It comes and goes."

"Douglas?" Ronen asks. He scoops the last of the rice onto a spoon.

"My partner, remember?"

Judith and Ronen nod and grunt, their mouths too stuffed to speak. Luna notices that Flynn has finally filled his plate, but moves the food around instead of eating it. "He'll think I'm off my head with this deal, but that's only until he meets you." He tips his hat then, as if he actually is introducing them to Douglas.

"When will that be?" Judith asks. Her voice is so plastic, Luna can feel it scraping against her ear.

"He's had a few legal tangles. You know what they say?"

"That crime pays," Judith says. Luna has heard this joke so many times, it's all she can do not to roll her eyes. She buries herself behind a thin takeout serviette, more like a piece of paper, and coughs.

"Well, you would certainly know," Flynn says. "Haven't met a lawyer who isn't one of your guys and they sure do get paid. You must be dealing with one for your real place. Renovations are a bitch. This is some rental."

"Absolutely," Judith says. She widens her eyes at Luna, daring her to correct the impression she's given Flynn about the house, as though they're slumming it while they add a new floor to their mansion over in Rockcliffe Park or on Prince of Whales.

Judith and Flynn drench their egg rolls in plum sauce at the same time.

"Our guys?" Ronen says.

"Lawyer after lawyer, every single solitary one of them. Your guys." Flynn points his finger at them like a gun. Bang, bang. He blows on his pointer finger.

"Maybe you weren't looking hard enough," Luna says. This is the first thing she's said to Flynn since she's walked in and she regrets it. Better not to give him any of her energy. She must preserve what she's got.

"Can't argue with that, my girl." Flynn rolls himself a cigarette. "A second look is always worthwhile." He raises his eyebrows at her. "You're not too warm in all that? Put the heat up, you'll be more comfortable."

"She never does," Ronen answers.

Judith scrapes her fork too hard against the plate and Ronen gets the message. He focuses on his food. Judith turns to Flynn. "So, you're fine with the nights. I'm a little tired by dinner time."

Flynn drains his cola. "You're a daygirl in a night business," Flynn says. "Lucky for you, I'm a nightman. And Douglas too. We'll slam him right in, go twenty-four hour."

"That would be perfect," Judith says.

Ronen's mouth hangs open in happiness. Luna can tell her brother thinks they're on the way to Easy Street.

"You won't even feel the place soon enough," Flynn adds.

"How do you mean?" Ronen asks.

"Like he said." Judith shoots a look at Ronen.

Luna's the only one not celebrating, everything around her begins to melt. She's terrified her mother will whip out a contract, nail it on the table between the unused chopsticks and the dirty plates. Ronen might do it faster.

"Something I learned from my mother," Flynn continues.

"What's that?" Judith asks. She leans forward.

Luna doesn't know what he said before with that stupid cigarette hanging out of his mouth, stinking up the kitchen even more. He rolls the empty cola can on the table where it picks up their leftovers, bits of rice stick to it. Luna looks away, her mouth dry, but she can't get up for water, something weighs her to her seat.

Flynn holds up one hand, remembering. No one says anything for a minute. "About grabbing things with two hands or letting go," Flynn says, smoke trailing out of his nostrils. "You have to learn to tell which is which. That was my mom, all right, a little like you, Judy."

Luna cannot believe this is happening. The surprise partner this afternoon, the late-night dinner, the reminiscing. The long, cold bus ride home, the disappointment that the car did not belong to her father; the short, red, low-cut dress, the high heels, the ashtray. Her head's a jumble, but it's all there.

Should she say it right now? Okay, mom. Enough. She'll do the night shifts, no matter what. Get this guy's ass out of here and change the locks first thing in the morning.

Somehow Ronen's facing her across the table. She hadn't noticed him change seats. He tries to catch her eye, to transmit hunches, intuitions of his own. But his expression is too genuinely happy, and Luna clears their plates instead, dumping them into a garbage that strains against the added weight, unable to find anything to smile back at her brother about.

Chapter 11

Ronen was right about the pinball machines. They sure attract teenagers, all of them with long hair who look as though they've come from or are on their way to juvenile detention. They line up at the pinball machines and buy cigarettes and snacks while they wait.

Even after Ronen has gone home, Luna can still hear the clink of the coins popping into the stomach of the pinball machines. She's been here every night for a month. Like a ghost, Flynn vanished just as mysteriously as he came—overnight. Luna hoped he'd never return. Her plan worked and her mother and brother don't guilt her anymore. Pinball machines have their own music. Clink, clink, clunk is now a rhythm in her dreams.

Luna's completes her college applications at work or late at night with Aiden over the phone. Mr. Betel's a deep sleeper.

But this cashier job has taken her usual strained existence to a whole new level. Sometimes she's at the store until 1 a.m. after a full day of dealing with requests for more light bulbs, towels and city maps. It takes time to clean up, cash out, and lock up, and Luna has to race to catch the last public bus home. Her mom isn't treating her to a taxi.

Now Luna removes her sketch pad and colored pencils, which she keeps under her brother's free weights. She's sketching what she calls an elegant fantasy bird step-by-step, whenever it's quiet. The two ellipses she needs for the head and body are already done. She concentrates, careful not to press too hard on the pencil, adding a beak to the small ellipses, which is more egg-shaped. Then adds three quick lines for the neck. Now she considers the wings. Smooth curves. That will work.

She's debating about a curvy crest and tail when two teens Luna doesn't recognize stroll through the back aisles with their hands deep in the pockets of their oversized jackets. Both have shaved heads and earrings in one ear. That's not unusual, but the umbrella one of them is carrying is a red flag. There wasn't a cloud in the sky all day.

"Hey, what's going on back there?" Luna says.

There's the sound of giggling but nothing more. Luna's mouth is dry. She throws her shoulders back.

"You plan on stealing?" she calls.

One of the girls saunters up to the counter. "I was wondering about your specials?" she says. Her open umbrella blocks everything behind her, including her friend.

"The lunch counter's closed," Luna says. "Mind opening your umbrella outside?"

Luna tries to look behind her, but the girl waves a newspaper in her face and she still has her umbrella open in her other hand.

"I'm looking for the French edition for my Old Man, got it around somewhere?"

"No," Luna says.

There's the ringing of the bell over the door and the girl's friend is gone.

Whatever she put in her pockets is gone with her.

"I'll check the place across the street for the French one," the girl says. "*Au revoir.*" The girl fits her open umbrella through the door. The bell chimes after her.

Such is Luna's panic that she puts a foot forward to chase them. She hurries to the entrance. Her mind races. She gets hit by a car running blindly behind them and bleeds to death on the street; they have accomplices waiting outside with machetes or screwdrivers in their pockets; by the time she locks the store they'll be long gone and someone else will be in here stealing even more. Still, she can't let them steal from her.

Luna swings the door open and plows into someone.

"Whoa," Aiden says.

Aiden. Luna squeezes her eyes shut for a second but when she opens them, her friend is still there. Luna has forbidden her to come here. She feels naked. There's nowhere to take cover.

Chapter 12

"I hope you're not upset I came," Aiden says stepping into the store.

"I wouldn't say upset." Luna wishes she had something to do with her hands.

"Going somewhere?" Aiden asks.

"Just checking the door," Luna answers.

Aiden strolls around the aisles with her hands in the pockets of her ankle-length leather jacket with fake fur collar and cuffs. Luna guesses it costs as much as every item she owns. As usual, Aiden's covered in sterling silver jewelry and looks elegant and sporty at the same time. This makes her all the more out of place here.

She has a silver ring on every finger, some of them have two. All from her dad's shop.

"Mystery of what Luna's life is like after work solved," Luna says. She feels her face grow hot. Her friend's checking out every inch of this grimy, sad place.

"Are you angry with me?" Aiden says.

"Why would I be?" Luna says. She takes the broom from the corner and tidies the floor.

"What did you say?" Aiden asks. "Is it always so noisy here?"

"It's a popular hangout," Luna says. She focuses on sweeping the dirt into the dustpan, tipping the dustpan into the bin. "They can stay back there for hours with those dumb pinball machines."

"Maybe that's why I almost got stabbed by an umbrella," Aiden says, coming back to the cash where Luna is cleaning the counter, wiping down the register.

"What?" Luna drops the box of chips she was moving out of the way. The box slams to the floor.

"These two girls," Aiden says. She bends to help her friend pick up the box of chips. "Bad running style." She tosses her black hair over one shoulder. "Pupils seriously dilated if you know what I mean. You sure it's safe here?"

Luna looks at her friend and Aiden blushes.

"Sorry. I sound like my dad," Aiden says.

The back of Luna's neck is covered in sweat. She busies herself organizing the chips on a shelf. This is the last place she wants her friend to be. It's easier for her to navigate her life if it's compartmentalized. There's no point in saying that. She smooths her sweater down and wipes her palms on her jeans.

"Something to drink?" Luna offers. "Maybe a Coke?"

Aiden sticks out her tongue and makes a sour face. Luna should know better.

The running track champion can't win on soft drinks.

"I mean fresh orange juice? Well, sort of fresh. Water?"

"Both."

"Watch the cash a second."

Aiden nods and stands behind the cash register.

One of the teenaged regulars, who goes by the name Ivan, told Luna many of the teens around here use aspirin and cola to get high. Aiden's comment about those girls' pupils has given Luna an idea. She charges down to the cola aisle. There's a space where two cola bottles would have been. Those girls stole from them.

She swallows. She isn't about to share this information with Aiden or Ronen or her mom. She doubts Ivan, who claims to be eighteen, but looks two years younger with his dark hairless skin knows either of these girls.

Then Gustav saunters in. He's huge, French Canadian, with a face that looks like it has taken one too many punches with his crooked nose and dented chin. He bragged to Luna that he's the leader of the gang that hangs out at the shop.

For half a second, Luna considers pushing him back outside. The idea of Aiden meeting Gustav magnifies her embarrassment. The last time Gustav came in he offered her shots of vodka from a bottle with no label. She talked her way out of it without sounding like a wimp, but just barely.

"Came for your demonstration," he says. His pronunciation is French Canadian. He drops the 'n' and the tion turns into an 's'. Demonstrah-seyoh.

"Demonstration?" Luna asks.

Luna shoots a look at her friend, who raises one eyebrow. She notices Aiden's fists are clenched. She's not used to boys who look like Gustav. Her boyfriend Isaac picks her up in the same model BMW as her dad.

"Figured last time you were chicken to admit you don't know how to drink," Gustav says. "That's okay, *mon petite chou.* Your buddy, Gustav's here."

It's an effort for Luna to keep the horror out of her expression. She's already exhausted from the shift and it's been less than an hour. Who is she kidding? Between work, running the house and this dump, she was a wreck when she woke up this morning. She looks at her watch. Three more hours to go and it's getting worse every minute.

"You want to handle your liquor, don't you?" Gustav asks.

"Not really," Luna says. She laughs, but it sounds more like a hoot and Gustav frowns at her. She has no desire to upset a gang leader, not in front of Aiden. It's impossible to tell what an insulted Gustav might do and maybe it's not a coincidence he showed up right after those shoplifters left. Maybe he came to warn her about talking if she figured it out. Maybe her imagination's on overdrive. That's what her mother would say.

"*Attention, s'il vous plait,*" Gustav says. He straightens and bows as though he's about to perform. "Step one, never light fire to the shot," he begins. He takes out a bottle of vodka and two plastic shot glasses. He plants them near the cash register.

"Sorry," he says to Aiden. "Didn't know there would be company."

Aiden sweeps her hand into the air as if to say no problem. She keeps her eyes on Gustav.

"No sipping, no nose-holding, no gagging, no wincing. With me so far?" He looks from Luna to Aiden.

"Got it," Luna says. She wishes someone would come in and interrupt Gustav.

Anyone. Aiden would be calmer if there were others around.

"And for god's sake," Gustav continues. "Don't hold it in your mouth. *C'est compris?*"

The words get lost are strangled in Luna's throat. She has to bite her tongue not to kick him out. He waves the bottle in the air and she hates that she's tempted by it. It would make it easier to finish her long, lonely shifts, to forget about those two shoplifters and what might have happened and what might come next.

She's heard you get used to the taste. But Aiden doesn't drink and wouldn't understand if her friend did. Luna doesn't drink either. This place is making her unrecognizable. She has to hold on until she can create her own world, though she can't picture what that would look like. She hasn't mailed one college application yet.

"Only newbies drink anything but straight up," Gustav says. He pours two shots and downs his.

"Go ahead," he says to Luna.

"No," Aiden says.

Gustav turns to Aiden. "What are you guys, babies?" He sticks his thumb in his mouth and chuckles. Luna notices a knife in his back pocket. She takes a step back and nearly trips over her own feet. Aiden shoots her a glance but she forces herself to smile. Gustav's busy lighting a cigarette.

It nags at Luna that if she turns down Gustav's offer, he'll be in here teasing her daily, making bottle and thumb sucking noises and that might be just the start. She'll appear as threatening as a feather. His gang will have free reign in here. She can't explain this to Aiden.

Gustav refills his shot and pushes Luna's closer to her. He gulps his second one.

"See how I ride out the burn? No chasers. That's why you only drink with pros. Like me," he says. He points at himself with his thumb and pours a third shot.

This time he catches Luna's eye.

"I'm two ahead of you. Need a review of the lesson?" His face is too close to hers. She smells the vodka on his breath mixed with tobacco.

"No. I got it," Luna says. She resists the urge to clean the shot glass. She closes her eyes and downs it.

"Yum," Luna says, though she wants to gag. Her throat burns. She stops herself from cramming a piece of chocolate into her mouth or opening a ginger ale. She forces herself to gaze at Gustav away from Aiden. She counts the earrings he has in both ears and has to stop herself from checking for tattoos under his ski jacket.

Gustav gives her the thumbs-up and pours her another.

"Can't overdo on the shift, eh? *Salut!*" He clinks her glass. Luna squeezes her eyes shut and swallows the second one.

"That's enough," Aiden says. "This is crazy."

Aiden reaches for Gustav's bottle, but he pulls it away, throws back his head and laughs.

"Get your own. Wannabe!"

Gustav wobbles left and then right and finally, marches out of After Hours but his smell of alcohol and cigarette butts lingers. Aiden looks at Luna and Luna reddens. A wave of dizziness passes through her.

"You need water," Aiden says. They don't speak as Aiden pours a glass of water for Luna, who doesn't want another thing, but sips it. The alcohol sloshes in her stomach. She's warm and takes off her cardigan. She hates to admit it, but she's more relaxed now. Then all at once she's so tired, she can't stand. Aiden slides her chair under her before she can sit on the floor.

"I can't believe I encouraged you to work here, to help your mom," Aiden says. "I am so naïve."

Luna hears her friend. Every word. She feels an overwhelming sense of sadness along with her fatigue, but she says nothing.

"That guy was too comfortable," Aiden says. "Was that a real knife in his pocket?"

Luna looks at her friend.

"God in heaven, it was real. If you don't tell me what goes on here at night, I can't do a thing to protect you."

When Luna speaks again her voice is heavy with sadness. "I know," she answers.

Chapter 13

"I'm sorry about Gustav," Luna says. "He doesn't come in every night."

"You didn't do anything," Aiden says. "It's not like I've never seen anyone drink."

"Of course. I didn't mean that."

"You don't think he's coming back?" Aiden asks.

"Not tonight."

Luna doesn't ask Aiden why she's not meeting her eyes. She's not sure if her friend is embarrassed for her or embarrassed for herself that she's scared. It's going on 10 p.m. and by now the place is more like an arcade than a corner store. There are a dozen teens in the back, mostly boys, using the pinball machines. The air is full of cigarette smoke mixed with the smell of pot. After Luna uses the bathroom and splashes water on her face, she feels fine.

Aiden scans the gum options. She chooses a box of Chiclets. She hands Luna two Chiclets and Luna welcomes the fresh taste in her mouth after that cheap vodka.

Gum is the only junk food Aiden allows herself and she only chews it when she's nervous. Luna notices Aiden glancing at the front door, as though Gustav might return. The rest of the time her eyes are on the backroom, where the noise is growing louder.

"Your mom at a rehearsal?" Aiden asks between chews.

"Something like that," Luna says.

"And your dad?"

"Haven't seen him for a month or two."

"I'm sorry," Aiden says.

"Don't be. He fixed the chair in the kitchen last time he came." Luna flips the sign to 'closed,' pulls down the shade, and turns the lock.

"Hey, you're done?" Aiden asks.

"I am so done," Luna says. "Early night, everybody." She heads to the back of the store and unplugs the music. For a second, there's silence, then the half a dozen boys on pinball machines continue to play. Luna unplugs those, too. She raises her voice over the pings and pongs of the games.

"You got your quarter's worth," Luna says. She doesn't look away from the boys in faded jean jackets and torn leather ones. There are two girls in black leather miniskirts, who look like twins, hanging off the tallest boy in the crowd.

"Closing early tonight." Luna claps her hands and flicks the lights on and off. She stands as straight and as tall as she can. She's five foot three, but she's taken to wearing high-heeled boots on her shifts.

"No way, man," the tall boy with the Walkman calls.

"Yes, way. Please use the back door to the parking lot."

One by one the boys leave, some of them throwing their cigarettes out on the tiles and grinding them with their heels. None of them picks up an empty chip bag or soda can and Luna notices that some of their garbage has price stickers on it from the store across the street. When the last boy is gone, she locks the back door and returns to Aiden.

"Cashing out."

"I can help," Aiden says.

"Nothing to do. Slip outside while I turn on the alarm and stick close to the door," Luna explains. There's no way she wants her friend to see how little they've earned.

A look of disappointment passes over Aiden's face, but Luna waves her friend out. Aiden finishes her orange juice, pays double for it and the gum. She ignores Luna's attempts to reject her money, grabs her coat, unlocks the door, and leaves.

Luna realizes too late that Aiden isn't disappointed, but scared of waiting outside alone and afraid to admit it. She wants Luna to think she can be supportive, not a wimp. Luna won't leave her for long.

When her friend's gone, Luna sinks in the chair behind the cash. She counts the money in the register. It's the same amount as when she began her shift. She sold zero with the exception of Aiden's gum and juice. It cost her mom more for the heat and lights and whatever those girls stole.

A cup of ice water never sounded so good and Luna gets herself one. She needs to calm down. From shift to shift, this place attracts more and more bored teenagers looking for trouble. It's developed a reputation. Aiden is right. Gustav is super comfortable here. Is this what she wants? She'll be doing shots with these guys, so they won't beat her up or rob her?

The cold water only partially works, but Luna can't leave Aiden alone on the street. She's already knocked on the glass part of the door twice. Luna puts on her coat and gloves. Once she locks the cash, the storage room in the back and turns off the lights, she goes outside, locks the door, and sets the alarm.

Luna slips her arm into her friend's and they march down the street toward the bus stop. It dawns on Luna that her friend was willing to bus to this scary neighborhood to visit her. After Luna's description of the place, she figured her seventeenth birthday present, a Volkswagen Beetle, would get stolen.

Aiden sings "Call Me," a Blondie pop tune and twirls around. The girls bump hips. They hold hands and sing at the tops of their lungs.

Aiden leaps into the air with exaggerated gestures. She's Blondie on the stage with thousands of adoring fans.

"Oops," she says, crashing into a woman holding a bag of groceries. "Sorry."

"Watch it," the woman snarls.

It's so hard to see in the dark. But someone sees them. A car honks across the street. They look over. It's Aiden's father.

Chapter 14

"*Abba,*" Aiden begins. She uses the Hebrew term for father, too.

"Don't move," Mr. Betel says. He parks his car and crosses the street in five giant steps. He points to the After Hours sign. Aiden's father is as tall as Ronen, but broader. Decades of swimming has given him a wide, muscular back. His only concession to the cold is one done-up button in the middle of his sleek coat.

"You said you have a meeting with your track coach. Odd because she had no idea what I was talking about."

"You phoned my coach?"

"I didn't have to," Mr. Betel says. "She phoned to invite *you* to a track meeting. I told her I'd look around and this is where I find you," Mr. Betel continues. "In the projects. At night. And I'm supposed to trust you on a trip to Morocco with your boyfriend's family?"

"You're using this as an excuse to say no."

"It's not an excuse, it's evidence."

Luna hears the anger in her friend's voice. She regrets not sending Aiden home the minute she walked into After Hours. The sky is pitch black and there are few stars to light up the street. The street lamp right outside the store is broken, so Mr. Betel's shadow is long and dark.

The only good light is the flashing red "True Convenience" sign across the road where the parking area is well-lit, and the parking spots aren't full of chip bags, broken bottles, and cigarette butts. There's a giant life-sized Santa Claus by the entrance with Merry Christmas Specials printed in neon lights.

"You've been looking for a reason not to let me go with Isaac," Aiden answers. Her eyes are full of protest and her jaw is tight. "I came to help my friend."

"Normal people don't work in this neighborhood. Not at night and the ones who do are called cops."

A group of teenagers smoking, chewing gum and talking at once pass by. Luna recognizes Gustav and looks away.

"*Mon petites filles,* Aiden et Luna," Gustav stands on his tiptoes and calls.

"Salutations!" he says, waving his vodka bottle in the air.

Luna cannot remember introducing the two of them. She must have still been in a trance from those two shoplifters. What a stupid thing to do.

Mr. Betel's cheeks turn even redder. "You know him?" he asks Aiden.

"What if I do?"

"How often do you come here?" Mr. Betel takes step closer. The keys to his BMW jingle in his hand. "Luna, do you smell of alcohol?"

"No, Sir."

He sniffs the air. "You stink of tobacco, that's undeniable. You sure that's all?" He smells Luna again.

"Stop interrogating my friends, Abba."

"You want to dive into what I can and cannot do?"

Mr. Betel stares at Luna and points to the car, which he's had one eye on the whole time. Aiden takes small steps toward the car, her head turned to Luna. Her footsteps echo in the night.

A police car whizzes by, sirens blazing followed by a car full of teenagers, pop music blasting out the windows. A squirrel dashes across the street and a truck slams on the brakes. The driver curses out the window and tosses out a beer bottle. It smashes on the pavement.

"I'll bus," Luna says.

"Your decision," Mr. Betel says. "Plenty of air freshener and mints in the car."

"Stop," Aiden says.

Aiden looks at Luna with apologetic eyes before she yanks open the car door and gets in. She slams it shut. She sits in the backseat with her arms crossed over her chest, pouting, and glaring at her father. Mr. Betel follows his daughter to the car, gets in, revs the engine, and zooms off.

For half an hour Luna stands at the bus stop in the dark alone, with clenched fists, jumping at every sound, and trying to control her breathing. What had been a clear night is now cloudy, so there isn't even light from the moon.

Luna doesn't dare sit on the broken bench that smells of urine. She blocks out thoughts of Aiden and the conversation that must be taking place in her friend's living room right now, a continuation of the strangled talk in the car.

Finally, a bus rumbles up the street. Luna flags it and it screeches to a halt. She hops on and makes her way to the back. The bus is empty. There's a Sprite bottle rolling up and down the aisle every time the bus turns, leaking everywhere.

If Luna can squeeze a drop of luck out of this miserable evening, her mom will be out with her actor friends and she'll slip into her room and keep the lights off without having to explain why she's home early. She has a high-powered flashlight for reading under her blanket.

It's not the first time she's wanted her mom to think she's not home. If her mom is home, she'll tell her she threw up and couldn't sit in the shop another minute with such a bad stomach. She'll throw in that she might damage the goods if she's sick on them.

The lights in the bus flash once, twice, and go out. The heat was never on, but without lights it's colder. Luna zips her coat to the top. The bus driver picks up speed, making her head spin, and when she glances at him, he signals to her with his upturned palm that there's nothing he can do about the cold and the darkness.

Chapter 15

It's been a week since Luna's seen Aiden, who hasn't appeared to visit her at work or taken any of her calls. She can only phone Aiden if she disguises her voice or uses their old signal: two rings and hang up, repeat. Neither has worked. Aiden's father must be on to their code.

Each time Luna prays to someone invisible in the sky that Aiden will pick up, but it never happens. She concentrates on the brass menorah on the shelf in the living room and asks for Aiden to call her while she lights the Hanukkah candles and recites the blessings.

Candle-lighting is supposed to be done after sunset, but now that she works nights, that's impossible and she's too nervous to light candles late at night and leave them burning while she sleeps.

She's sure her mother ignores the menorah on purpose and Ronen lost interest in Jewish holidays after his bar mitzvah. Stephanie brought over an overflowing basket of Moroccan doughnuts, called *sfinge*, this morning apologizing that she couldn't find anything particularly Yemenite to make for Chanukah in her Middle Eastern kosher cookbook.

Stephanie's pastries weren't as light and airy as the ones Aiden used to drop over and they were a little too sticky, but Luna devoured three in a row anyway, missing her friend.

Hanukkah is a holiday of light and miracles and she longs for both. It's already the sixth night and nothing. The phone might as well be unplugged. That invisible someone is too busy for her. It's not yet Christmas vacation. Still easy to transfer to a Montreal university and have plenty of the year left.

The next day on her nightshift at After Hours Ronen bursts in. Luna was about to hang more dead-leaf green and red streamers on the walls over a giant poster of a cowboy snowman complete with a lasso hanging on his twig arms, red kerchief, vest and matching hat.

Unlike True Convenience across the street, their Christmas decorations (which her mother insists are winter decorations) only arrived today. Her mother bragged about saving thirty percent ordering so late and getting a bonus artificial raven leftover from Halloween, which Luna keeps imagining is watching her.

"They broke in again last night. Stole baby aspirin and Coke," Ronen says.

The worry lines in Ronen's forehead run deeper than usual. He's upset about the lost revenue. He takes the streamers out of her hand and hangs them for her.

Good. Finally, he's getting it. Luna thinks this, but zips her mouth. This latest scheme makes her miserable and has cost her best friend.

The sooner it's over the better. Except that means her dreamer mom will come up with a more alarming one.

"How'd they get in?" Luna asks finally, pretending sympathy.

"Broke the door," Ronen says.

Luna remembers those girls, the shaved heads, the earrings, which she realized later were actually razor blades. She curses under her breath. The forest smell of Ronen's cologne is strong and it only makes it harder for her to speak to her brother. He must be going on a date with Stephanie while she's trapped here. They'll be laughing any minute now at a party with people their own age, while she has to use all of her willpower not to lock up the place and run.

Ronen runs his fingers through his hair, a signal he's about to break. For all of his bicep curling and squats, Ronen avoids confrontation. He tells Luna about his nightmares of being on duty when there's trouble. Luna points out that it's his genius pinball machines and the types they attract that make the waves around here and keep regular customers away. He responds by telling her that's a low blow when he's confessing something so personal. Luna just crosses her arms and shakes her head and looks miserable.

In the last week Luna has figured out who the main teen drug dealer is in the backroom, found no less than five stolen bicycles parked outside the shop (the owners came looking for them accompanied by police officers), and watched while regulars graffiti the walls across the street after they urinate on them.

The neighborhood teens have cased the place and realized the dark young girl is a much easier dupe than the tall, blond guy with the free weights under the counter, so Ronen has little to worry about if there's a larger plan at play. Luna doesn't say any of this. It would make it too real, too hard for her to stay.

"Keep a sharp eye tonight," Ronen says. "You'll be okay, here?"

"Worried about me?"

"A little," he says.

"I'm good. If it gets too intense, I'll close early."

When Ronen leaves, the door closes so hard the raven falls to the floor. Luna's left picking up the creepy bird with her bare hands. She chucks it in the trash. She's not standing on a ladder for that artificial thing with its expanded wings and black eyes.

The door opens and an elderly woman walks in who reminds Luna of the photographs of her grandmother her mother has in a few frames scattered on her bedroom dresser. The lady has the same horn-rimmed glasses and bad red dye job. It's obvious by the way she walks that her knees can barely hold her weight.

"Can I help you?" Luna asks, wishing for a moment that it was her grandmother. How she would have loved to have one. Her heart lightens at the idea.

But the lady either ignores her or doesn't hear her. She wouldn't be the first senior citizen Luna's met who keeps her hearing aid off.

Luna stares at the stranger's arthritic hands as she pulls a carton of milk out of the fridge. They're red with sores that look redder against the purple bruises. She drifts back to one of her mother's favorite stories, imagining this woman in her grandmother's place.

"I wanted to wait for you both, but I'm bursting," twenty-two-year old Judith says. She clasps her hands in front of her chest and stands on her toes.

"Someone's excited. All right, tell me?" Mrs. Possenheimer answers in a shaky voice.

Judith holds out her arms like a dancer about to fly across the stage. "I got an offer. London. England not Ontario."

"What?"

"A scout came to my play. *Rumpelstiltskin.*"

"What's a scout?"

"Mom, he offered me a scholarship to a drama school. He could have chosen anyone and he bet on me. This is it. My ticket to Broadway."

To hear her mother tell it, her parents slammed the window shut on their daughter's dream before it barely escaped her mouth. They died before Judith could fly off to London and after the medical bills and funeral costs, there wasn't a dime left to pay for a trip across the ocean. The scholarship was only partial and didn't cover living expenses. The letter from the scout yellowed in Judith Possenheimer's top drawer and acquired the damp smell of old news.

The bell over the door brought Luna back to the present. She looked left and right and even walked to the back of the store, but the old lady was gone. For a moment, Luna was terrified she'd had a heart attack or a stroke and she'd find her on the floor, gasping for breath at the end of an aisle. Instead, she found a $2 bill on the counter and a space in the fridge where two cartons of milk had been. The woman had tipped her four cents.

"Maybe mom's right," she says to no one. "I go so far away in my head; I don't know what's happening around me." Luna opens the till and deposits the $2. "Maybe I'm just a worrywart, convinced an old person can't even buy milk without dropping dead."

A strange feeling comes over Luna speaking out loud to herself in the empty shop. No one's coming here tonight. The regular teens would have showed up by now. She has to get busy, flee her own thoughts. She cleans the glass on the front windows and the door in wide strokes until it gleams. The sidewalk out front is soon spotless, free of cigarette butts and junk wrappers.

Then Luna grabs the broom and runs it along the ceiling, destroying all cobwebs. She draws the line at checking for moldy stuff in the refrigerator. She does enough of that at home and if her mom figures out she's doing it here, it will become a permanent part of her to-do list.

While Luna's wiping the cash register, some big guys who could be dead ringers for Gustav's younger brothers, enter the store and saunter to the back room where the pinball machines are kept.

Customers must cut through the middle of the store to reach the converted storage room that is now the official pinball room. It has an exit to the rear yard, so teens can smoke joints between games.

Luna doesn't identify the two boys. It's hard to recognize people wearing masks and long black coats. One is taller than the other, but with covered faces height isn't much to go on.

When they troop to the back, Luna has a pit in her stomach, dead center. She stands behind the cash register and pretends to rearrange the bright red and green Christmas candies that arrived this morning in large glass bowls next to the plastic elves, candy canes, and reindeer.

Out of the corner of her eye Luna watches the two boys. Those aren't Christmas holiday accessories they're wearing. A line of anger pulses through her.

Out of nowhere, the two boys reappear at the cash register. They have the jitters; their movements are jerky. The taller one waves a knife through the air, jabs it at the cash register, then at Luna. It has a long blade in a brown leather case. Her stomach is in knots, her heart flaps in her chest. She's as scared as she's ever been.

The shorter one stands, unmoving beside his partner. Luna can only pray they don't cut her up. *Please God. Please God. Go away. Go away.* She can't keep her eyes off the sharp blade.

"Okay, okay. Easy now. Here's the money," Luna says or maybe her Guardian Angel says it for her. She's so boggled she can't spit out a syllable.

Luna reaches into the till and hands them the few stained bills; some are taped together. She gives them $200. The boy with the knife slices the air with it again and they both leave. As soon as the door closes behind them Luna runs to lock it and presses her body against the cold of the glass door, sinking to the floor with her head in her hands. Hot tears stream down her face and her knees knock together. She takes deep breaths. She has never felt so alone and helpless.

The cops tell her the next day those boys used the blade to jimmy open the pinball machines first. So, her mom didn't risk her daughter's life over a measly $200, more like $400.

> *A little girl*
> *Went to school*
> *The doors are locked*
> *The girl sews*

Chapter 16

"Come on, Luna, a few more weeks," Judith says. Luna's mother's hair is rolled in hot pink curlers and she has cotton between her toes from her fresh home pedicure. The paint on her toes is as pink as the curlers in her hair. The sound of the commercial for *Simon*, the new electronic memory game, invades Luna's bedroom along with her mother. Ronen blasts the TV as loud as he blasts the car radio. Judith doesn't bother to close the bedroom door.

"Please," Judith adds.

"No way," Luna says. She breathes in to calm herself. In and out. "Can't I even dress after my shower in peace?" She stiffens and pulls her towel tighter around her and crosses her arms at her chest. Her wet hair has given her arms and neck goosebumps.

"Last callback, promise." Judith's smile is so wide, Luna thinks her face will crack if she stretches it any more. "You're not hurt, right?"

"This isn't an audition," Luna says. "And I don't want the booking."

Judith glances around the room and doesn't say a thing about the mess, even though they both know it's normally neat as a window display. Luna looks at her mother, who has been prancing around the house as the "Mad Woman of Chaillot" for the last few weeks in a dress past her ankles and a wide-brimmed hat topped with plastic flowers.

There are still a few towns out of the 89 in the province of Ontario that missed her theater group's autumn run. It unnerves Luna how well her mother plays an eccentric madwoman, even if she's a French countess from another century.

"You were so brave, such a star," Judith says, her open hand pointing to the sky. "I can forgive you for being oversensitive and emotional for a day or two. We closed for the weekend, but we have to open tomorrow."

Judith reaches out and touches Luna's cheek. "You've always been a quick thinker. Having you was like finding a lucky penny. I looked at you, shiny and perfect." Judith sings in her fluttering voice, "See a penny, pick it up, and all day you'll have good luck."

Luna yawns, stretching her mouth extra wide. She reaches both hands straight up and to her sides and catches her towel before it falls.

"That's why I named you Luna. You were as shiny and perfect as the moon in the sky."

"That's the French," Luna says. "In Hebrew Luna is a dweller. *Lalun.* Dwell. Remember?"

"You get that from your father. I've never been good with that language."

Judith tugs at her curlers in Luna's mirror. Then she picks up Luna's brush and pats the bed. Luna sits and lets her mother comb her hair.

"I was so exhausted giving birth at 42. But look you were worth it. Little dweller."

"Won't work, Mom."

"I let him choose both names. Ronen means to sing, you know. Isn't that pretty?"

"Of course, I know. Can I dress alone?" Luna says. She can't believe her mother is missing a rehearsal. She never misses rehearsals for anything. That means bankruptcy is their next destination, not that they've ever inhabited any other place. After an official declaration of bankruptcy, it's more Tupperware and silver polish demonstrations until her mother's next business.

Luna cannot deal with her confused emotions. For a moment she forgets that she's cold and wet from the shower thinking of what's ahead for her mother and by extension for her. She notices the perspiration rings around her mother's armpits and the sweat on her upper lip. Her mother's working hard at trying to convince her to spend nights as a cashier in a dump after spending her days as a clerk in a dump.

It's easier not to think about it. Finally, her mother puts down Luna's hairbrush and leaves. Luna closes her bedroom door and doesn't move until she hears her mother go into her own bedroom. Luna looks around for a pair of jeans and a sweatshirt, but there's nothing clean. Her mother hasn't bought laundry detergent for weeks and Luna's been on a housework strike.

Luna kicks a pile of dirty clothes across her room and scoops it into the overfed hamper in the hallway. Then she drags the hamper to the tiny basement and stuffs it into the machine.

In the kitchen, Luna measures half a cup of baking soda. Once the machine hits the rinse cycle, she'll add half a cup of vinegar. She's not asking her mother to go to the store for detergent again and she's not shopping. When she runs out of condiments for the wash, she'll use her mother's favorite shampoo.

Luna returns to her room and closes the bedroom door behind her. She'll wear a housecoat. It's early enough for her to get in some drawing before bed. Her mother knocks on her door again.

"If you say all's well that ends well, I'm not opening," Luna calls to her mother through her bedroom door.

"Then I'll just come in," Judith says. She opens Luna's bedroom door. She's changed into regular clothes, taken out her curlers and the cotton between her toes, and washed her face and neck. Luna can see the water in the crevices where her mother's neck's still wet and the grey roots of her hair.

"Please," her mother says.

With her housecoat on, Luna leans against the wall and closes her eyes.

"You know my answer."

The image of the knife sends tremors through Luna's knees, and even the presence of her mother is a comfort. She inhales her mother's strawberry-sweet perfume, the one she associates with eighth graders, and she feels better, which makes her feel worse.

"It won't be for long," her mother says.

Luna stiffens.

"Am I asking so much?" Judith asks.

Luna sits on her bed, reaches for her sketch pad and doodles. She must block her mother out. She feels herself weakening.

"Another month. What's the big deal?"

"We can't manage a store, mom," Luna says. "A month won't change a thing, but it might get me beat up or robbed again. Get a regular job that ends at 5 p.m. like normal people."

"Are you saying we're not normal? Millions of people own corner stores. Are they all not normal?"

Luna continues to draw on her sketch pad.

"We can't walk out on a lease. Don't I do things for you all the time?"

Luna looks up from her sketch pad. She presses her pencil so hard the tip breaks.

"We can split the evenings. Half, half," Judith says, as though they're talking about a chocolate bar or a pizza. "You're my girl, you know that? Ronen's older but am I asking him, no."

"Well, maybe he deserves the honor," Luna says.

She shuts her eyes, so she won't see the knife inches from her face or hear those voices that wake her up at night. Judith sits next to Luna on her bed and rubs Luna's back and shoulders. Luna hates herself for letting her, but it does make her feel better.

"Lightning doesn't strike twice, right?" Judith asks. "The worst is over. Did I tell you how grateful those seniors were for that new billiards table?"

And before Luna knows it, she's agreed to go back to the corner store for the evening shifts. Her mom never sticks out a project for more than a few months and the convenience store must be on life support by now. Luna must ride the latest family business wave and ignore the trembling inside.

Chapter 17

After her mother leaves, Luna longs to speak to Aiden. She heads to the phone, then hesitates. Part of her isn't so sure Aiden will be her cheerleader this time. Maybe she shouldn't tell her about the robbery. Maybe watching Luna drink with that Gustav guy has made Aiden change her mind about Luna and the person she really is. The thought makes her skin go cold. Luna looks at her own wrists, all three silver best friend bracelets from Aiden.

Impossible. Her one true friend isn't going anywhere. Aiden's father grounded her and took away her phone privileges. Her dad has enough money to make a donation to the university for her absence and get her private tutors for anything she's missed. That's all this is and it's almost over. Mr. Betel must recognize that Aiden is an adult now. Teenage punishments have an expiry date. Besides, she's just realized how she can return to the corner store and protect herself and Aiden is the one to help her.

The ring of the phone in the hallway brings her out of her head and back to reality. When no one answers it, she hauls herself off her bed and opens her bedroom door. Her mother is nowhere around. She grabs the receiver and pulls the cord into her room.

"Luna," Aiden says. "I only have a few minutes."

"I'm so glad you called," Luna says. She twists the cord around her fingers. "I need to ask you something important. You said you wanted to help me deal with the family business."

"I don't think I can now."

"What do you mean?"

"It's too late."

"Aren't you the one who says it's never too late? Your dad's the man I need."

"You're not listening."

"Let me just tell you this great idea," Luna says.

"It doesn't matter. Don't you get it?" Aiden sobs. "I'm so stupid. You said not to come, but I wanted to see it for myself. He still holds this ridiculous grudge against your dad. His dumb pride and honor. I know you hate when I mention that, but that doesn't make it disappear."

"I've grown up since then." Luna winces at the mention of the memory. She tells herself Aiden's not crying, nothing's that wrong. There's a silence on the line.

Luna fumbles for words.

"Promise me we won't grow apart," Aiden says.

A knot of sadness forms in Luna's stomach. And that's when Luna's body tells her that not only will she not be getting pepper spray to help her face returning to After Hours, she's lost Aiden.

"Montreal?"

"Meet the new number 36. Track."

"You've been there this whole time?"

"Most of it. Oh no, he's back. Don't forget what I said. Promise me now. Say it."

"Promise."

The line goes dead and Luna hangs up the phone, returns it to the hallway. In her bedroom, she picks up her sketch pad and finishes a drawing of those two teenage girls who stole the colas to get high. She designs both of them as exaggerated cartoons as though she's trying to make herself laugh, like they were nothing but a prank, a childish dare, not a warning.

Chapter 18

Two weeks later, it's mid-January and Luna and Stephanie meet at the running track after work. Running's not Luna's thing. Ronen offered to take the evening shift at the corner store if Luna would "bond" with his girlfriend. Work at After Hours is Luna's most dreaded part of her day, so it was an easy deal to make.

Ronen's insistence that Luna spend more time with his girlfriend is a message. Something's up and this "you should bond more with Stephanie business" is part of it.

Luna ignores her intuition and tells herself that working at the corner store is making her paranoid. Aiden is gone and she needs to trust someone. She even ends up taking her brother's advice about her pepper spray idea.

"Chances are whoever it is will wrestle it away from you and *you'll* end up with the burning eyes," Ronen said. "No offense, but you've got no upper body strength." He flexed his bicep muscles.

"Are you suggesting I get some?" Luna asked.

Ronen handed her a three-kilo weight and taught her how to breathe and work her biceps at the same time. Luna felt ridiculous and laughed him off. He shrugged and gave her a smile that told her he knew he was right. So, whenever she has an extra half hour, she's doing all of the upper body exercises he demonstrated behind the closed door of her bedroom.

Now Luna nods in acknowledgement and gives Stephanie the thumbs-up. She follows her grueling pace without complaint for a third time around the school racetrack. The sky is overcast. It's minus eighteen degrees, and there are mounds of fresh white snow pushed up to the sides of the field. Luna's cheap synthetic running pants make her feel sticky and suffocated.

Luna's clothes and hair, slick with perspiration, cling to her skin. She's never imagined she could sweat so much in January outdoors. She's lost her admiration for Stephanie's top of the line breathable work-out outfit, which she matched to her eye shadow and mascara. No doubt her brother's girlfriend's comfortable running shirt and pants are a contributor to her desire to do yet another three-kilometer run. Luna should have predicted that.

Sweat rolls down Luna's skin in thick, salty beads and her heart throbs inside her chest. She began at a jog, which wore her out too fast. She settles to stumbling along behind Stephanie, barely keeping up.

Soon, she tells herself. Almost time to catch her breath, fill her water bottle, get rid of the stinging in her leg. She's okay with the idea of weight lifting to help protect herself from creeps at her mother's corner store, but running is over the line.

Stephanie stops, bends, and breathes deeply.

"You've earned the right to eat as much chocolate as you want," Luna says between pants. "Wish I had some."

"You sound like your brother," Stephanie says. "We did great time today." She jogs on the spot as she speaks.

"We're done?" Luna says. She looks at her watch. "Let's get inside."

Now that Luna's not moving, she's turning into an icicle.

"Almost," Stephanie says. "Thirty percent of fitness is flexibility. Stretch time."

"I'll throw in a good word to the flexibility gods," Luna says, looking at the sky, which is the same white color as the ice at the edges of the field. "I can't feel my toes." Luna finishes the last drop from her water bottle and wishes she'd brought a thermos of hot chocolate instead. She was an idiot to think she'd want a cold drink out here after a run. The school was locked an hour ago, so she can't even warm up. The car is her only option. Bonding time is over.

"Whoa!" Stephanie freezes. "Oh my god."

"God told you running around in the dead of winter is crazy?" Luna says. "Great. Let's go!"

"It's him," Stephanie says.

"Are we talking about the same thing?" Luna asks.

Luna looks over and it's clear the answer is no. Stephanie's reacting to something that makes Luna wish the ground would open up and swallow her.

Chapter 19

"Don't look now. It's Ian."

"Who?" Luna asks.

"Shoot. This isn't how I planned things. You look like crap."

"What plan?" Luna asks. "And thanks a lot." She digs her hands into her pockets.

"I mean compared to your usual self," Stephanie says. "I planned to invite you both over at the same time to my place. I was working on it."

So, this is Ronen's message. Hook up with Stephanie because she's looking out for her by scanning the local selection for a boyfriend. He thinks Luna needs a replacement for Aiden.

Luna feels apologetic. She misjudged her brother and Stephanie. She thought they were planning to abandon her in Ottawa now that it's been a year since she finished high school. In Ontario there's still grade thirteen, so most high school graduates are nineteen. This whole time they were only trying to get Luna to trust Stephanie enough to let her play matchmaker. Working at that store *is* making her paranoid.

"Can you look without staring?" Stephanie asks.

Luna gazes across the track field. Someone's waving at them from the other end. It may be sweet for Stephanie to be working on setting her up with someone, but it doesn't mean Luna's interested. Her summer fantasies about meeting a boyfriend this year are a million miles away.

"I'll do the intros," Stephanie says. "You look casual." She waves and rocks on the toes of her runners.

Luna has no idea how to look casual. She touches her ankles windmill fashion as she used to watch Aiden stretch out after a run and feels like a dunce. Her eyelashes are stuck to her face in this cold.

"Had to happen sometime in such a small city," Stephanie adds.

"What had to happen? Who is that guy?"

Ian isn't much taller than Luna and she's sure he's staring at her. She's wiped out, a rag. She would never want to meet any guy this way, not even on a dare.

"So lucky," Ian says. "Didn't think anyone would be out here in the deep freeze." He looks at Stephanie, who is stretching her back like they're on the beach. "Come on," Stephanie says. "It's not that bad."

"Not for you," Ian says. "You haven't changed."

Luna looks away. This guy is cute and if he thinks Stephanie's a freak, wait until he finds out how she spends her evenings. The usual feeling of shame that overtakes her when she meets someone new crawls up her spine. Soon it will cover her completely like a bad rash, Levi-itis.

"Ian, meet Luna Levi. Luna, this is my new neighbor and old family friend from Winnipeg."

"Nice to meet you," Ian says with barely a glance at Luna. "Are you leaving soon?"

"Right now," Stephanie says. She circles her wrists.

"Could I hop a ride? There was this guidance counselor meeting, part of my internship process." He holds up two fingers of each hand to emphasize admission process. "My mom needs the car and I just got uninvited."

"Sure," Stephanie says. She stretches out one quadricep and then the other. Luna's dying to do the same, but not with this audience. The sting in her leg has turned into a cramp and she can't feel her nose. She'll have to bear it until she gets home.

"Steph," Luna says. "I'm turning into a snowman."

"To the rescue," Stephanie says. She points to the parking lot on the other side of the field and they start walking. She winks at Luna. "Ian's still checking out schools for his guidance counselor internship, but I think he might end up with you, I mean, where you used to study last year."

"I heard," Luna says. "Not heard exactly." She stumbles over her words. He might think she's been talking about him. What a dumb thing to say. She laughs as though she made a joke. Ian looks right through her. Luna has no time for snobs. She pulls her hat lower over her ears and rubs them.

"Luna was at the top of her class," Stephanie says to Ian.

"School's easy for some people," Ian says.

"Others are just smart," Stephanie says.

Luna wishes Stephanie would shut up. Ian has black wavy hair sticking out from under his winter hat. His best feature is his full lips, even if Luna's his height on tiptoe. She wishes she'd stop noticing. Ian chats to Stephanie but Luna tunes out. She concentrates on staying on the dry part of the path.

"Huge interview tomorrow across town," Ian says.

"Stressed?" Stephanie asks.

"If I want to have my choice of schools, I need to ace them." He holds his gloved hands together in prayer. "Need help from a higher power."

Luna understands why Stephanie likes Ian, besides his good looks. They're on the same wavelength. Stephanie's forever trying to tap into otherworldly influences.

Stephanie has her head stuck in her gym bag. "Here they are," she says, jiggling the keys. "Let's pick up the pace."

"I'll sit in the back." Ian pats his knapsack. "Next to my luggage."

Stephanie nudges Luna in the ribs and Luna returns the dig.

"I was sweating like a pig there for a while," Stephanie says. "We'll be warm as toast soon."

Ian lags behind them and Luna hates the idea of him watching them walk. At the parking lot, he knows which car belongs to Stephanie. How often has he spent time in the car, sitting where she often sits, in the same spot?

But when they reach the car, Ronen's there leaning against the trunk with his arms across his chest. Impossible. Ronen's watching the store for her for once in his life. He promised.

As she comes closer, Luna sees his clenched fists, the pained look in his eyes. Something's up. Something bad. She has to stop herself from turning around and running away.

<h1 style="text-align:center">Chapter 20</h1>

Ronen's appearance strikes Luna like a thunderbolt. She stumbles over her own feet. No one glances at her. She hears the conversation around her as though she's far away. Stephanie and Ian debate like two internal immigrants.

"Ottawa's between Montreal and Toronto," Stephanie says. "Best of everything."

"Winnipeg," Ian begins. "Is the heart of the Canadian prairies and the summers are hot."

"Winterpeg, you mean," Stephanie interjects.

"You're a traitor to your hometown. Like we're not freezing our butts off here," Ian answers.

If Stephanie answers, Luna no longer hears her.

"Off work early?" Stephanie calls to Ronen as she gets closer to him.

Ronen gives her the thumbs-up.

"Great. Joining us for dinner?"

Ronen shakes his head. Luna realizes how bad Stephanie is at reading her own boyfriend's body language. Or maybe *she's* hyper tuned into the body language of her brother from years of living on eggshells.

"We were about to get something to eat," Stephanie says. "Come on."

Luna wishes for something, anything to happen, so she won't have to hear whatever it is her brother came to tell her. There's a ball of dread in the air between them. She wraps her arms around herself.

"Sorry," Ronen says to Stephanie. "Can't."

Stephanie pouts. Ronen kisses her on the cheek. "You're not why I'm here. I'll explain later. Let's go," he says, looking at his sister.

"Hey, Ronen," Ian says.

"Buddy," Ronen says. He shakes hands with Ian. "Sorry, in a hurry."

"No problem."

"Luna," Ronen says. "Say goodbye."

Luna looks around in confusion. She cannot believe it. Ian and Ronen know each other. Luna wishes they had stayed to run around the track a fourth time. She'd rather brave the cold than hear her brother's news.

Ronen taps his foot, looks at his watch.

"I guess we'll catch up later," Stephanie says to Luna.

"We got to go," Ronen says.

"I made dinner plans," Luna says. "Can't it wait?" She looks at her brother's face and regrets her words. She couldn't think of another way to stall. Now Stephanie and Ian are both frozen in place, waiting for Ronen to speak.

"We have to beam out. Now," Ronen says. His eyes plead with her to shut up. Luna turns to Stephanie and Ian. "Bye, Stephanie. Nice meeting you, Ryan." Luna says.

"Ian," Stephanie says.

"That's okay," Ian says.

"Ian," Luna says. She coughs. "Sorry."

Ronen hooks his arm around Luna's and leads her away. Luna can't help but look back. She watches Stephanie open the trunk, toss in her gym bag. Ian's already seated in the passenger seat with a book open on his knees. He's bundled in a scarf and gloves, both look thick and expensive, something a mother would choose.

Stephanie opens the door, gets behind the wheel, starts her old Chevrolet, buckles in. She turns to say something to Ian, who laughs. They're both rubbing their hands together, waiting for the car to warm. Finally, Stephanie pulls out of the lot and heads down Greenbank Road.

"I knew I'd find you," Ronen says. He stomps his feet in the cold.

"You dropped me here," Luna says. She holds up one hand in a stop motion. "Why aren't you at work?"

"No work tonight," Ronen says. "I'm freezing my butt off."

"There's work every night," she says.

"Not tonight."

Luna gazes at Ronen's fatigued expression, realizing his exhaustion. Otherwise, his appearance remains unchanged. He wears stonewashed jeans, a snug sweater, likely layered beneath a tight ski jacket. He's unshaven, but that's not uncommon in winter.

"Can we at least get into Warp and out of the rain?" he says. "I parked halfway across the world."

Rain is falling in a light mist, often a prelude to a downpour at this time of year. The sky's been black since 4:30 but the school grounds are well lit. There's a flash of lightning, a roar of thunder. Luna doesn't bother to cover her head with her hood. She looks around the empty fields as if someone will save her from whatever Ronen's about to say. But there's no one but an older couple walking their German Shepherd through the misty rain and snow. No signal for Luna in that.

"Come," Ronen says.

Luna watches her feet walk to the car; her dusty canvas sneakers now splattered with raindrops next to Ronen's polished black leather boots. Ronen walks like someone in a hurry, maybe to compensate for a girlfriend who is always late.

Ronen opens the car door for her. A bad sign. He's not that polite. He can only be stalling. Once they're seated and the engine's running, Luna puts a hand on her brother's arm.

"Tell me," Luna says.

"It's Mom," Ronen says.

Luna coughs into the back of her hand. Her mouth opens but no words come out. Her mother's not as young as she used to be. She never exercises and her idea of a salad is a leaf of iceberg lettuce cut to the size of a piece of Melba toast. Luna takes a minute to prepare herself for the worst.

Chapter 21

Ronen stares straight ahead. He takes off his gloves and rubs his hands on his knees, revs the engine. He passes his gloves to Luna, who puts them on over her own.

"Is she okay?"

"Physically, she's fine."

Luna feels her shoulders relax. They're not on the way to the emergency ward. "But?"

"It's both of them. Abba, too."

Luna lets her head rest back and closes her eyes. She feels better. It's not serious. She's aware of the windshield wipers swish against the glass. The rain falls harder.

"Ready to listen?"

Luna covers her eyes with her hands but she's listening. Her heart beats in her ears. Her emotions can go from zero to ten when she's around her brother, just like that. She must regain control.

Ronen takes a deep breath.

"Remember Angelo Anastas?" Ronen asks.

Luna thinks for a minute. Ronen cleans his rear-view mirror, puts the windshield wipers on high speed. The swishing sound fills the car now, joins the patter of the rain in a winter concert.

"Is he that Greek guy?"

"Greek chef," Ronen says.

"Didn't we go to them for Thanksgiving once a hundred years ago? Amazing food."

"That's them."

"So?"

"His wife left him and dad's been living at his place. Around the corner from his nightshifts."

"Wherever those are these days," Luna interrupts Ronen. She purses her lips and her nostrils flare. Ronen had her all worked up for nothing. She hates losing herself like that. He scared her.

"This is the big news? Mom didn't know where Abba was and she's juggling the store and the damn play and the whole time he's been out in the boondocks, so he can walk to work and gorge on gourmet moussaka, while I wash our clothes in vinegar to save a few bucks?"

Ronen wipes the windshield from the inside using wide circles. Luna can see him trying to control his facial muscles.

"You're not listening," he says.

"I heard enough," Luna says. "Maybe I pulled a muscle." She closes her eyes and rests her head on the leather seat. "And I want to hear how you know that Ian guy."

"What you want is not why I'm here."

Luna feels as though she's been slapped. Her instinct is to tell her brother off, but something in his face holds her back.

"You're right about one thing. Abba did show up today with moussaka for a celebration."

"Mazal tov!" Luna says. She takes off her shoe and rubs her frozen foot with her warm hands. She reaches for her bag and takes out dry socks. She puts her wet socks in the bag and puts on the dry ones. She angles her runners under the heater, so they'll dry. "Sorry, I missed the party."

"Angelo had a hard time when his wife left him," Ronen speaks with his eyes on the road. "She jerked him around, the usual. He wants to get back into the restaurant business and—"

Ronen's words have sucked the air out of the car and sent Luna thinking about all of the signals she misread today. This morning her mother made her breakfast.

Strawberry yogurt, chocolate chip pancakes. Her favorite.

Her mother never prepares breakfast and on the rare occasions she does, it's out of a box and into a toaster. But Luna was so happy she didn't have to work at the store tonight, she accepted it, though it's never that way. Each action means something else. It's like living in two languages, one spoken and one intuited.

Luna leans her head on the cold window pane. She rubs her temples with her fingers. "No, no, no."

"Angelo talked Abba into partnering with him or Abba talked mom into it or mom talked Abba into it. I swear, I don't know, but they're in it now."

Luna wishes she could sleep for a century. Nobody says anything for a minute. Already Luna sees the 'for rent' sign on the dirty, cracked After Hours door still stained with Gustav's vomit.

"Partners need money," Luna says. Her voice is low. She's so tired of this. She'll never get off the carousel her parents have put her on. She'll merry-go-round forever with Ronen in front of her or behind her. A wave of dizziness passes over her. She wants to wash away in the rain.

"Partners get loans. In dad's name this time. Mom's credit is shot." Ronen puts his face in his hands. "And maybe a little extra cash thrown in with this loan."

"Extra," Luna says. She hugs her knees to her chest and rocks in the car seat like a child, her seatbelt tight around her, though they haven't moved. She wants to feel happy that After Hours is out of their lives, but something in her brother's voice roadblocks her.

"Maybe I got some calls. It's not like I sit by the phone, so might have missed a few."

"Calls from?"

"Inspector types."

Time slows down while Luna's mind races. She must decipher her brother's cryptic language. Are creditors inspectors these days? Are more visitors calling than usual? She hasn't noticed, but with work all day at the motel and working for her mother all evening, she can miss important things.

"Maybe I've been ignoring the phone."

"You always ignore the phone," Luna says. She doesn't add they've been trained since childhood to disregard the phone and the doorbell, as though they're evil intruders. Snubbing the ringing of the phone and knocking on the door is their way of guarding the borders of their lives against unwanted truths.

"Not always," Ronen says. "Answered it the other day."

Luna feels as though someone has hit her in the gut with a hockey stick. Ronen's tone of voice is the same synthetic one she uses for debt collectors.

"So," Luna asks. "It was for you?"

"I hung up the first few times. I was like, I don't owe you anything. Screwed-up credit card companies with their broken computers. But they kept phoning back. Like there aren't a thousand Ronen Levis."

Ronen stops talking. There's a line of snowplows in front of them, inching along. Luna tries to put the pieces together. He wouldn't admit it, but their mother's terrified both of them into ever taking out a credit card, so that part's true.

"Anyway, the guy proved it to me over the phone. He had details and he mailed a copy of the contract. I checked the mailbox every day, so mom wouldn't get to it first. You know how she attacks the mail."

The mailbox is a third border to be guarded. Luna nods and clicks her tongue against the roof of her mouth. Her mother's like a starved eagle spotting a mouse when it comes to the mail, swooping for it first. If she's in town she knows the mailman's schedule by heart and often they don't get mail when she's away. Maybe that's why her father changed his mind about putting his letters in the mailbox as soon as she returned.

Luna's always suspected her mother of stopping the mail when she's not around. Perhaps, Judith's opened a postbox somewhere and fills out a quick change of address card before she drives over the Ottawa border. Her children can't get near anything but junk mail if she's home.

"My signature was there in black and white," Ronen says. He takes a deep breath.

Luna's on the edge of her seat. Her brother's words are like a poisoned needle above her elbow, the signature he describes something he's already been injected with that he now passes to her.

"Luna, she forged my signature."

"Mom?"

Ronen hunches forward. His face shadowed white and red by the lights from the snow plow in front of him.

"Dammit, Ronen," Luna says. She stamps her foot on the floor of the car. "She put a credit card in your name and ran it up?"

"Pushed it to the limit," Ronen says. "I can't remember what the inspector guy, whatever he is, said I owe, but it's in the thousands." Ronen's bangs the steering wheel with his fist. "What do I buy? Tell me. Less than nothing."

"Jesus Christ," Luna answers. She feels a surge of rage. "She doesn't stop for a minute to think about what this means for your future. She's impossible."

"Call her what you like," Ronen says.

"The family goldmine closed overnight, didn't it? She let you show up to that locked door today. Then what? You jumped in your car, raced home and found them splitting a fancy meal? Don't tell me. Mom left at the normal time this morning and hung out at the wig maker or that tailor she uses for her costumes or god knows where—"

"Stop, Luna. Please."

"Why for heaven's sake? Why can't we ever—"

"Because I can't. Do you want to drive in this weather?"

The rain has turned to hail. The banging on the roof like an attack.

"No," Luna answers.

"Then stop. I can't do this."

Ronen rocks in his seat the way he used to as a five-year old. Three-year old Luna would lie awake at night and watch her brother bang his head into his headboard until he slowed and finally collapsed into sleep.

Now Luna bites her lower lip. Neither of them says anything for a moment. It's hard enough for Luna just to breathe. It's pitch black outside. Her workout with Stephanie seems like last week. Luna checks her watch. They've been sitting here for half an hour. She has to get out of this car.

"What kind of restaurant is this?" Luna asks.

"Big. Two floors. Heart of the city."

Luna thinks of Ian's description of his hometown: heart of the Prairies.

"You sure Angelo asked them to partner with him? Those two? Maybe she was celebrating *his* new restaurant? She can't cook, she sucks at numbers. Abba sucks at showing up."

Ronen closes his eyes and Luna reads the answer in his body language. She hates him for not letting them say anything real, but the betrayal is too great, the greatest it's ever been.

"I get it," she says.

"Thanks. I appreciate you not rubbing it in about what can happen when I do want to buy my own place or take out a loan for something."

Luna puts her hands over her ears, though Ronen has stopped talking. How naïve her parents are, how easily taken with any new idea. Poor Ronen. Her mother has already set him down a path full of traps. What's the use? The cold glass on her forehead feels painful and good at the same time. She presses her whole face to her ice-cold window, numbing her skin.

There's a tap at the window. A police officer stands outside. He motions for them to roll down a window. Luna beats Ronen to it.

"Good evening, folks. Everything all right?" he asks.

"Perfect, Officer," Luna answers. "Thank you."

"You'll have to move along. This is private school grounds at this hour," the policeman continues.

In a minute Ronen and Luna are on Greenbank Road. Luna can't tell where her brother's driving, but it's not in the direction of their house.

Chapter 22

Luna understands Ronen's giving her time to prepare herself before she has to go home. She swallows, but it doesn't help the feeling of her throat being squeezed. She studies her brother's expression while he drives.

Ronen's old enough to be free, to leave. Stephanie's family moved here from Winnipeg when she was twelve. That's how she knows Ian. Luna wants to ask her brother if Stephanie ever talks about going back there, if they whisper about returning there together, but her brother's too tense. His hands grip the wheel and he's blinking too much. Plus, he hasn't turned on the radio. Ronen always turns on the radio.

It's too much for Luna to believe her brother's holding back tears, so she doesn't. That would mean things have reached the kind of bad that draws blood and leaves permanent scars.

"Is there more or not?" she repeats.

"Well, there's the new loan that can't be great since the place went bust," Ronen says. He presses on the gas and they speed up. He slows as they reach the speeding limit and lets another car pass. He's allowing Luna to digest the news in pieces, he's trying to be kind.

"No more After Hours?"

"You were planning to eat with Stephanie and Ian. Still hungry?"

Luna takes her skin off the cold glass. She sees the red splotches she created in her side mirror.

"Food factor?" Ronen asks. His smile is small, but it's there. "Resistance is futile."

Luna's not hungry, but they can't circle the city forever and the minute she walks through her own front door, whatever she feels now will penetrate deeper.

"Food factor high," she answers in her best Captain Kirk voice. "Let's give it all we've got."

Ronen flashes a real smile at her and does a U-turn. Luna feels better, but the moment is thin. At least she'll have more time to absorb this news if they can stay out of the house a little longer. Her mother has hopped from one bankrupt business to another and now she's maxed herself out, and talked her husband into taking a loan.

Luna has no doubt her mother leaped at the idea. She was bound to get bored of the corner store goldmine idea in less than a year.

The bank loan wasn't enough money, so Judith stole Ronen's ID and took a credit card in his name and ran that up to its zenith, too. That's fraud or something Luna learned about in an introduction to business high school course. The same course that taught them to fill out checks, though Luna never needed a lesson on that.

She's watched her mother burn through checkbooks as though they're cooking fuel.

Luna will be her mother's next target when the restaurant implodes. Maybe she's already started practicing her daughter's signature too. It's not as if she doesn't have access to her ID. Luna can't let this happen.

Judith knows nothing about running a restaurant and some lonely old friend has charmed her and her father into believing she can not only run it, but partner with him, take on half of the expenses, sink herself in debts.

"What's done is done," Ronen says. "We'll only make things worse fighting with her."

"Is that your way of saying you're not planning to mention this credit card?"

"Her denying it will only make it worse."

"For who?"

"For me," Ronen answers.

Luna has nothing to add to that. She twists her watch on her wrist. She bought it for $20 and Aiden replaced it for her graduation with a silver one and she struggled to tell her friend this cheap one *is* her, it's the one she *should* wear. Now she sees what Aiden saw. It's more of a toy than a watch.

Ronen pulls into a Swiss Chalet. The smell of chicken roasting on a spit fills the air, even from inside the car. When Luna gets out into the parking lot, the hail hits her like a bucket of ice water.

Chapter 23

A bang on the window makes Luna look up from where she paces on the sidewalk. Aiden waves and signals she'll be out in ten minutes. Luna gets it. Mr. Betel's around. Luna must disappear.

It must be bad if Aiden's worried about her dad checking the driveway when the family's only minutes out of their mourning period. The latest news about the Levis' new restaurant is floating around the community airwaves. Funerals and shivah homes can be good places to gossip. Luna rubs the back of her neck. She shouldn't be worrying about things that may not even be true. She focuses on putting one foot in front of the other.

Luna walks to the corner, head down, her hands deep in her jacket pockets. She waits, her back to the road, her eyes lowered. Once she's out of the line of vision of Aiden's father, she looks around. She's always loved how the wide tree-lined streets in Aiden's neighborhood are decorated in nature's gold, orange and yellow. She soaks up their natural brightness, hoping to erase the toxicity of Aiden's dad, who would be sending her get-lost vibes if he knew she was here. Five minutes passes. It feels like half an hour.

"I thought my aunt would never leave," Aiden calls out her car window. "My dad's put me on a timer. Let's hit Elgin Street for a quick breather."

Luna hops into Aiden's Volkswagen and they speed away.

"Sorry about the wait at the corner thing," Aiden says. "My dad."

Luna holds up her hand and her bracelets jangle. "I get it. Your dad's buddies with all the bank guys. I can imagine."

"So, something is up," Aiden says.

"How's Montreal?"

"It's great." Aiden says. She whisks in and out of traffic. "Nice girls, super professional track team, and teachers are okay, too."

"So, I can stop feeling guilty?" Luna asks.

"For what?" The car slows. Aiden glances at Luna.

"You know what."

"None of this is your fault. My dad was waiting to pounce."

"Guess so."

They don't speak as Aiden eases into the turning lane.

"The truth is I like getting away from my father. Not being watched 24/7."

"I'm happy for you," Luna says and she means it, even though it hurts.

"Are you?" Aiden asks.

"Freedom from overbearing dad. What's hard to get?"

"And what about your freedom?" Aiden says.

Luna licks her lips. She flicks on the radio. Country and Western music fills the car and Luna doesn't bother to turn the dial. It's a message to Aiden. She's not ready to talk.

Soon they're strolling on one of their favorite places, an elegant street that runs north/south through the city's downtown core. Luna plods forward shoulders down, appearing to hug the sidewalk as though she'd like to vanish as they head south, towards the business district bursting with shops, restaurants, and bars.

"This is the most sophisticated street in the city," Aiden says. "Don't you love it? Feels so good to be out after being plastered to a tiny chair for a week."

"It must be hard to know your grandmother's gone," Luna says. She takes out half a roll of Lifesavers from her corduroy pocket, tears open the end, and pops the remaining candies into her mouth, crunching loudly and avoiding eye contact.

"I'm lucky I had that last trip to Vancouver. We talked so much. She still had her strength then. You know she never liked my mom, too dark-skinned," Aiden says. "But nobody's perfect, I guess. She gave me so many blessings and her engagement ring. I'll show it to you when we get home."

"She never liked your mom?" Luna says.

"My grandmother was very light-skinned. She wanted my dad to find a light-skinned Moroccan girl like her but he found a super dark one instead."

"That's us," Luna says. Luna and Aiden are often mistaken for sisters—or used to be when they lived in the same city. It was common for girls in their high school to ask them which tanning salon they use to get such "even tans." Aiden insists Luna looks Moroccan and Luna counters Aiden looks Yemenite.

The girls continue to window shop, arms linked. There are enough people around to create energy, but it's not crowded this first Sunday in February.

Staring hard at Aiden, the underlying contentment in her face, the confidence that surrounds her, Luna's heart wobbles. She hates playing the role of the damsel in distress, casting Aiden as her savior. She's not her mother.

"So, this is it," Aiden says. "My first year's well underway. You'll catch up to me soon."

"You bet," Luna says.

Luna doesn't want to say she'll have to quit her job, maybe by next week. A restaurant is full time. Luna fiddles with the silver bracelets on her arms.

"Hot chocolate. My treat," Aiden says. She stops at an outdoor kiosk and buys two large hot chocolates with extra whipped cream. She hands one to Luna and takes a long sip.

Aiden downs her drink and Luna wishes she would schlep it out instead, but that's never Aiden, who does everything decisively with confidence in minimal steps.

"Whatever it is, you can tell me," Aiden says.

Luna hugs her hot chocolate.

"And I love you no matter what, *chabibi,* friend," Aiden continues.

"Thanks."

"You going to tell me what's wrong?" Aiden asks.

"There's a lot in the way," Luna answers.

They both flop onto the nearest bench and Luna takes the opportunity to close her eyes and collect herself. Ronen's been up every night this week all pumped about this new restaurant her parents bought.

This time he has no choice, he's a partner now, unwilling or not. He'll never say a word to their mother about the credit card. He'll find a way to pay back the loan and keep his mouth shut. He's too well-trained to keep his parents' imperfections buried, another one of Ronen's code words, imperfections.

Last night Luna sat with her fists in her eyes listening to her brother drone on about the cascades of money he anticipated flowing in through their new family restaurant. Her mother promoted him from extra to main character in her mind, the restaurant their new set.

Now, when Luna opens her eyes again, Aiden's using the nearest display window as a mirror.

"Before you ask, no your boobs don't look too big in that tight sweater," Luna says.

"Not sure I agree," Aiden says. "And you look like you need more than a hot chocolate." Aiden says. "Should we get Beaver Tails to go?"

"Extra-large," Luna says. She can smell the fried doughy pastries from here. There must be a street vendor nearby.

Ten minutes later Luna's enjoying a hot pastry covered in maple syrup.

"Did I tell you there's this gorgeous new guy?" Aiden asks. She eats her pastry like a rolled-up pita. "A little on the short side, but you look good in heels."

"I have bad memories of needing to wear them at After Hours."

"You can take mine."

"Ian Angel, right?"

Aiden slaps her hand against her cheek. "You know him?"

"Stephanie's new neighbor from Winnipeg," Luna says. "Her hometown."

Aiden clears her throat.

"Seeing a lot of Stephanie?"

"Kind of."

"Getting tired of waiting for her to show up?"

Luna stops drinking her hot chocolate and puts her hand on Aiden's arm.

"It's true, she's not good with time, but she has other qualities."

"Like what?" Aiden asks. She puts the last bite of her pastry in her mouth.

"Is it upsetting you? Me hanging out with Stephanie," Luna says.

"Never," Aiden says. "She's practically part of your family, right?"

"If you ask my brother, yes."

"I'm not asking your brother," Aiden says.

"She's around more than my father," Luna says.

Luna throws the rest of her pastry in the garbage. There's too much sugar in her mouth.

"So, Stephanie's introduced you to Ian?"

"I don't have time for guys." Luna won't tell Aiden she met Ian and he ignored her. More pity is not what she needs. Besides, trouble is cascading her way.

"I've seen him more than once," Aiden says. "Make some time."

"He sounds very together," Luna says. "Something I'm completely not."

"How many Sephardic guys do you think you'll find in this town?" Aiden says.

Luna looks at Aiden. She notices a new pair of earrings with a matching necklace. All gleaming silver. Her boyfriend Isaac made them himself under the trained eye of her father. It's no problem for Isaac to drive two hours every weekend to visit Aiden. Anyone would prefer the privacy. Now they can go out alone without her dad's presence always a possibility. At least someone benefited from that stupid corner store.

Luna pours the last of her hot chocolate onto the snow and tosses the cup. The last thing she needs is to get rejected by a stuck-up snob everyone's falling all over. She gets it. Ottawa has a small Jewish community and local Jewish girls are always on the prowl for new guys, and Sephardic ones are as rare as unicorns. But Luna has much larger problems. Aiden sits beside Luna and puts her arm around her shoulder.

Luna's eyes fill with tears.

"Speaking of time, I won't have much soon."

A flicker of concern flashes in Aiden's face. "What now?"

"It's not fair what she does to me."

"I know, sweetheart," Aiden says.

Luna feels herself beginning to cry and she pretends to look for something in her purse. She pops a piece of gum into her mouth.

"Not another pointless store?" Aiden says, squeezing Luna's shoulder.

"A restaurant," Luna answers. "With this guy, Angelo." She stares at her shoes, swings her legs back and forth like a toddler.

"And you're the waitress?"

Luna spits the gum out. "You know my mom's thing about honor and family," she says. "Her whole culture is about respect, family loyalty, putting the family first." She digs her heels into the sidewalk.

"I thought that was your dad's thing," Aiden says. "Your mom's different. You have to put her first and she puts you last. There's a word for that. Manipulation."

"She says her parents did the same."

"No, she says she did the same for her parents," Aiden answers. "Put them first. Except they were sick and it was her choice."

Luna shrugs. "You don't know how hard this is going to be. I can only imagine it myself."

"I'm sorry," Aiden says. "I wish my dad wasn't so tough. Half our house is empty. I could move back here and you could live with me. We could be sisters."

"That's even more of a fantasy than my mom leaving me out of her plans."

"Maybe this time the business will work."

"Now who is lying?"

Luna's voice cracks. Aiden holds out her arm and Luna takes it. The friends hug.

Chapter 24

"My dad's expecting me back," Aiden says.

The girls head to the car. Traffic's heavier than usual at 4 p.m. for a Sunday and they pull into the Levis' parking lot later than they planned. The sky darkens further. Aiden looks at her watch.

"Let me pop in," she says. She gets out of the car and locks it.

"It's not worth the risk," Luna answers.

"Just for a minute. I forgot. I have a surprise for you," Aiden says. "Stop thinking I care what your house looks like."

Aiden grabs Luna's hand and they walk to the front door.

"So where are Judith and Angelo?" Aiden asks.

Luna searches the parking lot.

"My mother's Oldsmobile's nowhere," Luna says. "Don't worry. No way she's home if her car's gone."

The front door isn't locked. Another sign Ronen's the only one home.

"What time change?" Ronen is saying when Luna and Aiden enter the living room. "Is there ever on-time with you? Should I be pleased about changing my plans? Maybe this is passive aggression. Maybe *you* don't want this relationship to work out."

Luna and Aiden exchange looks.

"Smells great," Aiden says. "Stephanie was here."

Stephanie's graduated from making perfect Yemenite *jachnun*, a pastry dough layered with ghee, rolled into a jelly shape and cooked overnight to superb *malawach*, a sweet flaky flatbread, and *kubaneh*, a slow-baked Yemenite brioche. Stephanie doesn't read between the lines when it comes to her own boyfriend. She's forever calling Luna exotic-looking, lamenting that Ronen got all the light European looks, and doesn't get it that her boyfriend hates to be reminded that his absent father's roots are North African. Even a plate of food in his own living room is too close. Yet she persists, determined to master Yemenite Jewish cooking and equally determined to get Ronen to embrace it.

Luna feels sorry for Stephanie when she sees the rejection on her face yet again after surprising Ronen with fresh toppings for the *jachnun* she made the night before. She'll stand there with a tray of freshly grated tomato and hot sauce (called *zhug*) or strawberry jam and honey looking as though she's on the verge of weeping.

Ronen will close his eyes and massage his temples as though the presence of fresh food prepared by a loving girlfriend gives him a headache.

"You're here," Ronen says instead of hello. "Aren't you banned for life?"

"Focus on your girlfriend, Ronen," Luna says. "You don't see Aiden here."

It looks as though Ronen hasn't shaved in a month and his plain white t-shirt hangs too low over his jeans. Ronen sticks his tongue out at his sister in response. Then folds his arms across his chest, showing off his biceps.

Upstairs, Luna can feel Aiden's eyes on her bedroom. Her room is what she'd call a level two mess if the rating scale was between one and three—clothes, textbooks and scuffed shoes lay across the floor in random piles. There are teen magazine pages taped onto the walls (a juvenile obsession Luna can't break) and cassettes in small towers against the wall on the floor. She did have time to make her bed this morning. She's grateful for that.

There are also no signs this is a Jewish girl's room. Besides the mezuzah on the front door, no one would guess a Jewish family lives here. Aiden's house is the complete opposite with menorahs, Sabbath candle sticks, shofars, dreidels, prayer books, and every other popular Jewish object anyone has ever made into art displayed on every living room wall and shelf. The Levi's don't have a display shelf, not even for their small brass menorah that's stuffed in a cupboard.

"Don't tell me?" Aiden taps her chin with her pointer finger. "Ronen's roped into this restaurant idea? Thinks it's his ticket to millions?"

"You're still the best prophet."

"Why thank you," Aiden says.

Luna sits on her bed with her chin in her hands and stares out the window. She needs the moment to pass, so Aiden will stop probing. Luna can't tell her that her own mother stole money from her brother. The shame is too great, even between best friends.

"Almost forgot," Aiden says. She digs her hand into her purse and comes out with a small jewelry box. "I told you I had a surprise."

"Overkill," Luna says. "You already updated my friendship bracelet."

"Late birthday present number two. Happy twentieth," Aiden says. "Sorry, it's only now."

"It's February, only a month late. You don't live around the corner anymore," Luna brings her hands together. She loves Aiden's presents. "And all I got for you was perfume."

"I love *Giorgio Beverly Hills*. Wear it every day. I want you to wear something every day from me, too."

Aiden pushes a box into Luna's hand. Luna takes the box and opens it. She pulls out a silver *hamsa* pendant on a silver chain. A *hamsa* is a palm-shaped amulet thought to protect against the evil eye, a popular symbol in Muslim and Jewish Sephardic and Yemenite cultures.

"This looks antique," Luna says.

"I had Isaac copy one from my grandmother. She must have had a dozen of those and she gave them all to me on that last visit. I want you to have one."

"You designed this for me?" Luna says.

"Well, Isaac made it."

Luna turns it over and finds her name engraved on the other side.

"To protect you against the evil eye," Aiden says. Luna meets Aiden's gaze and her friend's eyes tell her that Aiden believes she'll need protection. Luna's too scared to ask Aiden what she knows. Maybe Aiden's father did tell her something. Luna thinks again of her mom's new restaurant business, the one she forged her son's signature for and knows nothing about running.

Luna turns around and lifts her hair. Aiden claps the necklace around her friend's neck.

"Tell Isaac he's a master designer," Luna says. "I love it."

"May you only have a good eye on you this year, my friend, and forever,"

Aiden says. Luna squeezes her hand.

"Is that a blessing or a prayer?" Luna asks.

"Both."

"Then, *amen*," Luna answers. She's more moved than she's been in a long time. "And whatever you ask for me may you receive for yourself."

"May it be His will, *chabibi*," Aiden returns.

Aiden glances at her watch and her expression changes. Luna senses her friend's panic. She doesn't blame her. Aiden can hardly spit out a sentence around her father these days.

"I hate that I have to go," Aiden says.

"Me too."

"My dad's still directing my life," Aiden says. "Wait for me to contact you. It might be a while."

"My mom's directing mine," Luna says. "I know how to wait."

Chapter 25

The front door of Judith's new restaurant had already closed behind her when Luna hears it open. Stephanie Bakerman grabs her shoulders from behind and steers her into a corner behind the coat racks.

"You just carry on," she whispers. "You can't control this."

Luna has one eye on her mother in a green Peter Pan outfit, at least it's a dress and not a costume. She turns to Stephanie. "Thanks."

"I'm with you," Stephanie says. She slips off her coat and passes it to a waiter running the coat check. Luna does the same. The place is full of families with young kids and there's jazzy music on low.

"I've been around enough of your mom's opening nights. Too many," Stephanie says. "To think it started out with home Tupperware parties and jewelry potlucks in someone's living room and now it's come to this after that crazy corner store."

Luna swallows. Stephanie remembers everything. Luna wishes she had a potion to cure that.

Stephanie sticks her hand in her pocket and pulls out a letter. She waves it around. "There's a top makeup school in Toronto with my name on it. Either Ronen comes with me next fall or he can check his mailbox every day."

"Is that the plan?" Luna asks. "By the end of the summer you're gone?"

"It's the only plan," Stephanie says.

"You'll remember to call?" Luna notices Stephanie's on-trend makeup: blue eyeshadow and fuchsia lipstick. Her long curls unaffected by the wind and rain and the stylish braided bandana around her forehead. There's no doubting that whatever this school is in Toronto, she's an ideal candidate.

Stephanie grins to soften the sting. "You think some of your family's reputation hasn't rubbed off on me? It's better for both of you to get out of here."

"We all need somewhere to go then."

This is a good thing for Ronen and Luna wouldn't want to blow it in a fit of anger by blurting something she shouldn't. Her mom can manipulate Ronen better than Stephanie.

"Now you know," Stephanie says. "I'm not a secret-keeper."

"Like us you mean?"

"Yes, actually."

"Maybe my family's discreet?" Luna says.

"Right. In the same way your mom missed her Oscar," Stephanie says. She squeezes Luna's arm. It doesn't take the edge off. Luna hates that Stephanie's touched a nerve, her family and their endless supply of secrets. Her mother and her inability to keep her childhood dreams and adult disappointments to herself. Even Aiden's never brought things to the surface like this. Or maybe she has. Luna's snowed under with mixed feelings, a place she knows well.

"There must be dorm schools with scholarships somewhere," Stephanie says. Luna can't believe Stephanie doesn't put the brakes on. She's starting to suffocate in this corner. "Look at your jogger friend, what's her name?"

"Runner. Aiden." Luna's hand immediately goes to her necklace.

Stephanie slips a lipstick out of her purse and adds another coat. "Yeah, I hear her dad's never letting her back home. Schools like that are all over the country. They offer grants, scholarships."

"Got it," Luna says. She feels the twist in her smile and inches away from Stephanie. She waves at her mother, who is eyeing her from a distance. Her mom's eyeshadow is as powder blue as Stephanie's. Her mom's makeup is always for an audience. "We're missing dinner," Luna says.

"That's the idea." Stephanie whispers in Luna's ear, "I'm weaning Ronen off this. High school's long over."

It's on the tip of Luna's tongue to fill in the blank, to say it's his family she wants to wean him off, he left high school years ago at sixteen. But she pulls away from Stephanie and joins her mother behind the bar. Judith pours Luna a *Seven-Up* and adds a shot of grenadine. The Levis don't drink, something both of her parents have always agreed on. There are crimson and black streamers that read 'grand opening' and 'opening night' crisscrossed on the ceiling and free appetizers on a food table. Luna can't make out what all of them are, but there's a lot of parsley and dill and the herbal smell of bay leaves.

Luna notes the rainbow-colored popcorn for the younger crowd and the spicy chicken wings and dips for the adults. Waiters trail the dining room with free trays of soft drinks and the waitresses totter around in three-inch heels.

Luna loses track of Ronen and Stephanie within the first ten minutes. Stephanie's plan is working. They slipped out. Luna has to give Stephanie credit. She doesn't want Ronen to get attached from day one. At least her brother has someone around who cares enough to save him.

Luna spends the next two hours with her mother introducing her around to the people "who made this evening possible." She greets various bankers from the loans department, food suppliers, even electricians and plumbers. Her mother doesn't stop for a minute, so Luna's stomach remains empty until she finally retreats into the hot kitchen, the only place her mother will most likely avoid. The kitchen's not center stage. She digs around until she finds a dinner roll and a few pats of butter. She makes herself a plain sandwich.

The chaotic dance of the dinner rush ended at 8 p.m., two hours ago. A motley crew of misfits floated around Angelo, the chef, and the only person Luna recognized, cooking the food, deadlifting frozen chickens, stooped over the freezer, tasting a dozen dressings all at once.

The opening night's winding down to a few stragglers lingering over their coffees and Luna can't wait to go home, but so far no one with a car's going her way. Now Luna can hear her mom and Angelo arguing from the back of the restaurant's giant kitchen. She wipes the sweat from her upper lip.

Luna laughs at the time she wasted showering before she came. There are rings of sweat under her armpits. She needed another shower ten minutes after she walked into this place.

"What did you say?" Judith yells.

Judith and Angelo are downstairs in the storage room, but the door's wide open. No doubt anyone else poking around downstairs or using the washrooms on the bottom floor can hear them, too but awareness of anybody and anything around them was never one of her mom's strong points.

"Why did you have to flirt with that bank guy?" Angelo growls. "You got no respect."

"What guy? You imagine things," says Judith. "There are dozens of men here. I'm drumming up business."

Luna can hear Judith's high heels clacking on the tiled floor and Angelo's footsteps following them.

"Do you have to dress like this is one of your kiddie shows?"

"Now you're being ridiculous. You need some fresh air. You've been working too hard. I'm doing what I have to do to make this work."

Luna can't hear anything more except the occasional rattle of boxes. Oh God.

She doesn't want to know what's going on. She wishes she could fly out of here, but she's stuck waiting for a ride.

No doubt Chef Angelo *is* exhausted after bearing the brunt of entertaining the 100 people who showed up in a snowstorm for the opening and he's easily calmed. She wipes her hair off her face and paces. She did as her mother asked and showed up at the grand opening. Now she wants to go home.

Chapter 26

Luna gives up on her mother and Angelo. She's melting in the restaurant kitchen. She leaves and pours herself a glass of Sprite at the bar, fills it with ice and drinks it in one gulp. The drink menu catches her eye. She cannot believe her mother has gone from serving bacon lettuce and tomato sandwiches to Singapore Slings.

"Need a hand?" someone asks.

Luna looks up and it's Ian. She feels a nervous twitch run from her thigh to her ankle.

"A waiter or help in the kitchen?"

"I don't know," Luna says.

"I'm super organized and I worked at a place like this back home."

"You could leave your name and number."

Luna can't figure out if Ian remembers their meeting. He's still nice to look at, especially in the zip-up sweater he's got on. Luna wishes he wasn't.

"Pen anywhere?" he asks. "Paper?"

Luna glances around and finds a mason jar full of matches. She passes one to Ian.

"This will do," she says. She finds a pen behind the bar and slides it over to him. She stares at the walls, at the floor, at the ceiling. There's no way she wants this guy working for her mother. She'll throw out that matchbook as soon as he leaves.

"Who's this?" Angelo asks. Luna hadn't noticed him come behind the bar.

"Ian Angel," Ian says. He holds out his hand for Angelo to shake.

"Could use a job. Anything?"

"Wash dishes?"

"Sure," Ian says.

"Age?"

"Nineteen."

"Make sure you leave your number with lovely Luna here. Might take me a week to phone but I'll get to it."

Angelo shakes Ian's hand.

"Don't forget," Ian says as Angelo returns to the kitchen.

Luna can't wait for Ian to leave. He turns to her instead.

"I'm sorry I was so distracted when we met."

"Did we meet?" she asks. She taps her chin with her finger. "Oh, yeah. I remember now."

"I deserved that," Ian says. "I was stressed out, had a big fight with my mom. Major anti-social of me."

"That's okay," Luna says.

"Cool this is your place."

Luna can't think of a way to respond.

"Luna? Where are you?" Judith calls. For once Luna's thrilled her mother's calling her. She can't wait to get away from Ian.

"Hold up," Ian says. "Do you work here all the time? What about your brother?"

"No, not sure, excuse me."

Luna turns and leaves the bar. As she hurries toward her mother in the kitchen, she concentrates on the background music, which had switched from jazzy to the top 100 pop hits. Tears for Fears' hit song "Shout" takes over her thoughts.

As soon as she enters the kitchen, she takes the matchbook with Ian's number tears it to pieces, and throws it in the garbage. There's no way a cute guy like that will stick around once he figures out who she really is.

Chapter 27

Luna's at the beverage station. It's here that everything related to drinks hot and cold is stored for easy refill by the waitresses. There are spaces for sugars, creamers, straws, stir sticks, tea bags, serviettes and anything else a customer at a restaurant might want with his beverage.

Meters away, Luna's mother's behind the bar noting their stock of ice, olives, maraschino cherries, limes, lemons, different sized toothpicks, and miniature decorative umbrellas for alcoholic drinks. Her brother's playing a video game.

"You saving the straws?"

"Course, mom."

"Rinse and right back in the box. What do those dumb waitresses know? Every morning your father drops off the rounds. Saving us a fortune."

"Rounds?"

Luna twists her bracelets. If she wants to see her father, she should skip sleep in the morning and hop over here. She can no longer remember the last time she saw her father in person. Sometimes she forgets about him for a whole week and then something will remind her: a torn jacket in the hall cupboard, a broken comb in the bathroom drawer, a bottle of aloe vera hand lotion. Then her throat burns with acid for a little while or the room swims around her. Maybe she was supposed to write him back and when she didn't, he got angry.

"First McDonald's, then Burger King, Harvey's," Judith answers. "Straws, sugar, salt, pepper. Those dumb restaurants put it all out there for the taking, so he takes it."

"Why not?" Luna asks. Her heart sinks thinking of her father, in his silent role, like an extra in her mother's film. He loads his pockets with ketchups, salts and peppers from fast food restaurants every morning, pulling in and out of parking lots, filling up.

"Just make sure you clean the used stuff good. Shine it up."

"Right," Luna answers. She shakes her head and pins the hair off her forehead.

It's minus ten outside, but she's sweating in here.

"You listening? I'm not talking to your backside."

"Course, mom."

Luna keeps her eyes low until her mother strides through the swinging doors to the kitchen. She searches inside of herself for much needed strength and she finds it. Passover is at the end of March, not that they'll be even a mention of the holiday this year. She can swing lighting Hannukah candles on her own, but making a Passover seder requires a family.

A symbolic box of matzah will probably be the beginning and end of the holiday for her. She closes her eyes and lets herself drift. She remembers the seders when they were little. They would sit on huge colorful cushions on the floor around a low table her father brought from who-knows-where, Yemenite style. They ate *charoset* her father called *duka*, a mixture of dates, nuts, ginger, cardamom, wine, raisins and other spices spread on leafy green vegetables.

Luna's mind was quieter now, filled with the happy memory. She allows herself to feel hopeful. Maybe she can find a job as a counselor in a sleepaway camp somewhere far away. For the first time in her life, she's old enough to make a plan that excludes her family. She has to find the time to do it and the energy. Or maybe it's the belief that she can get away that she lacks.

"You can't run a restaurant any better than my ex," Angelo, the chef, screams.

Bursting through Luna's warm thoughts. Angelo's cliché huge belly has doubled in size since their opening night in February and the matching double chin that droops down to his grease-stained white apron is now a triple one.

Luna rubs her forehead with her palm. The words penetrate. She's never heard Angelo so angry.

"Will you cut that out!" Judith yells back. "We screw up and we'll both lose our shirts."

"*Malaka*, we already lost them. You've made sure of it with your crazy zigzag spending. One day you overorder and a week later you're running around cutting the lights as if that will make up for it."

"*We* aren't losing nothing," Judith says.

"Losing isn't enough for you. You have to lose B-I-G. Malaka."

"Who you calling malaka? You dumb, greasy Greek bastard," Judith fires back.

"You're the grandma of malakas and don't think I don't see you sneaking bags of stuff in here. Why do the waitresses need matching vests, eh? It's a uniform, not a costume. Tomorrow you'll have them in bunny ears and tails."

"Very funny. It's bowties tomorrow and it's classy, that's why," Judith answers.

Malaka is Greek for something not nice. *Idiot* or *dummy* wouldn't scratch the surface. The part about her mom charging nonstop useless items to the company credit card as a business expense is true. Updating waitress outfits is another one of Judith's new expensive past-times.

"Why do you think Nir was sleeping at my place?" Angelo asks. "He ran away. He left you with VISA, so he can close his eyes at night."

Luna cannot see Angelo, but she's certain he's cleaning his personal knives one by one, the ones he won't let anyone else touch. Soon he'll reach for the wooden box he keeps them in. He won't be slicing steaks today.

"Get it through your big fat head," Judith screams. "My husband never left me. You live close to his work. He never got used to driving on ice. He's from the Middle East."

"You believe that? He drove a tank in a war; he's worried about ice!"

Luna can see her mother aiming at Angelo, right above his ear with her pointer finger.

"Worry about your ex-wife."

"Nir's a smart guy!" Angelo says. "But he doesn't talk much. If I would have known what I know now."

"Then what?"

"*Audios, malaka.* Know what that means?"

Judith's runaway spending starts with hiring double the staff they need, ordering triple the food and bringing in expensive singers to entertain on weekends downstairs in the part of the restaurant they call The Cavern for evening entertainment.

Angelo could leave and save himself from losing his house in Kanata and his car. Houses are cheaper outside of the city and he didn't mortgage his home when he bought into this place. He was smart about that.

Luna's seen the tiny back office, rustled through the mail. Bills are piling like snowdrifts on the side of the highway and her mother's dream of a successful restaurant will take its place with the others. There are dozens of letters her mother burns when she thinks no one's looking. She feeds unpaid bills to matches and convinces herself that copies won't arrive.

In her mind, Luna's transfixed by the orange flames as her mother sets fire to the neat computer-generated first reminders and second reminders and final reminders with the red stamped capital letters: Payment Due.

"Don't worry, Mom," Ronen booms, as he pulls the levers of the Pac-Man game at the entrance of the restaurant. "Let him go. Luna! More quarters."

"Get your own quarters," Luna says.

She's sick of that damn game. Luna walks over and pulls the plug on the machine.

"Ronen didn't do anything to you," Judith says.

Luna ignores them both. She straightens as she continues to set the tables for the dinner crowd. She spaces the tables so people aren't on top of each other and to prevent a table for two from being overwhelmed by a large table. The lights are still dim from last night, so she brightens them.

Angelo taught her to dim the lights as the night wears on to keep the atmosphere gentle and calm. Calm people eat more. Bright lights make customers tense. With all of the screaming and slamming that just went down in the kitchen, Luna could turn on search lights.

"Who'll be the cook now?" Luna asks.

"Don't worry. Any slob can cook," Judith answers.

Luna can't think what the customers will eat, given the chef deserted, but she sets the two dozen tables. The fork on the left, the knife on the right, blade facing inward. One kiss-red linen napkin, matching red candle in the center, tall clear water glass, oversized metal soup spoon next to the knife.

Angelo finishes packing and huffs to his station wagon with two overflowing boxes under his sweaty armpits. He's still in his long white, stained apron as he drives off. His tall white chef's hat left behind on the pavement.

Chapter 28

Luna strains to listen over the elevator music that pumps through the place as she sees her mother beside the Pac-Man machine talking to her brother. If it was up to Ronen the whole restaurant would be filled with video games, Asteroids, Pac-Man, Space Invaders. Angelo put his foot down, insisting on only one machine.

"So, you like him?" Judith asks. "Here's to our new partner."

Like who? Luna missed that part of the conversation. She watches as her mother puts her hand on her son's shoulder.

"I *always* liked him. Oh, man. Game over."

Fear spreads through Luna. Her mind switches to crisis mode.

"Leave that for a few minutes, will you? Let's go to his place to seal it," Judith says, grabbing her son's arm and pulling him out the door as the three evening waitresses show up to work the nightshift.

"Where's Angelo going?" asks Yvette. Her blonde hair is piled high on her head. She must have crossed paths with Angelo in the parking lot.

"Hi ladies," Luna says, with fake enthusiasm. She ignores the question. The answer is too depressing and they'll find out soon enough. Judith and Ronen don't bother saying hello to their own staff, let alone respond to questions.

Luna was worried about how they'd manage without a chef a minute ago, but now she doesn't care. There's a much larger problem rocketing towards them. The words 'new partner' roll around in her head. Her mother's determined to prove herself. There's someone waiting in the wings and Angelo's barely screeched out of the empty parking lot.

If there's a fresh deal going down, tomorrow Luna will have to live with a whole foreign element in here. Anyone fished out by Ronen and Judith must be all wrong.

"I asked you a question," Yvette says. She snaps her gum. "Why was Angelo carrying all of those boxes?"

Yvette has a right to know what's going on, but Luna cannot bring herself to speak.

My mother got sick of running this place fifty-fifty with Angelo within a week and began looking for a richer partner behind his back. They probably plotted to bankrupt the place so that Angelo would take off. My mom always thinks there's something better around the next corner and she just threw the chef out on the street. You might be unemployed tomorrow.

"We'll have to ask my mother when she gets back," Luna says.

That satisfies Yvette and she returns to help the other waitresses. One vacuums the floor, while the other wipes the menus.

Luna twists one of the red cloth napkins between her fingers. She blinks back tears and considers pouring herself a drink at the bar.

"You guys wouldn't care if the boss's daughter takes a drink on her shift, would you?" Luna asks.

She glances at the waitresses, but not at anyone in particular. Yvette laughs, the other two shrug their shoulders.

She usually flits around the restaurant like a robot following whatever orders Angelo barks at her. Well, no one's in charge now. Her mother doesn't count. And she couldn't care less what the others think.

Luna marches to the empty bar, unscrews a bottle of vodka and pours a shot glass full. Screw them! Her mother, her father, Angelo, Ronen. Her mother has her here until 3 a.m. sometimes. It would serve her right if she worked drunk, wobbled around on other people's toes, puked down a customer's blouse.

Without Angelo they're below zero. An Arctic fishing hole offers more security. She'll have no way of saving money for college during another one of their brilliant searches for a slashed-price rental when they're kicked out of their home in a month or two. She might be homeless by summer, the talk of the town again.

Luna pours a shot of vodka. She used to watch the regulars at After Hours downing shots outside between joints. She remembers standing at the cash register at the After Hours listening to Gustav's lesson on shot drinking. She knows how it's done. One time won't kill her. She downs it. It burns from the back of her throat to her stomach, but it releases some tension. Once her coughing fit is over at the shock of the taste, she feels less murderous.

A vision of Aiden comes to her. She lost her. Aiden's having a grand time in Montreal and now she's in Toronto for the provincial track meet. Luna should be a part of that, but instead Aiden's there with her new friends, ones her father approves of.

Luna will pour herself a dessert vodka shooter and down it, just this once. In light of Angelo's sudden departure to wish him well on his journey.

"A good eye on you, Angelo," she whispers, twisting her *hamsa* necklace.

Lucky guy.

Chapter 29

The next day Luna places the photo of Aiden winning the track meet in Toronto in a transparent frame. Aiden stands on a platform holding a gold trophy and smiling. Luna flips the frame and reads her friend's note: *Your victory energy is magic.* Aiden didn't set out to run a race but to win.

Her happiness for her friend isn't enough to get her mind off her troubles. Ever since her mother mentioned this new partner, Luna's whole body's been on high alert. Beware signs flash in her head. The weight of her problems wraps itself around her ankles, but she fights. She can't go under. Every time she thinks she's getting close to the finish line; it moves out of reach.

Outside it's an early spring day for March. For a few minutes Luna watches the dark green leaves blow on the green ash trees under a blue sky from her bedroom window. She craves coffee. Sugary doughnuts. And fresh air. Soon she's on her way, hurrying, head down, refusing to look left or right, willing herself blind to anything that might stop her. The busses don't tempt her. She wants to use her arms and legs after sleeping off her exhaustion for almost a whole morning.

A steaming, sweet coffee and a buttery, creamy doughnut are the only things on her agenda before she has to face whatever her mother's bringing into her life. Luna has to be at work for the early evening shift. But not now. She's stolen a few hours for herself. She swings her arms in exaggerated motions, snaps her gum, and stamps her running shoes on the hard pavement.

Luna tries to think warm, happy thoughts to ward off what's waiting for her at her mother's restaurant. She dreams about drawing. Sketching the blooming flowers and getting it just right, the hardness of the graphite in the pencil in her hand, the control of her hands over her drawing. She can't go to a place close-by. Someone might see her. She chooses one in another neighborhood. The coffee shop is farther than she estimated on foot. It takes her a full hour to find it on four-laned Robertson Road. She doesn't care. The exercise clears her head.

The place is in full swing when Luna thrusts the door open. People huddle in orange, indigo, and forest green workout outfits. The floor's dirty from the comings and goings of hungry, impatient customers, many clutching briefcases, their eyes on the menu printed overhead. A girl with a pinched mouth and blue-streaked hair attempts to keep the floor dry with a mop.

Luna thanks her and slips her a dollar. She knows all about underpaid waitresses. She sips her coffee and licks the thick doughnut cream from her fingers. But the bad feeling that something awful is coming at them won't go away. She passes her hand over her eyes. Rubs her temples. She'll forfeit the syrupy smell of warmed pastries, fresh coffee, and hot sugar soon enough. She must enjoy it now. Her walk has made her hungrier than when she left the house. She sucks on her finger in an attempt to extract one hundred percent of the sweetness.

Luna takes her sketch pad out of her knapsack and unclasps her hamsa necklace. She hasn't worn it since Aiden gave it to her. Stephanie saw it and congratulated her on her authenticity and going back to her North African roots. Embarrassed, Luna took it off after that.

Luna doesn't want to represent a whole group of people, only herself like Ashkenazi Jews when they wear a Star of David or the two letters *chet* and *yud*, which spell the word *Chai,* life in Hebrew, another popular necklace charm. No one congratulates Ashkenazi Jews on returning to their Eastern European roots when they wear Jewish charms.

But today Luna thinks her reasoning was flawed. She loves the necklace. End of story. She noticed it on her desk and put it on. Now she sketches the bottom half first, making a deep bowl shape. It looks like a tulip. Then she moves on to drawing three erect fingers, pointing straight up. Shoot. She didn't bring another color to add a jagged edge.

"It's Luna, right?"

Luna looks up from her hamsa drawing. Ian's thick wavy black hair falls in ringlets behind his ears. He's wearing a soft blue ski jacket with the sleeves pushed up to the elbows.

There are thousands of people out there and the chance of anyone one of them showing up in this doughnut shop in the middle of the day who know her are next to zero. Yet, here's Ian where he's not supposed to be. She came for a refuge from her life, if only for an hour. No one is supposed to find her here. She's invisible. Luna closes her eyes and reopens them and he's there, like a candle in a window.

Chapter 30

"A touch of doughnut cream," Ian says. He points to Luna's chin. She wipes it on the back of her hand and tries to remember if she did anything to her hair before she left the house as if that would help after an hour's walk in the wind. Oh god.

"Remember me?" he says, extending his hand. "I see you like to draw."

"It's nothing," Luna answers.

Luna stops drawing and shakes Ian's hand. Her body tingles when her skin meets his and she can't ignore it. She shoves her sketch pad back in her bag. "I guess your mom never needed any more workers?"

"Nah," Luna says. She prays she's not turning red.

"I didn't even get a shot."

"There's busier places."

"Or I'm not making the right impression?" Ian says.

Their eyes meet.

"Ouch," Luna says.

"Caught you," Ian says.

"You did," Luna says. Her anxiety skyrockets.

"Levi, am I pronouncing it right?" Ian continues. "With the emphasis on the second syllable? The Yemenite pronunciation?"

"How did you know?" Luna asks.

"My aunt's married to a Yemenite guy and she's taken on customs I don't think he even knew he had. She even passes around a snuff box on Sabbath afternoons."

"My dad used to take out snuff on Yom Kippur right at the end of the fast," she says. "And take the evil eye away with an egg right before the beginning, pass it over our foreheads then crack it in water after the fast to make sure the evil eye was gone."

"I'll have to ask my aunt about that one," Ian says.

Ian smiles and Luna smiles back though she keeps her hand half over her mouth. She's not used to sharing old Yemenite customs of her father's with anybody.

Here in Ottawa, Yemen may as well be Venus or Pluto.

Luna feels more cheerful than she has since Aiden gave her the hamsa necklace. Maybe she misjudged him. Maybe she's so highly strung, so far away from sharing anything with someone her own age that she'll crack if she's not careful, like the egg on the Eve of the Day of Atonement, one for her and one for her brother.

"My brother would hate it if he knew anyone recognized his last name as Yemenite. He calls himself Ronen Levi with the English pronunciation."

"Yes, he said so."

"Right." She squirms in her seat. She's so stupid for bringing up Ronen. Talking about her brother is not inviting. She has to steer in reverse. No way Luna's letting Ronen hijack the conversation. She focuses on staying centered.

An awkward silence falls between them. Luna tries to channel Aiden. What would she do? When things get awkward, think of something that makes you smile, Aiden would say to her.

But one smile per conversation is more than her usual quota these days. Now all she can think of is how she tossed Ian's number when he came in for a job at the restaurant. Ian excuses himself and helps a waitress with a heavy box of supplies. Is he try to get away from her or just very polite? She forces herself to stop watching him as he holds the door open for another waitress carrying boxes and returns to her sketch pad.

"Mind if I sit?" Ian asks a few minutes later. "This coffee's burning my hand off."

"Of course, sorry," Luna says. She didn't notice he was holding hot coffee. She scoops her hair back into a ponytail and ties it with an elastic from her wrist.

"It's nicer when you show your face," Ian says.

"Thank you," she says.

"Thought you might like a fresh one." Ian puts his coffee down and takes another out of a take-away bag. "I'm sorry for how I acted that time on the track field."

"Don't apologize. I didn't even notice."

Ian looks at her and tilts his head to one side.

"Okay," Luna says. "Noticed a little."

This cute guy slid into the booth across from her and bought her a coffee. He has complimented her and apologized. He has had to move to another province and fought with his mom about it.

Now he's offering her one of his four chocolate doughnuts. He takes them out of the paper bag one by one. She chooses a chocolate doughnut, though she can't imagine eating it. She cannot get more cream on her face or turn down his gift.

For a minute they both sip their coffees and Luna nibbles at her doughnut while Ian downs his and begins another. One of the fluorescent lights above their table flickers on and off. A waitress stops at their table and refills the napkin holder. A second one heads to the bathroom with giant rolls of toilet paper in one arm and a bottle of Windex in the other. The smell of cleaning fluid overpowers the aroma of coffee and doughnut. Ian looks right into her eyes. Speak, Luna. Talk!

"So, you moved from Winnipeg?" Luna says. "With just your mom." She's so stupid. He's already told her that.

"Yeah. My parents divorced and my mother got a government job, and everyone in Fat Cat City works for the government, right? So here we are."

"Fat Cat City?"

"That's what Winnipegers call people from Ottawa."

Luna laughs. "Fat Cat City where us fat felines prowl," she says.

"Where you all have a direct line to the prime minister," Ian says.

"Like it," Luna says.

The doughnuts are a distraction. Luna cuts what's left of hers in half with a plastic knife. Then in quarters. The idea of having an honest conversation with this guy makes her want to sink to the floor. He'd run for his life. Then another voice. He's new in town. He hardly knows anybody. It's no big deal he's talking to her. He's that lonely.

Luna rubs her temples with her fingers. The coffee shop has emptied out. A waitress has put on the radio. Queen's Freddie Mercury belts out: "Another one bites the dust."

"Sorry. Did I say something wrong?" Ian asks. "Before about divorce? Your parents aren't?"

"Divorced?" Luna asks. "No such luck."

"Interesting answer," he says.

Luna looks at her hands. She's usually more careful with strangers.

"Why do you ask?" she says.

"Well, either something I said upset you or you just realized you don't like chocolate," he says. He hands her a napkin. Luna looks down again and sees she's shredded her doughnut. It's all over the table.

"Oh my gosh," she says. "I can't believe I did that."

Luna does her best to clean her hands. She shouldn't be here with this nice guy who she has now lied to twice and misjudged. Whatever's waiting for her at work, the last thing she wants is publicity. He hasn't been in Ottawa long enough to hear about her parents. Otherwise, he'd have spotted her and taken his coffee and pastry to-go. She glances at the clock. She has a meeting with her mom's new partner. The thought adds ten pounds to the worry in her gut.

"Have to go to work," she says. "It was nice to meet you."

She grabs her knapsack which has her work uniform, her ugly black skirt and crimson blouse, stuffed inside. The colors of the restaurant—the tablecloths, the napkins, the staff uniforms—are crimson and black. Dark, menacing colors.

"Hey, I was only kidding," Ian says. "Need a ride?"

"Enjoy your coffee. Don't rush out of here for me."

"I can't think of a nicer reason," Ian says.

Luna looks at the floor. She'd love a ride. Outside, there's little brightness left. Or she's blind to it. She imagines walking out of here with Ian. If he can appear at a coffee shop on a random day, her mother can too. Curvy women with large busts, red lips, and behinds that stick out with dyed blonde hair might transform into flashes of her mother at any time, if they've still got a wiggle when they walk. Tall men with broad shoulders, low hanging stomachs, and bow-legged knees become mirrored shards of Angelo.

"It's a small community here. Even Stephanie's family is away this week. Show me around?"

"Can't," Luna says. She has to work tonight and tomorrow night and every night until the restaurant collapses. She cannot get tangled with anyone, not today, not tomorrow. Not until she's managed to alter her entire universe. And anyone who knew what her life was like would run in the opposite direction.

"Tomorrow?" Ian says. His voice is like a warm blanket on her shoulders. She must fling it off.

"I work a lot."

"I have the new Elvis Costello in my car," Ian says. "The tape recorder works."

"Thanks, but I'm fine. Good luck finding a job."

Luna rushes outside before he can say anymore.

Chapter 31

The next day Luna's at her usual spot, the beverage station, polishing a heap of teaspoons and trying not to think about Ian, who must believe she's the least friendly person in the world. The front door opens.

"Luna!" Judith calls. "Come."

Luna's mouth runs dry. Her mother told her last night the new manager starts tomorrow morning. It's already late afternoon and he hasn't pitched. She's been hoping the deal has soured. Maybe Ian brought her some luck. She shakes her head. She's thinking like Stephanie. Maybe the guy wised up, checked out her mom's track record, or bumped into one of her ex-partners before he thanked his good fortune and fled.

"You hear me?" Judith calls again.

Luna drops the knives and makes her way to the entrance on lead legs. If she could she'd walk in reverse, run home, pack a bag, and keep running.

"Meet our new-old partner," Judith says. "You remember Flynn?"

Flynn whistles at Luna instead of saying hello. Luna rocks on her heels. Shock fills her, then recognition and fear. The atmosphere is intense as her eyes meet Flynn's. She feels an instant chill as he looks at her. He hasn't changed at all. Same jewelry, same suit, same expression like he can see her naked.

"Luna," Judith says. She nudges her daughter in the ribs.

"Hi," Luna manages to croak.

"Come on, Flynn," Judith says. "Mountains of work to do."

"This time's the charm, Judy," Flynn says. "Restaurants are much more my speed." He winks at Luna as he follows her mother into the kitchen. She wants to spit.

Ronen laughs from his usual spot by the Pac-Man machine. "Don't be so nervous. We're starting fresh." He calls Luna over.

"Relax, little sister," Ronen whispers in her ear. "I got a phone call from Toronto today."

"What? Is there yet another savior on the way from Toronto?"

"No, no, no," Ronen says. He stands too quickly. "Who said anything about saving?"

"So, what then? Is Angelo coming back?"

Ronen shrugs. "Don't think so."

"Then what are you talking about?"

"You're thinking too hard, Luna," Ronen says. He sits at the table behind him.

"Oops." He stands, cola dripping all down his butt. "Klutz."

Luna stares at him. She's sick of everything. Tired of spending so much of her energy trying to decipher her family's secrets, decode their messages, and sleep in their messes. She's had it up to here crunching on the matza she purchased alone. Nobody even bothered to mention it was Passover or comment on the cracker-like bread she purposely put in the center of the kitchen table to remind them. What's the use? The holiday has come and gone. Nothing matters to them anymore except this restaurant.

"Soaked through," Ronen says. "Coke flood. Listen, Steph's coming by with dinner, no fooling you. That was the call. I was just kidding about Toronto."

Luna puts her hands on her hips.

"You should take off early and be there."

"I just walked in," Luna answers. "If I get dinner it will be at 1 a.m."

"We'll save you some then. I'll finish up here, changing my shirt first."

Ronen saunters off to the bathroom fussing with his wet clothes. Luna stares after him, her arms crossed at her chest. Through the window a police car siren flashes red across the wall accompanied by a piercing wail. The sound fills Luna's ears, so if her brother had a message for her, it's drowned out.

Chapter 32

Every time Flynn's in the restaurant, he blabs about his business partner, Douglas. This means for the last month Luna hears about Douglas from morning until night. This happens every day after work and on weekends, unless she can beg a day off. Aiden says her father's watching her more closely than ever and she's sent several apology letters special delivery, but that's cold comfort for Luna.

There are only a dozen payphones in Aiden's dormitory for 200 students and Aiden often has to wait hours in line for a few minutes on the phone with a long list of people to call starting with her father and then her boyfriend, so phone calls to Luna are inconsistent. She's not allowed to leave the dormitory at night to use public phones, not if she wants to keep the budget her father's got her on. Often Luna's so tired from work that she can't say more than how are you and goodnight when Aiden does reach her.

The only bright spot is Ian who has become Luna's friend now that Aiden's gone. He's as happy to have someone in the city as Luna, who keeps her usual boundaries. He has his internship as a guidance counselor most of the day, but there's a space between late afternoon and early evening when they listen to music mostly in his car or grab an early dinner, which he insists is a late lunch. She never invites him to her house and she has to work every night. Visits to the restaurant are off-limits.

Luna's brain struggles to process the amount of damage this Flynn can do and that's before his friend shows. She turns to her notepad and her pencil that she always keeps in her bag, even at work.

She draws an isosceles triangle with a 'u' shape at the base and a cupid's bow across the triangle. After adding a curved line and erasing the sides of the triangle, she has the outline of a perfect pair of lips. She adds lip wrinkles and blends and shades and darkens. It doesn't take her long before she realizes she's drawn Ian's mouth. She swallows. She's never kissed a boy before. Another humiliation to add to her long list.

Luna stares at her sketch and runs to the bathroom where she stuffs her drawing back into her bag. She returns to the bar and tries to get a hold of herself, but her hands tremble at the idea of Ian kissing her and her kissing him back.

For once no one's paying attention to her. There's only one other waitress who has been fussing with the vacuum for the last twenty minutes and Gears, the new cook, doorman and everything in-between, is in the kitchen, chopping feathers off chickens with punk music on full blast.

Luna spots Flynn's black Cadillac pulling into the driveway and any thought of romance with Ian vanishes. She prays Flynn's trying to freak them out, intimidate them with his creepy Douglas tales. Her mother insists that's the case.

She tallies how much of what she's heard in her life she's wished to be the work of someone else's active imagination. Luna takes a beer from behind the bar, pops it open and takes a long sip. Beer isn't alcohol, at least not while she's forced to work here.

There was a time when Luna had looked at her post-graduation year as the entrance to adulthood and, by extension, freedom. How could she have made such an incorrect assumption? Things are worse than ever.

Luna's pulled in two directions. She doesn't want to set foot in the place, but when she's not here, she breaks into a sweat, freaking about what the hell might be happening. Then, as soon as she's back behind the restaurant doors, she berates herself: *family loyalty will get me killed.*

For Luna, it's astonishing how Judith reacts to information about Douglas, her voice breathy, her eyes wide like a model in a shampoo commercial.

Luna bites her nails listening to Flynn yakkety-yak about his adored Douglas. Luna grasps that Flynn believes women are aroused by his cheap, stinking cops and robber talk. Otherwise his stories are too bizarre, even for him. A restaurant manager who spreads information about a convicted hired killer on his way through the front door any day, any minute.

In her weaker moments, Luna tells herself her mother is right and Flynn's lying. She soothes herself with these words like cool talcum powder on a hot burning rash when she can't sleep for the nightmares. But Flynn babbles about Douglas more every day. It's obvious that Douglas, an ex-con even more dangerous than Flynn, is on his way. Her mother didn't just make a deal with one devil, but two, and the consequences of those choices now loom ominously over their lives. He must be getting closer. He's getting closer. Luna sleeps less and less.

Deep in her core, Luna knows it's all true. Every one of Flynn's stories is echoed in the newspapers and she's exhausted both her old high school and city libraries. It's only a matter of time until Douglas steps in and her mother disappears.

Chapter 33

The following week Luna's standing at the bulletin board reviewing her upcoming shifts. Flynn pins the weekly work schedule every Wednesday morning.

"What's this?" she says to her mother, who sits beside her assembling take-out boxes. Ronen's helping Judith, reviewing the orders for any missing items and placing them in take-out bags. They're both ignoring her as if it takes the most intense concentration to box chicken cutlets and fries and toss in disposable ketchups, salts and peppers.

"What's what?" Judith says. "Did I show you the note some guy left me on the back of his receipt the other day?" She flips up her collar prep style.

"Five times," Luna says. "I'm glad you're still getting phone numbers at your age, mom, but could you pay attention to me?"

Judith stops opening cardboard boxes and her blue eyes meet her daughter's black ones. Ronen continues to review his list.

"It says I have tomorrow night off. Since when do I get a free Thursday night? Is this a mistake?"

Luna notices Ronen sway backwards in his chair. She senses a rise of tension. Her brother's knees are pressed together and his head is lowered.

"Your turn for a Thursday night off, that's all," Judith says. "Ran out of plastics."

Judith gets up and heads into the kitchen. Luna can hear her moving boxes in the storage cupboard.

"I happen to have tomorrow night off, too," Ronen says. He still hasn't looked up.

"Is that so? As much as I'd love to be with you, maybe Ian's free," Luna answers.

Ronen clears his throat. "Hang out with me and Steph. Dinner."

"Since when? For what?"

"We missed your birthday, right? Come straight home after work tomorrow."

"My birthday was in January," Luna says. "It's May."

But Ronen's gone, takeout orders stacked in his arms, before Luna can say anymore.

The next afternoon Luna understands as soon as she walks into the house and smells the combination of lemon Pledge and Windex that something extraordinary has happened. Ronen has cleaned the house. It's either the end of the world or he has some big news and if his news compelled him to clean, it's not good news for her.

Luna lets this information sink in. She takes her time changing out of her running clothes. She's been running more since she met Ian or whenever she can. She rubs her feet that are still sore from standing for hours last night behind the bar, placing her running shoes in the hall cupboard. She goes to the bathroom and washes her hands for longer than necessary at the sink. She splashes warm water on her face and neck.

Luna hears the vacuum upstairs, the rumble of the washing machine competing with the purr of the dryer. Something's up. She hums to herself as she dries each finger and struggles to tame her curls, almost impossible in this humidity.

The smell of spicy food attracts her to the kitchen and repels her as a warning. Even this sad kitchen looks decent. There are no dirty dishes in the sink and the floors were cleaned with real cleaner. The counters are cleared and the broom and dustpan are put away, instead of leaning against a cupboard. The garbage can's empty and new. They accomplished a lot since she left the house an hour ago. Too much.

Luna tries to guess what disaster's coming. She has not had enough time to put all the pieces together. The place smells less like soft lemon Pledge and more like sharp bleach the longer she's home.

Luna sits at the table set for four. There's no one to ask who the fourth guest might be. She feels the heat from the oven. She tastes the floor cleaner in her mouth.

"I'm here," Stephanie says. "Needed a few things."

Stephanie's voice booms through the kitchen all the way from the front hall.

Luna stands to see her too wide smile, her hair too perfect for the humid weather. She's weighed down with shopping bags, three in each hand. Luna watches her wipe the wet off her sandals from this morning's rain and hang up her cotton pastel-colored cardigan. She puts her matching sunglasses in the pocket. Stephanie's face is flushed from the heat. June is around the corner.

"Give me a sec," Stephanie says. She zips downstairs with the bags.

Luna smells her vanilla perfume as she runs past. Two minutes later, Luna hears Stephanie stomp up the stairs.

"I bet you need a break," Stephanie says, coming into the room.

"What's a break?" Luna answers.

Stephanie laughs, but Luna isn't trying to be funny.

"Ian says he'll call you later," Stephanie says. "Ran into him at the store. I hear you're chatting all the time."

"Here and there," Luna answers. She cleans her nails with a toothpick.

"He mentions you whenever I see him," Stephanie says. "I've told him how amazing you are."

Luna sticks her tongue out.

"I'm totally with you playing the hard to get thing."

"No playing," Luna says. "I work every night in a gang hangout. He deserves better."

"That's temporary," Stephanie says. "Don't overdo the let's-just-be-friends thing. You're not the only girl okay with short guys and he's only three months younger than you and solid."

Luna makes a face. It crosses her mind that the fourth plate might be for Ian. She can't decide if she would like that.

Stephanie gets busy taking hamburgers and fries out of the oven. In a few minutes the table's decorated with small bowls of condiments, coleslaw and sour pickles. This is Ronen's favorite meal. No *jachnun* and crushed tomatoes today.

They're celebrating something and Stephanie's trying to relax Ronen or bribe him or compensate. Luna ponders the possibilities and tugs at her sleeves. She notices a stain on her shirt. Another thing ruined.

Ronen comes downstairs and smiles at his sister. She frowns. He sits next to Stephanie, who pats the seat beside Luna. But Ronen doesn't move. So, the couple sits across from her with one empty seat beside Luna.

"All here?" Luna begins as she helps herself to a burger and a huge pile of fries. She's starving. She can't stomach the cheap cuts of chicken at the restaurant and skips dinner most nights. Aiden's no longer in town to share her dinners. Whatever it is Ronen's about to throw at her, an empty stomach won't help.

"You planning to tell me what all of this is about?"

"Where are the compliments on all my blood and sweat?" Ronen asks. He speaks with a forkful of coleslaw in the air.

"The only things missing are the balloons and the cake," Luna says.

"Right, your birthday," Stephanie says. She sits on the other side of Ronen and munches on a pickle. "Happy twentieth."

Stephanie kicks Ronen under the table. "*Yom huledet sameach, achoti,*" Ronen echoes his girlfriend in Hebrew. "*Ad meah v'esrim.*" He adds a blessing that she should live until 120.

Luna mutters a thank you and finishes her hamburger. It's delicious, but she's not in the mood to dish out compliments. She can wait for what these two are really serving.

"Tell me already," Luna says.

Stephanie and Ronen stop eating. Ronen doesn't look at his sister. Luna straightens. Her patience is running out.

"You know Flynn?" Stephanie says.

"Yes," Luna says.

"And?" Stephanie says.

"And he's all the bad things my mother attracts," Luna says.

"This next one, this Douglas Bald, is worse," Stephanie says. "The worst."

"Tell me something I don't know," Luna says.

"All right," Stephanie says. She plays with her napkin and pushes her plate away. Ronen's already at the sink washing dishes. "Did you know he's getting out of jail like yesterday?"

Luna can't speak. Her hamburger threatens to reappear in her mouth. There's no point in arguing because she's right. Her mother keeps hitting new highs in catastrophe. Luna tries to predict what the coming weeks will bring. Her mind fills with fog. She has no desire to clear it. She'd rather get lost in it and stay there for a while.

"Mind getting the door?" Stephanie says to Ronen.

"What door?" Luna asks.

"It's for you," Ronen says.

There's the creak of the front door opening.

"Hello? Anyone home?"

It's Aiden voice.

"You invited Aiden?" Luna says. "She's come from Montreal on a Thursday?"

"Figured it would be easier to have a friend around when—"

"When what?" Aiden asks. She's brought everything beautiful about spring in with her. Tanned complexion, fire red heels and a long, indigo tunic. She commands attention in the room like a bouquet of flowers. Luna jumps up and hugs her friend.

Aiden has her own problems. She has to stop seeing her as a life raft.

"Those salads look gourmet," Aiden says. She pats her flat stomach.

"You sure your dad didn't hire a thug to follow you?" Stephanie asks. She forces a laugh, but her joke doesn't work and Aiden pales and glances toward the door.

"My dad thinks I'm shopping. I'll grab something from the mall on the way home."

"So, where were we?" Stephanie says. She flips her hair over her shoulder and fiddles with the gold Star of David hanging low over her ribbed shirt.

Aiden washes her hands and comes to the table.

"You know Aiden doesn't eat meat, right?" Luna says to Stephanie. Her voice is strained. Her eyes beg Stephanie to change the subject while Aiden's here.

"I'm great with these salads and fries," Aiden says.

Stephanie looks at her watch. "Didn't have time for a vegetarian menu. Actually, Ronen and I are in a rush." Stephanie moves her chair closer to Luna. She holds her attention with her eyes. "You know a guy like Flynn's introduced your mom to a whole new friend set and she's more desperate than ever," Stephanie says. "And this Douglas is the icing on the cake."

"Enough, Steph," Ronen says.

Stephanie clears her plate and Luna hears her go upstairs to Ronen's room.

The clock on the oven ticks in the silence.

"I'm leaving, we're leaving," Ronen says. "We got a free place in Toronto. Her grandparents need a house-sitter while they're in Miami."

"That's a five-hour drive," Aiden says.

"Half an hour on a plane. I'll pay Stephanie back for the ticket. Douglas was the last straw."

"For Stephanie, you mean?" Luna says.

Ronen looks at his hands. Luna exchanges glances with Aiden who excuses herself to go to the bathroom.

Ronen leans closer to Luna. "Stephanie thought we could wait until the fall but we can't. Mom's gone too far with this Douglas guy." Ronen rubs his eyes with his hands. "And we'd be crazy not to take this free apartment."

"It's too much," Stephanie interrupts. Luna never saw her return to the kitchen. "Even for your mom. This Douglas is really bad news. You could end up in jail. I can't risk that for us."

"You're leaving me here? Mom agreed?"

"Nobody asked her," Ronen says. "She knows what she's done. She can't exactly say no."

"Have a great new life in Toronto."

Aiden returns to the table. "Luna," Aiden says. "Slow down. I didn't catch everything, but I'm sure it's not that instant."

"We're leaving tonight," Stephanie says.

"I thought you'd become her *real* friend," Aiden says to Stephanie.

"I am. Always have been."

"Since when do real friends take off? Why not wait until the fall, see this through with her?" Aiden says. Her eyes are intent on Stephanie's face.

"Who played her up to Ian? Who comes over all the time with food and helps around the house like it's my own? It's easy to talk from your mansion or from your perch in Montreal." Ronen puts a hand on Stephanie's arm but she continues. "Did you stand up to your dad when he sent you away from your best friend? I bet he threatened to cut off your allowance or take away your car and you brushed up on your French *tout suite*," Stephanie says. "Let's go, Ronen." She stomps out of the kitchen without looking back.

Ronen looks from Luna to Aiden. He twists the buttons on his shirt. "Where would I be without Steph?"

Luna keeps her eyes on the table. The coleslaw's drowned in ketchup and the guacamole's turned brown.

"Why did you drag Aiden here?" Luna bursts. "Don't I get to decide anything for myself?"

"I thought it would help to have a friend when I told you," Ronen says. "It might have been stupid."

"Might?" Luna says. She swings her legs in her chair and rocks the table.

"I figured you could stay with us for the summer. There are way more places for you to work in Toronto, lots of Jewish camps that need counselors. I'm setting us up for before you come. Think of it like that."

Luna closes her eyes.

"I'm sorry, Luna," Ronen says.

With her eyes still closed, Luna hears Ronen walk up the stairs, call his girlfriend's name.

"I want to help," Aiden says to break the silence.

"You can't," Luna says. "Some things no one can help. It's not like I can't see how scared Ronen is of losing Stephanie."

"It's you I'm worried about," Aiden says. "Where are you going?"

"To find my notepad." Luna searches in her schoolbag for her notepad and charcoal pencils. She thinks best while drawing. At the kitchen table she chews on the end of a pencil and stares at the blank page.

It's Aiden's turn to swing her legs. She moves the salt and pepper shakers around on the table. She throws out the salads. Luna clears her throat. It's hard for her to concentrate with Aiden fidgeting.

"We don't *have* to talk," Aiden says.

There's a knock at the door.

"Let me get it," Aiden says. She rushes to the door.

"Isaac? What are you doing here?"

Luna can hear most of their conversation from the kitchen. She prays Aiden won't invite Isaac in.

"Came to warn you. Your dad's figured out you're not at a mall."

"What? How?"

"I don't know, but he's called me twice and I'm running out of excuses. You need to leave. I'll catch up to you."

Aiden returns to the kitchen.

"I heard," Luna says before Aiden can talk. "It's okay. Call you later."

"Promise?" Aiden says.

Luna nods.

They don't speak while Aiden grabs her purse and leaves with her car keys in her hand. They remain silent as Luna walks Aiden to her car. She can't help looking around for Mr. Betel. She watches Aiden drive away.

Luna returns to the kitchen ready to give it to her brother now that Aiden's not here to calm her. Instead she finds a spotless table. The countertops are clear.

"Ronen," she calls. "Stephanie?"

Even the air is still. She hears a bang and heads downstairs.

They don't have a basement but a spare room and bathroom one flight of stairs down with a back door. It's the same one they use to give debt collectors the slip. It's not closed. The spring wind blows right through Luna. She hugs herself and swallows hard. Ronen and Stephanie are gone.

Chapter 34

Luna has even less time now. Each absent person diminishes her energy bit by bit. Her mother, her father, Aiden, and now Ronen and Stephanie. She's been so busy that she's lost her favorite necklace; the hamsa necklace Aiden gave her for her birthday is gone. She's opened every drawer in the house, peeked under every bed, nothing. She feels robbed. She can't shake the feeling that a force of some kind made her necklace disappear, the way Mr. Betel zapped Aiden out of town with a stroke of a pen. Now a similar energy took away her good eye. Or is it a signal from the charm itself? Its vanishing is a way of telling her that she cannot be watched over, so it has left her for some other dimension of lost things.

Out on the street, a DJ's voice is booming out of someone's car. Luna opens her bedroom window wider, appreciating the company. She feels a stab of annoyance thinking about her brother and his girlfriend free in Toronto.

Ronen's called her a few times since he left, but she always tells him she's just on her way to or from work. She's not ready to hear about his new, mom-free life. Luna stops drawing and sticks her head out the window, so the sun can shine on her, but it's already a grey-blue dusk.

The sketch pad calls her back. As Luna doodles, a realization comes to her. She thought she was the lynchpin, holding the family together, and she drew strength from that. It gave her a map to follow. Now Ronen's proved her wrong, just like that. Luna feels the snap of truth in her bones.

It's Stephanie her brother's held on to. Luna's no one's captain. Her decisions, her actions, none of it influences anyone in her family. The four of them are in separate lanes. She sees that now. Her eyes puff with tears.

Luna understands why her father enjoys jewelry design. Just the thought of sketching and her shoulders relax. Luna tries to draw the view from her bedroom window again. She remembers her fourth-grade art teacher.

"There's nowhere in life that a black edge actually exists," Mrs. Sherman used to say. "In life color shifts. You must interpret these changes, on the page. Do you know what interpret means?"

Fourth grader Luna didn't know what her teacher was talking about, but twenty-year-old Luna understands every word and her mouth sours. She still cherishes the memories and the feeling of being a magician that came over her in first-grade drawing classes.

"Draw what's there, not what you believe is there, Luna," Mrs. Sherman said.

By the time Luna started high school, her drawing teacher had retired and Luna was into creating concepts and character designs. She still dreams of becoming an illustrator, sitting in a cool leather chair during her meetings in her private office.

In her fantasy, she'll spend time with important authors of children's books and graphic novels, who leave the depictions of their precious ideas in her hands. She'll consult with famous cartoonists like her new icon, *Far Side* creator, Gary Larson. They'll debate over sketches, consider revisions, and settle on characters that will become icons for children and adults worldwide. People will fall in love with the artwork of Luna Levi, write her letters of appreciation, and she'll respond to every one of her fans.

Luna uses an old spiral photo album as a surface to doodle on, half lying in bed. She's too tired to sit at a table. It's the only family album in the house. The neglected book has a floral plaid print on a black satin cover. The corners are ripped and if Luna didn't have the album to prove the Levis had ever done ordinary family things, she wouldn't believe it. She can't explain why she keeps it under her bed but she does, adding dust to the pages.

When she stares at the dozen photos of Sundays on Mooney's Bay Beach with her parents and Ronen, she feels no connection to any of the people in the picture, including the brown-skinned, black haired, overweight girl tilting her head to one side.

Now Luna rubs her eyes and drags her hands through the knots in her hair. It's all she can do not to drop her pencils and pull the blanket over her head. But she does have some beautiful pencils her parents once bought her as a birthday present.

They're super smooth to use and leave velvety marks on the page. They didn't even do that right, buying a girl not even bat mitzvah'd enough for a ten-year supply. Something they share, no sense of proportion. There's usually nothing of whatever you're looking for in the house, but if there's something, there's enough of it to last into adulthood. At least this saves her from spending her tips on art supplies.

Luna picks up a chalky white shade determined to get the willow tree outside, it's tapering finely-toothed leaves on paper. Instead she looks down and realizes she's sketched the restaurant in exaggerated lines. All she's missing are candles and cobwebs. She leans her forehead on the window pane. And then she sees the car with

Ian at the wheel.

Chapter 35

Luna jumps back from her bedroom window. It's too late. She can see Ian looking up at her. He waves. She returns to the window and waves back. She forces herself to smile, though it doesn't override the twinge in her stomach. That primal fear Luna has of anyone inside her home, as though they're pulling back the curtain while she showers.

Luna runs her brush through her hair and speeds downstairs. She shoves her feet into her sandals. There's no way she's inviting anyone in. He's seen the outside of her house, the unkept lawn, the weathered front door, the broken front step and rusty mailbox. It's more than enough. Then there's the real danger that Judith could appear unannounced with her ex-convict business partner.

Luna yanks the front door open. Ian's on her doorstep with his hands in his jean pockets.

"You're not at work," Ian says.

"Not now," Luna answers.

"Must be my lucky day. And yours," he says. He pulls his hand out of his pocket. "Found this." He opens his palm and reveals Luna's hamsa necklace.

"Oh my gosh," Luna says. Luna's hands fly to her neck and then her cheeks. "Thank you. I was so upset about this. You could have waited until tomorrow, but I'm so glad you didn't."

Luna turns, lifts her hair. His fingers rest on her neck as he closes the clasp and she feels his breath on her skin. With her necklace on, she faces him and forces herself to keep her eyes off his fingers. She fiddles with the charm.

"I stopped to pick up some doughnuts on Robinson Road and the manager said she'd found this a while ago."

"I remember something like that now," Luna says. "I was drawing there." She's aware of her loneliness leaving her and smiles at Ian, willing him to understand why she won't invite him in.

"Aiden was smart to engrave it," Ian continues. "The manager remembered I was there the day she found it and voila!"

A flash of an Oldsmobile catches Luna's eyes. Her smile fades. She clears her throat. The space created when loneliness left her fills with fear. She doesn't want to be here with Ian when her mother arrives.

"You free?" Luna asks.

"I was about to ask you the same thing. Feel like hanging at my place? My mom wants to meet you."

"What?"

"She doesn't know too many people here."

"Oh my gosh," Luna says. "You're worried your mom's lonely."

"More like, my mom's worried that I'm lonely and I want to take that weight off her. Make sense?"

Luna sees her mother park, open her door. Flynn's with her. Today he wears a tan cowboy hat with a silver buckle on the band and matching boots. The air goes stale. She must focus.

"Totally up for it." She reaches for Ian's arm. "Let's go."

"Really? I thought you might think I was pathetic."

She laughs instead of answering, trying to keep the nervousness out of her voice, while she steers Ian in the opposite direction of her mother and Flynn.

She concentrates on Ian's hands, his voice, his breath on the back of her neck only moments ago, anything to distract her from the ringing in her head that's getting louder the more she panics about what her mom and Flynn might be up to.

Chapter 36

Ian's mother sits on a white couch also dressed in white. She looks like someone in a magazine photograph in the sunken living room with her legs folded under her, scribbling in a diary, also white. When she realizes she's not alone, she startles and slides her diary under the couch. If Ian notices, he pretends not to.

The room couldn't look more different from Luna's own messy living room that until recently doubled as a bedroom for Ronen and occasionally her father, as well as a dining room. There's little to break up the white carpet and blank walls besides a metal side-table on bird-like legs.

Luna remembers this is a rental. The Angel family photos are probably crammed on a wall in Winnipeg in his father's home or packed in boxes, divided between two homes. Still, she's disappointed. She wanted to see Ian as an adorable kid in family photos. She'll have to wait.

For a second Luna smells the candy-sweetness that often hits her when she slides behind the bar at the restaurant, but that can't be right. The Angels don't stock maraschino cherries. Even when she's not at that horrible restaurant, its stench clings to her.

"*Neshamah*, sweetheart, you're back early." Ian's mother adjusts the oversized shoulders of her white blazer and tightens her belt in one lithe movement. "You could have given me a head's up. I would have bought real food."

"We're fine," Ian says. "There's plenty here. I want you to meet someone." He leans down and gives his mother a kiss on each cheek in the traditional Sephardi manner. "This is Luna Levi."

"Finally, you're here." Gal takes Luna's hand in hers. "Ian talks about you all the time."

"How nice to know, Mrs. Angel," Luna says. Ian's mother kisses Luna on both cheeks.

"Abi*gal*, gal not gail and everyone calls me Gal, but no one calls me Mrs. Angel anymore."

"Mom," Ian says. "You're family name's the same as mine." He puts his hand on his mother's shoulder.

"Only on paper and only for you," Gal says. "Nothing wrong with Berabi, my maiden name."

"We're one family," Ian says. His eyes plead with his mother.

She turns to Luna. "Aren't you beautiful, *bli ayin hara*, the evil eye shouldn't see you," Gal says. "I'm so glad I was here when you came."

"Civil servants are done by five," Ian says. "Where else would you be?"

"Here and there," Gal says, eyeing her son. She winks at Luna. "You could be this other girl's sister. We met her at synagogue when we first came, remember?"

"No," Ian answers. He picks up two square throw pillows from the floor and fluffs them on the couch.

"I'll straighten up later and yes, you do. What was her name? Such a lovely complexion, too. Aiden something, the one with the father who looks like a million bucks."

"*Ima*," Ian says, as if naming his mother will make her speak like one. He gives his mother a look and clears the used coffee cups from the side-table. He puts them on the kitchen counter with a louder bang than necessary. Luna can hear water running in the sink and the clink of dishes.

"It's been over a year. I have eyes," Gal says. It's hard to say if Ian can hear his mother while the water's running. "He's a widower, I hear."

Luna shifts from one foot to the other.

"Mmmhmm," Luna answers. She's close enough to smell Gal's floral perfume. She can't help preferring it to her mother's syrupy smell. What Mr. Betel thinks of her and her family is at the back of her throat.

"You must know them," Gal presses.

"Aiden Betel," Luna says.

"Yes, that's it." Gal smiles and Luna recognizes Ian's expression in his mother's face.

"The daughter, not the father," Luna says. "She's my friend was, is, I mean, she moved to Montreal a few months ago."

"That must be hard for you," Gal says. "Beautiful hamsa."

"It's from Aiden, actually," Luna says. "I almost lost it. Ian found it for me."

"What did I tell you? He's my whole heart."

"Snack on the way," Ian calls from the kitchen.

Ian returns to the living room with a bowl of fresh fruit and smaller bowls of almonds, walnuts, and cashews. He places everything on the table with side-plates.

Luna admires the pomegranate design on the dishes.

"My *neshamah*," Gal says and ruffles Ian's hair. "He's like two daughters. So good to his mother." She reaches for two plums and passes one to Luna. "Eat, my *metukah*, sweetheart."

Gal sits on the couch in the same place she was when they came in. "Everyone knows everyone here," Gal says. "But I don't think I've met your parents."

"They're very busy," Luna says. She rubs her palms on her knees. "Not too involved, I mean community-wise."

"I thought we said no third degrees, mom," Ian says.

"I was trying to get to know your girlfriend," Gal says.

Girlfriend? Luna keeps her eyes on the plates in front of her and prays her expression is neutral. She doesn't want to embarrass Ian, who sets his jaw and looks out the window, even though there's nothing to see in the darkness.

"Was I not supposed to say that either?" Gal asks.

"Honestly," Ian says. He picks up a white napkin, wraps the largest plum, and hands it to his mother.

Gal takes a bite and Luna accepts the plum Ian's wrapped for her. She notices Gal's manicured nails, a soft summer pink like the throw pillows.

"And you have siblings?" Gal asks.

"An older brother. In Toronto." Luna takes a bite out of her fruit that's so big she can't talk. Ever since Ronen moved, her father's been leaving notes for her on the fridge while she's at work. She understands they're a continuation of that first letter and she loves them. She has no idea where he's sleeping and she's never caught him sneaking in. She's sure he writes them in Hebrew because he doesn't want her mother to read them, so she keeps them to herself.

They're short:

My Dear Luna,

There should be no evil eyes on you, Amen or

May God put a good eye on you or

Make sure you rest, my sweetheart.

Only once he wrote: *I had another friend. Yehuda Azeulos. We were cornered.*

No way out, not alive. Someone had to be the sacrifice, to distract the enemy, so the rest of us could run. He volunteered. So brave. My God. He was a lion of a man, a tank.

He said: I'll be okay. You run.

There was no other way. He was shot in the kidney almost instantly. I drove to visit him in the hospital in Ein Kerem in Jerusalem. The hospital's 2,000 windows were covered with anti-splinter gauze, 15,000 sandbags, 400 yards of protective walls, 92 doctors, 17 surgeons. None of it could save him.

I think now: how did I find him? Hundreds of beds lined in rows, plasma, drips, forty tanks of drinking water in case supply was cut, eight emergency crews, nine operating rooms. They were even prepared for the Egyptians to use poison gas. I sat beside him and cried. He lived three days. I felt like such a coward.

You think anybody remembers Yehuda Azeulos? I see his face, I hear his voice telling us to go, go! God forgot about us that day.

You know, I still love you.

There's always a fifty- or hundred-dollar bill underneath the small square of white paper. Each note Luna slips in her top drawer in her room. They make her feel better, except that last one. That one was the only time she phoned Ronen and begged not to ask her questions, just to leave his receiver open, so she could hear him breathing until she fell asleep.

Luna finishes her plum and moves on to the salty almonds.

"Let me get out of your way," Gal says. "If you don't want take-out, there are homemade dips in the fridge."

"We can find the fridge and you don't have to move," Ian says. "We'll watch TV in the basement."

Ian motions for Luna to follow him down a flight of carpeted stairs where the light has been left on. The basement matches the living room. A roomy couch and small coffee table. There's a television in the corner, but Luna notices it's unplugged.

Ian follows her eyes and connects it.

"Sorry about that," Ian says.

"About what?" Luna says. "I loved the part about you speaking of me all the time." The word girlfriend she keeps close to her heart for now.

"I meant that comment about Aiden's dad. It's like she's always practicing the divorced woman role. She's not used to it. Neither of us are."

"Maybe *she's* not practicing anymore," Luna says. "Maybe she was scribbling about him in her diary. I can see women going for Aiden's father."

"Let's not talk about that," he says.

Luna realizes how selfish she's been acting as if she's the only one in the world. It hits her that Ian can't stop cleaning up and helping his mother, and she understands he feels he has to be perfect all the time. He cannot be a disappointment like his father. Ian pats the cushion beside him and Luna sits on the couch, leaving some space between them. He switches on the TV. For a few minutes he flips between channels.

"What will it be?" Ian asks. "Hillstreet Blues"? Or are you more a "Cagney & Lacey" type?"

Luna pauses. Perhaps, Ian does feel the need to be perfect around his mom, but she's not exactly normal. She takes a sharp breath.

"Not much time for TV," Luna says. "My mom's in a bad way."

"How bad? Is she sick?"

Luna closes her eyes. It was painful enough to say that one sentence to someone she likes and she needs to let the hurt move through her. There's no point in leading Ian on anymore, even one tiny step. Luna's spent her whole life putting up barriers for a reason. It wouldn't be fair, so it's now or never. She has to tell him the truth about what's going in on her life, so that he can decide if she's someone he wants to get involved with.

Chapter 37

The only light in the basement is from a thin overhead lamp, giving everything a yellowish glow. Luna's grateful. She doesn't need Ian to see her too clearly. It's cool down here and Luna wishes she'd worn something more than a t-shirt.

"How bad?" Ian asks again.

"She's not sick," Luna says. "She's in way over her head with a dangerous gang. She thinks she's in control."

"Violent dangerous?"

"Yes."

"Illegal dangerous."

"That too."

He reaches for her hand and plays with her fingers. Luna enjoys the energy from Ian's touch, but she fights it.

"There's this restaurant crowd," Luna says. "And everyone who comes in is now a regular. My mom's even started calling it a family." She snorts. Her mouth is full of unease. It fills her nose, her ears, her throat. There's no separation between her and her humiliation, but she forces herself to continue. As long as she doesn't look at Ian, she can speak.

"I get it," Ian says. He holds up his hand. "My family's not all kosher either. They've been divorced for a year and it sucked before that."

"I'm so sorry," Luna says. "But I can see how much your mom loves you."

"She's a great mom but I miss my dad. Don't let me stop you. You were in the middle."

"You sure?"

"My parents are already divorced. There's nothing to be done."

"I guess you're right. Well, this family's wrapped around my mom's new partner, Flynn." Luna says. She wrings her hands together. Her finger finds a hole in her jeans and she pulls at the threads. "Flynn has his own personal tribe. And he keeps telling us about this other guy, Douglas, a third partner getting out of prison any minute," Luna says. "I don't even think this Flynn's officially on any papers. I'm pretty sure it's my dad's name still on the lease and my mom's been stalling this guy because that's how she is. Maybe she thinks she can get him to take more than half. Who knows what's in her head?"

"Douglas may never show." His voice is soft. "You can find somewhere to work and spend the summer, let your mom deal with her own problems. We can watch TV and have a normal evening. It's allowed. You don't have to tell me anymore."

Luna rubs her temples.

"I want to tell you the worst part." Luna says. "Ronen and Stephanie, I get it, they ran, but I'm not a runner and there's no reason for you to be with me. Am I making any sense?"

Ian doesn't speak for a few minutes. "This requires food," he says. He races upstairs.

Soon Ian's back with two ginger ales and a vegetable platter with humus in the middle and smaller dips around the sliced carrots, cucumbers, and red peppers: *tehina, matbuchah,* eggplant.

"All homemade and this is for you," he says. "Always too cold down here." He unwraps a Winnipeg Jets sweatshirt he tied around his waist and Luna puts it on.

He eats a few black olives from the platter and pushes it closer to Luna. She opens her drink and sticks a slice of red pepper in the humus.

"Waiting for compliments," Ian asks. "My dad's recipe."

"I'll never eat store-bought hummus again." Luna takes another pepper.

The television's on low and the theme song to "Hill Street Blues" plays in the background. *Da, da, dum,* pause*, da, da, dum,* pause *da, da, da, da da, da, da, da, dum.*

"I used to play this game with my dad where we hum theme songs and have to guess," Ian says. "He's a big music fan."

"Like you," Luna says.

The muscles in Ian's neck tighten. He stares at the TV and sips his drink.

"You miss your dad?" Luna asks. Her voice is more emotional than she'd like it to be.

"Yes, like you," Ian says.

This line brings Luna's reality crashing down around her. She thinks she's confessing when he's had insider information all along.

"What do you know about my dad?"

"Just what Stephanie said. She also told me a lot about this restaurant. They're not coming back."

Luna takes a spoon and tries each dip and then starts from the first one again. She continues eating until the dips are half empty.

"She probably said more than you wanted her to, but I pushed her," Ian says.

"You shouldn't be anywhere near that place."

"It's going to explode." Luna takes a cracker and breaks it in two and then four. Soon it's inedible.

"This sucks for you," Ian says. He pushes Luna's hair off of her face. "Yes."

"Summer's coming. Maybe apply—."

Luna slides away from Ian. "To a dorm somewhere on scholarship. You *have* been talking to Stephanie."

"I can tell you that you're not the solution. I wanted to save my parents, too."

Luna lets Ian hold her hand and rests her head on the couch. She closes her eyes. The room fills with the squeaking of pipes and the running of bath water. Ian's mom must have gone upstairs. Outside a dog barks. Luna forces herself not to think of police, police cars, jails, criminals. She sees one of Flynn's groupies spit out a bloody tooth, struggle to his feet, get knocked down again, then his face ground into the floor with a boot.

"I've been keeping my tips when they're not looking," Luna says. "I deserve them. They pay me nothing. But who am I kidding? What will it pay for? Do I think I can cover the rent on our next place? I don't know when I appointed myself the responsible one."

Luna stops talking. She can't believe how easy it is to talk to Ian. She hasn't even told Aiden what's really happening. If she keeps opening up, she won't know how to put on the brakes and then there won't be anything ugly that isn't hidden and there's so much ugliness in her life. It will be impossible to cover it back up. It will blacken the whole picture of who she is.

Luna checks the time on her watch. Judith came home expecting to drive Luna back to work when whatever she was planning to do with Flynn was done. They must have given up searching for her by now. Let them. She's not working tonight. Ian rolls his empty drink can back and forth on the table. He finishes the other half of the vegetable platter.

"Humus was my dad's specialty. Both my parents are Moroccan, but my dad's the cook in the family. I'm supposed to be with him this summer."

"Nice to have," she says. She doesn't let herself think about the summer. It's enough to get through tomorrow. "My father's Yemenite and if he can cook, he hides it. My Ashkenazi mom serves food out of cans and boxes. Yemenites and Moroccans aren't the same."

"Are you saying the *Ashkenazim* are wrong?" Ian puts his hands on his cheeks in mock surprise. "That not all Sephardi Jews are the same? I thought not-white was not-white. Baghdad, Algiers, what's the difference?" Ian's voice drips with sarcasm.

Luna laughs. "I can't tell you how many times I've heard that we're all the same."

"As many as me."

Ian reaches out his hand and Luna lets him hold hers. Most of the people she knows don't realize that Middle Eastern and North African

Jews exist. One part of herself she won't need to explain. Too bad there are so many other parts.

"So, I have some other news," Ian says.

Luna plays with the buckle on her sandals. She cannot bear any more news.

"I reapplied at your restaurant. Gave my number to that Flynn you mentioned."

"You didn't?"

"Meet the new dishwasher. Whatever's going on in there, I don't want you to be alone."

"That's crazy. You're not working there."

"Why not? You do."

Luna feels as though she's on a rooftop, looking across empty air thousands of feet above ground. One of her feet dangles over a ledge, while the other steadies her on a steel cable only centimeters wide. If she shifts her body forward and grips her hands around a balancing pole, she'll make it over the gut-wrenching void.

If not, Aiden's warning in her last letter will come true. She'll spend her life trying to save people who express no interest in saving themselves. On the contrary, they're all convinced their path is the correct one. It's the rest of the world that doesn't get it. In the end, they'll all go down together.

"Ian?" Gal calls from upstairs.

Luna moves out of Ian's arms.

"It's getting late, no? Weekday tomorrow."

"We're coming."

Ian leads Luna upstairs by the hand.

"You'll come for dinner next time. Did Ian tell you he's an amazing baker?"

"No," Luna says.

Gal kisses Luna on both cheeks. "He's too modest. So nice to finally meet you."

Luna can't say she works every dinner shift, that tonight was a one-off escape from her real life. She hopes her smile is enough.

"I'll clean up downstairs when I get back," Ian says.

On the drive home, Luna remembers her gymnastic lessons as a girl. The secret to walking a tightrope is to lower your center of gravity toward the wire. A person is less likely to fall if their mass is closer to the ground. That's how she feels around Ian. Grounded.

The houses in Luna's row share one large parking lot. When they get to the parking lot of her house, Ian hesitates and leans over. Luna's nervous but Ian holds her hand and she feels reassured. She can't keep her eyes off his lips. She leans toward him and their mouths meet. Ian's kiss is delicate.

"Shit!"

Ian and Luna jump apart. She sees a man waving his arms out on the street.

"Someone's smashed my windows," Flynn shouts.

Luna exhales with annoyance. She can hear Ian breathing. She pulls away.

"Every window," Flynn yells again.

Luna peers out the window into the darkness. Flynn's voice is so loud Luna can't figure out why the entire neighborhood hasn't spilled into the street. Instead, it's deserted except for Flynn under a streetlamp standing in a puddle of broken glass.

Chapter 38

Ian and Luna open their doors at the same time and hurry to the front of Luna's house. Flynn's across the street on his knees, examining his car tires.

"My fucking car!" Flynn yells.

Luna's mind fills in the blanks. Judith wasn't upset that Luna wasn't home when she arrived with Flynn, but relieved. It gave the two of them a place to be alone and talk for a few hours, make future plans, review the accounts, maybe eat in peace for once without the drunks and the moochers and the hangers-on. They finished their evening just as Ian and Luna were making their way to Luna's on the other side of town.

Flynn told Judith he didn't need an escort to his car and it was time one of them checked on the restaurant. She could use a night off. Leave it to him.

But when Flynn returned to his parking spot, the closest one to Judith's front door, all four tires were slashed, the car windows were shattered on the street. And the words: *An Evil Eye on You* were graffitied in blood red across the roof.

Judith races out the front door and keeps running until she's next to Flynn. Her hair's still wet from the bath.

"Holy shit," Flynn says. He's quieter now, his hands are on his ears.

"There's my mother," Luna says to Ian. "You'd better go."

"I can't leave you," Ian answers.

"You have to. Please. I'll see you tomorrow." She leans over and kisses Ian on the cheek. "Please," she repeats. The familiar shame and humiliation wind their way from Luna's stomach up her throat, around her neck, tighten.

"If you're sure," Ian says.

"I'll be fine."

"I *will* see you tomorrow."

"Good."

"And Luna," Ian says.

"Yes."

"You're not alone in this," Ian says. "I'm with you. I mean it."

Ian brushes his lips against hers, squeezes her hand and gets in his car. Luna watches him drive off. For the first time she realizes that Ian is officially her boyfriend. What should be one of her happiest moments is washed out by the life her parents have created for her.

"Luna," Judith calls.

"Mom," Luna answers.

Judith crosses the street again to stand next to Luna, wiping any thought of a boyfriend from Luna's heart.

"There you are," Judith says. "I guess you saw."

"It's Abba, isn't it?" Luna says to her mother. "Him and his good eyes and evil eyes." Her voice is low.

"Shush," Judith says. She grabs Luna's arm. "You never said that, do you hear me?"

"Why not?" Luna asks.

"Are you crazy or blind or what?"

"What do you mean?" Luna asks. "Is Abba home?"

"No, your father's certainly not home and I don't know where he is. I haven't seen him and neither have you and he could be anywhere at all. Nothing to do with us and he's banned, do you hear me? Banned from coming anywhere near the restaurant or our house."

"Do you realize how crazy this all is?" Luna asks.

Flynn calls Judith over and she moans.

"Your father must have lost it completely," Judith says.

"Didn't you just say we never saw him?"

"If Flynn even dreams your father did this, god help us. Nir doesn't know who he's dealing with. Ill winds can blow in all directions."

Luna hears the anger in her mother's voice, but it doesn't erase the fear and sadness in her eyes.

<h1 style="text-align:center">Chapter 39</h1>

The next day Luna's behind the bar with her mother. Luna's working the cash register, her usual spot, and her mother's whipping up cocktails in a crimson silk blouse and black pleated skirt (Singapore Slings are the most popular). She flips open bottles of beer next to Luna in a cheaper version of the same outfit, except Luna's wearing Mexican-style sandals instead of pumps. To Luna's happiness and horror, Ian's in the kitchen manning the dishwasher.

There's the chatter of sloshed customers, clang of glasses on the counter, crackle of handfuls of ice drowning in liquid, the hiss of the coffee maker. There's music too. Blondie shrieks "Call Me" but soon the tone will change to Country and Western, the most popular local music, and Luna will be treated to Flynn Lee's "Lookin for Love" or Dolly Parton's "9 to 5."

Lit cigarettes wave in the air like tiny orange warning signals. Luna breathes tobacco all night, sometimes peppered with marijuana or hash. Mixed with the burning nicotine odor, there's cheap cologne, waxy lipstick, and drunk breath.

Luna's father's trashed Flynn's car again and now Flynn's on red alert. He has scouts everywhere. She doesn't know what scares her more, the idea of coming home to find her father and one of Flynn's buddies waiting for him or the idea of never seeing her father again.

Tonight, Flynn's promised a surprise. So, between worrying about her father and Flynn's promise, she's had a couple of shots. She won't let Ian see her and she's not drunk enough to blur her vision or make her stumble. The alcohol gives her fake courage.

Luna silently toasts to her father's good luck and then her brother's. Another shot. Another shot. She can't blame anyone for wanting to escape this unholy mess except when she does and curses them both for leaving her.

Then a guy in a pinstriped suit that stands out in a sea of jeans, mid-calf boots, and thin cable-knit sweaters strolls in. A hush falls over the room as one by one people come to attention. Luna's not one of those people. She continues to wipe glasses and slide checks under the till.

The stranger in the suit has grayish, wavy hair. He's classically good looking, a real Mafioso man, shorter and broader than Flynn. His name is Douglas Bald, though he has enough IDs in his wallet with alternative names.

"You must be Douglas," Judith yells above the noise. "Welcome."

"I do feel welcome. Thank you, kindly."

There's electricity in the air, on the ground, on the long black marble bar counter, everywhere. There's something about this Douglas that makes everything around him hum.

Luna has never wanted to kill her mother before. She puts two cups of ice in a blender. Crushes it to bits, pours rye and ginger ale over it, and downs it in one swallow.

Bang. Boot. Smash. Crash.

There's a major brawl in minutes. Luna was so hyper-focused on her mother's cornball reaction to Douglas's entrance; she missed the start of the very thing she's been terrified of for weeks.

Luna's struck with terror when Douglas pounds a guy's head with a telephone receiver. Blood gushes down the side of his temples over Douglas's hand onto the counter.

"Mom!" Luna screams.

But Luna can't find her mother. She weaves around the restaurant searching for her. She gives up. She has to get Ian and get out of here.

In the kitchen, Judith's on the phone in what they call the back office.

"There you are. Where's Ian? Where's everybody?"

Judith hangs up without even a goodbye.

"They heard the cops were called and took off." Judith runs her hands through her hair. "Ian's somewhere."

Luna can't figure out what her mother's doing in this back office when the cops are on their way. Her mother has her purse over her shoulder.

"Flynn's been running the place for almost four months," Luna slurs. "This hole is crammed with bikers. Half the customers salivate over Flynn like lap dogs. Now this piece of I-don't-know-what shows up."

"Have you been drinking?" Judith looks up from the open ledger on the desk.

"I'm amazed there's a hair left on my head." Luna hits the wall with her fist. "Why the hell aren't you doing more to take control of your own damn business? Don't you see what's going on? You'll end up with nothing in the end like always."

Luna stumbles forward and her mother catches her.

"You're talking nonsense. How can you be so good at school and so bad in real life? Flynn's my friend, yours too if you'd let him. You cannot be here like this when the police show up. Let's go out the back."

"Why?" Luna pulls out of her mother's grasp. "You don't want the police to see me serving alcohol to biker gangs? Worried they'll think I'm one of the hookers or strippers?"

"There's no time for this." Judith puts on her best angry expression and links her arm in Luna's. She drags her daughter to the back door.

"Stop." Luna unhooks herself from her mother and heads back up. "I'm waiting for Ian."

"This isn't a joke. Let's go." Judith unlocks the back door and opens it. It leads to a back alley and then the main street.

"Whatever's bothering you?" Luna raises an eyebrow. "Flynn's got you covered."

Judith whirls around. She puts her hands on her hips. "What do you mean?"

"You think these guys are amateurs? I got enough fake IDs, no one will ever think I'm Luna Levi."

"Very funny."

"Go check the officer drawer. Where you were. Left-hand side."

Judith's expression darkens. "You shouldn't be in that office. Don't move."

Luna watches through the window as her mother bolts back to the kitchen. In another minute she'll find a tower of IDs, not that Luna's ever accepted one from that creep, but she can be anyone from nineteen-year-old Alena Archibald to twenty-five year old Brit Efergen, courtesy of their fake business partner. Judith returns to Luna with a counterfeit ID in her hand.

"Smart cookie. And you say Flynn's not a friend. Look how he protects you? But to be on the safe side, I took them with me." Judith pats her purse. "If the police find those, you'll be in trouble, too."

"You're serious, aren't you?" The tone in Luna's voice is one of exasperation. "Is there anything you can't talk yourself into?"

Luna takes a step backwards toward the office door.

"We should still go," Judith persists.

"I'll stay," Luna says. Her conviction is fueled by the need to know what her mother was doing in that back office. If the police do show up, there's enough of a brawl going on out there to keep them busy for a while.

"Are you kidding me? Come on." Judith's eyes dart everywhere now.

"I'll catch up."

"Dammit." Judith stamps her foot. "I mean it."

"Ian will drive me home and my friend Flynn's sure to be around."

"At least keep this on you." She hands Luna a fake ID. Her mother leaves without bothering to close the back door. She opens the gate that leads to the alley.

Luna doesn't see her get into her Oldsmobile and drive away, but she hears her.

Chapter 40

The locked door of the back office attracts Luna's attention. Why is this the first place her mother would run when the cops are on the way? She opens a few kitchen drawers searching for the keys, while she tries to visualize what her mother did with them. She saw her mother put them in her purse, but there must be duplicates.

"Looking for something?" Ian's holding a set of keys.

"Where'd you get those?"

"Had to call my, mom. I had this crazy idea that the cops coming here would be on the news and she'd freak. But I don't hear a single siren."

"Don't worry." Luna snatches the keys from Ian's hand. "We're on their regular route."

"I found them in a kitchen drawer," Ian says. "The keys."

"Thanks." Luna struggles with the key.

"Don't give me too much credit, I was looking for the dishwashing soap."

The lock turns and they enter the small room. Luna flips the light switch. Ian's right behind her.

It looks like an ordinary office. Lots of papers. A rotary telephone. Phone books, broken pencils and a couple of pens. There's a large calculator on its side. Luna open drawers, one after the other. She spots the fake IDs and notices the depth of the drawer. She pushes the IDs aside.

"What are these?" she asks Ian. Her heart begins to hammer. She has a pretty good idea what the answer will be. She opens the drawer on the other side of the desk and shoves the first layer of papers to the side, too. She opens a garbage bag next to the desk that looks ready to be tossed in the dump.

Together there are hundreds of watches. She picks them up one by one. All of them have price tags in the thousands of dollars.

"Guys like this will tell you they fell off a truck," Ian says.

"How do you know?"

"My dad's a criminal lawyer."

Luna feels the weight of Ian's words. The voice of a police officer reaches them in the kitchen and snaps her to attention. It's too muffled to make out what they're saying. Luna begins to sweat.

"We'd better get out of here," Luna says. She doesn't feel drunk now. She flings the watches back in their place and turns off the light. She tries to lock the door, but her hand's shake.

"Let me," Ian says. He locks the door for her and puts the keys back where he found them. "I'm sorry, *metukah*, sweetheart."

Luna sucks on her lower lip. Her mother has graduated from ignoring her father's kleptomania to dealing in stolen jewelry.

"Hey," Ian says. He takes a tissue out of his pocket and dries her eyes. "We have to get out of here."

Luna nods. She can't speak.

"Let's go. Now."

Ian grabs Luna's hand. They hustle out the back door and out the gate.

The streets are deserted. It's after midnight on a weekday.

"My car's another couple of blocks," Ian says.

"Don't mind," Luna says. "So, you agree?"

"About what?"

"They've got my mom acting as a front for a stolen goods runner."

"Looks that way."

"It's not the part she usually auditions for."

"I didn't think so," Ian says.

"She's so naïve."

Ian doesn't respond.

"You're not so sure about that. You think she's taking a cut?" Luna walks faster. Her mind reels. "You think that's why my father threatened them? Cause he's worried they sucked her in? What the hell is she doing?"

"I don't think she knows," Ian says. "You should sleep in my basement tonight. Your place isn't safe."

Luna spots Ian's car up ahead. Instead of feeling exhausted, she's full of adrenalin. The walk's helping her clear her head.

"Thanks," Luna says. She doesn't say she can't imagine sleeping. "I have to speak to my mother."

"No way your mother's home and you don't know who might show up at your place." Ian hooks his arm in Luna's.

"I can't allow things to get that chaotic. I'm sleeping in my own bed."

The streetlamp ahead of them is broken. It illuminates the street on and off. The sidewalk is remarkably clean. There isn't so much as a stray cigarette butt or it's just so dark.

"Then I'll sleep on the couch at your place. I'll think of something to tell my mom. Don't bother saying no."

Luna has no energy to argue. Only a few more steps and she can collapse.

Chapter 41

Ian let's Luna lean on him as they walk. She wishes she could tell him how amazed she is that he can read her moods. She has too much fear of the inexplicable to express any of her emotions. There's no way she can rationalize her mother's actions. They're too far off the mark and the lines move too often. Luna can't keep up.

Soon she can close her eyes, rest her head against the cool leather of the car seat and feel the motion under her. As hard as it is to believe, she has a repairman coming to fix the oven tomorrow and a guy on his way to check a leaking toilet.

Luna hears familiar voices. She gazes across the street and sees silhouettes she recognizes.

"Wait," Luna says. She unhooks herself from Ian's arm, stops walking and leans against a brick wall. She motions for Ian to stand beside her.

"We should move," Ian says.

A late-night bus drowns out his next words. A taxi driver honks and yells something in French out his window. Luna holds her fingers to her lips. She hears her own breathing in her ears.

Ian whispers in her ear, "We really can't stay. My mom will be so worried."

Luna shakes her head. It's a clear night. The moon's full and the black velvety sky's full of stars. She points across the street where Flynn and Douglas smoke cigarettes and talk on the corner. A cat screeches and races down the sidewalk. It takes Luna a minute to realize it's a porcupine.

She grabs Ian's hand and together they find the darkest part of the street and cross to the other side, trying to make themselves invisible. They're meters from Douglas and Flynn. Luna prays they're drunk and unlikely to pay attention to their surroundings. She sucks in her breath and crouches low against the buildings and listens. Ian stands with his back flat against the wall.

"When are we squeezing them out already?" Douglas says. "I'm tired of the partner act."

"We're not," Flynn says.

"Come on. Enough playing house. She's just an old pair of tits," Douglas answers.

A wave of dizziness almost knocks Luna to the ground. She feels Ian's arm around her waist. Don't move. Don't breathe. Don't blink.

"I thought they were padded up," Flynn says. "But Judith's broke. She's got these two kids and this ex-army husband who lost his marbles in a sand dune somewhere."

"Who gives a shit?" Douglas says. A cigarette dangles out of the end of his mouth. Luna can hear him slap the brick wall.

"Stealing from the poor's not my line of work," Flynn says. "I don't loot veterans either."

"Since when?"

"Since never."

"What are you saying?" Douglas says.

"I thought we had them at this corner store and kept my eye on her when that Angelo got to her. He made a mint in his last two places, was in the papers. Figured anyone he'd partner with had to have their share. But his wife was right. The guy's burnt out. Lost it. He was already way off the mark when he signed with Judith. I enjoy ripping off the rich. This isn't it."

"You want to renege on our deal for a piece of ass?" Douglas says. "Another couple weeks and she'll sign the whole place over to us. We got the best location in the city for a song."

"That's not it, brother," Flynn says. "I don't put women and kids on the streets or ex-soldiers."

"After all the work I've done you're going to shit it all down the drain? This is bullshit."

"Fuck you! Okay, so she's kind of like my own mother. But the truth is I screwed up. I'm no scumbag. I nailed them as rich Jews and they're just poor losers."

"Bullshit," Douglas says. "This place could be ours like that." He snaps his fingers. "She's as dumb as a brick, ready to take the rap for those watches."

A car pulls up and Douglas and Flynn jump in, still arguing. They speed into the night.

Luna inhales through her nose, counts to ten, exhales through her mouth, counts to ten. She rakes her hands through her hair. She watches a grey squirrel mark his territory, waving his tail, and barking warnings at intruders. The last squirrel she noticed was roadkill.

"Luna," Ian says. "Jesus Christ. Let's go."

"Oh my God," Luna says.

"We have to get off the street," Ian says. "Now."

He grabs Luna's arm and they don't speak until they get to his car.

"Buckle in tight," Ian says.

Luna notices Ian drives over the speed limit and glances into the rearview mirror the entire ride to her house.

Chapter 42

The next day Ian drives Luna to work. She's determined to find out more about those watches. Ian insists she can't be there alone and won't take no for an answer.

They arrive early and Luna realizes she's forgotten her key. When no one responds to Luna's knock. They pace in front of the door, rapping on it every few minutes. They can see Flynn's black Cadillac. Luna can't tell if it's the same one her father trashed or a replacement, but he's in there. Finally, Luna goes to the payphone across the street and slips a quarter in the slot.

"I'm outside," she says when Flynn answers. She forces herself to keep her voice calm, normal, just as it would have been if she'd never heard Flynn and Douglas talk last night. For once she's happy her mother's an actress and prays she's inherited her acting skills.

Flynn doesn't bother to respond. The phone goes dead. A minute later he's at the door.

"No key today?" Flynn says. "We don't open for an hour."

"Must have left it at home."

Ian and Luna walk into the empty dining room. Flynn's eyes are red and his lids are puffy. Luna's always thought of him as a drinker and she doesn't know what he smokes, but he's taken it up a level lately. An Export A cigarette dangles out of the corner of his mouth and there's another behind his ear. Luna can see the empty jade green pack on the bar.

"You don't have one of those headache tablets on you?" Flynn rubs his temples.

Luna hands him her bottle of aspirin.

"That's my girl," Flynn says.

He pops open the lid and pours two aspirins into his palm, downs them and chases them with a sip of his Labatt's beer with the same green label as the cigarettes. There's a newspaper spread open on the bar and a pizza box. There's a bag of zucchini sticks in wax paper next to an empty beer bottle lying on its side. A piece of Boston cream pie is uneaten next to the pizza. Luna notices the berry red logo on the empty paper takeout bag that reads *Larry's Lounge*. Flynn ordered food from Richmond Road to his own restaurant.

"I'll get started on the dishes," Ian says.

"See you soon," Luna says. She widens her eyes at him and he winks at her. This is his way of telling her he understands he has to stay cool, no manly defending of his girl in front of Flynn, nothing that will raise his antennas. Luna wishes Ian would stay with her, but that's not usual behavior.

"Thanks again for the pills. Feel better already," Flynn says. "Don't want you banging down the doors again. Remember? New schedule. You're lucky I was here."

"Don't know how I forgot," Luna says. "We'll keep ourselves busy, I mean, I'll stay busy." She pats her bag to indicate she brought her drawing.

"Doesn't mean you can go home early and I'm not paying your boyfriend for an hour we're closed if he can't be useful in the kitchen starting now," Flynn says. He looks at her for an extra minute.

"You banged on the door like someone's after you. Gears will be here any minute. Need him to check something?"

"No," Luna says. "I mean, yes, everything's great. My mom's away. You know how it is?" Luna knows she's babbling.

"Just keep smiling at the customers," Flynn says.

"Of course," Luna answers.

Luna has no idea what Flynn would do if he found out she'd eavesdropped on his conversation last night with Douglas. She worries it's printed on her forehead and he's just biding his time until he lets her know. The thought makes her want to vanish.

The restaurant only opens at 6 p.m. these days. Flynn's right. She barely slept last night and then had to act normal with repairmen all day and pay them out of her own pocket. Luna had forgotten. She was so stupid to come in early. She won't get near that back office. It's only putting her higher up on Flynn's radar. The types who frequent the place aren't interested in breakfast or lunch and the alcohol's way more of a draw than the food. Even the boss orders in.

Luna forces herself to smile at Flynn, but he's not paying attention to her anymore. He's returned to his late lunch or early dinner. She's still shaken from last night's revelation. She had a liter of water, downed two aspirins and flopped into bed. It worked. She felt fine this morning until she remembered the conversation between Flynn and Douglas. The plan to take her mom for a ride's been in the works all this time. She can almost feel her heart shriveling at the humiliation.

A car screeches into the parking lot. Luna sees Gears driving his car outside and waves. He waves back. She hates to admit it, but she feels safer when Gears is around. Or she did. Everything's different today. Gears might be on Flynn's side or Douglas's. Is he part of the group who wants to rip her mom off or who feels sorry for her?

She eyes Flynn, who has one hand holding a phone and the other flipping through receipts. When he returns her stare, she rushes to the bathroom and splashes her face and neck with cold water. She's rattled enough to think he can read her mind. When she returns Flynn and Douglas are deep in conversation. They stop talking as soon as they see her.

Luna and Ian have barely been there for half an hour when the door swings open. It's dusk and hard to make out anything beyond a shadowy figure. Luna was setting the tables closest to the bar. Ian had gone into the kitchen to bring her more cutlery.

It takes Luna a full minute to recognize it's her father. She can't remember the last time she saw him. Her blood goes cold and she has to stop herself from crying out. Nir Levi stands in the doorway of his own restaurant with a sawed-off shotgun. He wears his usual blue and white checkered button down with pushed-up sleeves, paper-bag colored shorts that reveal his hairy legs, and navy loafers without socks. He takes a single giant lunge forward.

"I'll kill all of you pieces of garbage," he says. "Get out of my restaurant. Get the hell away from my family." He points the gun at Flynn and then quickly at Douglas, both of whom were setting up the bar.

"Who the hell are you?" Flynn says. He looks at Luna with questioning eyes and Luna can't stop blinking. She cannot do what her brain wants her to do. She cannot create a distraction, so she can give her father the message to leave. Instead, she's as frozen as the Ottawa canal in January.

"I'm the asshole who trashed your car," Nir says. "Twice."

Nir smiles at the word twice, but it's not a happy smile. Luna's body trembles and she can't get her breathing under control.

"Hey buddy, the car was a write-off. No hard feelings," Flynn says. He waves his cigarette in the air and laughs so that his shoulders rock back and forth. "You did me a favor. Insurance paid me double." He straightens his collar. He stands and raises his hands.

"*Yalah*! Get out," Nir says. "Now!' Nir takes two more giant steps forward.

The air changes. Luna feels as though she's turned into a zombie. She mustn't look at her father in a way that arouses suspicion. She cannot warn him. Her inability to act is like a throbbing bee sting in her palm.

Ian squeezes her hand but she's sweating so much it slips. She can't remember him returning from the kitchen but he must have because there's a pile of clean cutlery on the table. Luna can hear the beating of her own heart. Someone has turned on the jukebox. Kim Carnes screams about a woman who has Bette Davis eyes.

"Let me take that for you," Flynn says. "Easy fella. No one wants this to turn bad. Just take it easy."

Luna can't tell if her father's eyes are shiny or not. Her mouth is so dry. The song ends abruptly. Maybe someone pulled out the plug.

Luna's too terrified to turn her head and see who is moving where. She only has eyes for her father. Could he know? Has he discovered Flynn's plan, too?

"Come on," Flynn says. "Just put the gun down and we can talk about what's bothering you."

"Stay away from me," Nir says. He leans forward but does not move more than that. "I know how to use this."

"You don't really want to do that," Flynn says. His hands are up in the air in front of him, his palms wide. Flynn's wearing more jewelry than usual. Three rings of gold necklaces, two bracelets. His shiny grey suit matches his shoes and his belt.

When Flynn lunges forward, Luna bursts. "Abba, no," Luna exclaims.

"What did you say?" Douglas asks. He had been silent until now. Luna had forgotten he existed. "You know this guy? You look like you've seen a ghost. You do know this guy, don't you?"

Nir looks at Luna and it's obvious he didn't notice her before.

"What are you doing here? You shouldn't be here," he says. "Oh my god. I could have shot you."

Nir begins to shake. Flynn takes advantage of Nir's distraction to jump aside and grab the barrel of the gun, sending it clattering to the floor. Flynn kicks it under the table and nods to Gears, who is flexing his knuckles.

"No," Luna screams. Her legs can't hold her. Ian holds her up and whispers something in her ear she can't make out.

Nir starts his run before turning and throwing open the door with one hand. He disappears into the darkness outside.

"Let him go," Flynn says.

"We'll have to tell Gears to start coming in earlier," Flynn says. "He'll probably come back. Recognize him, Luna?"

"No," Luna says. She realizes that if Flynn and Douglas ever met her father it was close to a year ago now and not more than once or twice. Even she was aware enough to notice her father looks older, greyer and thinner than he did last year. She leans heavily on Ian. It takes all of her willpower to stop her knees from shaking.

"Gears will find out. You'll get on that, Gears, my man."

A little girl
Went to school
The doors are locked
The girl sews

Chapter 43

Mom's been away since that night Douglas showed up at the restaurant and it's Luna's responsibility to find her father and warn him. A repeat of yesterday can't happen. This is what she tells herself on her way home.

The pain in her head and her anxiousness makes the bus feel as though it's the longest ride of her life. As she opens her front door, the phone rings. She leaves her key in the lock and dives for the receiver.

"It's me," Judith says.

"Mom. Where are you?" Luna asks. She can't stop herself from locking the door, sliding the curtains shut, closing the windows, blocking out all of the sun from the room. She tosses her bag on a chair and scans the kitchen for anything edible. "Do you know what's going on?"

"Of course. Aren't you going to ask me about my performance?"

Luna draws a long breath. "I don't think you do. Abba's lost it. He came into the restaurant yesterday with—."

"Shush," Judith says.

"But."

"I mean it. Stop worrying over things that don't concern you. I'm calling so you can wish me luck and to tell you I might be delayed. I thought I would get the machine."

"Are you kidding?" Luna says. "You purposely called when you thought I wouldn't be here?" She opens the fridge. Nothing.

"I'm taking care of everything. Look, they're calling me. We'll speak later."

Luna's left holding the receiver in her hand. It rings again before she has time to think.

"Ready at 4?" Aiden asks.

"You came through," Luna says. She swings the fridge door open again as though something tempting snuck in there in the last twenty seconds.

"Do I ever disappoint?"

"You're a star."

"Have to go," Aiden says. "Big line for the phones. Have to leave Montreal soon to make it."

Aidan hangs up before Luna can say goodbye. The fridge is a write-off. She looks at her watch. Ten minutes are left to eat and drink a cup of coffee. If Aiden's picking her up in three hours, there's no time for the short nap she'd planned. She'll have to push her exhaustion aside and search for her father now.

The headache tablets worked. Luna sighs. She's turning into her mother. Someone who always has a headache. Luna gathers some of her precious tip money to bus around the city, while she chews on the last dry onion bagel in the breadbox. Her father hasn't told her where he's working or sleeping for months. She'll start close to home. Outside as she walks, she calculates how much time she has to check all three YMCAs. Not much.

Luna's mind races with possibilities. Maybe her mom spoke to Flynn and he told her what happened. She figured out it was her own husband and then what? Maybe Judith had the sense to come home and scare Nir out of his wits, inoculate him against this idea that he could save his family and she returned without ever telling Luna she was in town. She wishes she could discuss it with Ronen, but she still hasn't had more than a two-minute conversation with him. It's too painful.

Luna rounds the corner and she's at the YMCA on Carling Avenue. Her father loves the indoor pool and uses it for next to nothing in return for taking Christmas and Easter holiday shifts guarding the door. No luck. No one has seen him, at least no one who was willing to admit it to her.

The YMCA has two more locations much farther away. She hops on a bus that's mercifully empty and finds herself on Bank Street, one of the largest commercial streets in the city, just south of Parliament Hill. She's too preoccupied to enjoy being out around expensive restaurants, busy offices and nightclubs. At the front desk of the YMCA, Luna fails again. No one has seen Nir Levi.

It's less than a ten-minute walk to Argyle Avenue, her last shot. Now she's close to the Nature Museum and Ottawa University. She wishes she could disappear into both, get lost in a place that has nothing to do with unhinged fathers and indecipherable mothers, but instead she finds herself in a rerun at a front desk receiving the same short, polite sorry and shake of the head.

The clerks even look the same, all three of them speaking to her from behind today's copy of *The Ottawa Citizen* and Styrofoam coffee cups. No one has seen Nir Levi they tell her. Happy to pass on a message if he does come in, would she like to leave her name?

Luna falls down a well of disappointment and crashes into a poodle-haired woman carrying a giant thermos.

"Watch it!"

"Sorry."

Luna can't take her eyes off the heavy metal thermos as it rolls toward the exit. She hears the thud of the gun as it hit the floor, her father's panic. All of it comes flooding back. Flynn's voice. Nutcase.

There's a quieter, parallel voice in her head telling her how ridiculous it is that she thought it would be a matter of rounding the corner or hopping on a bus and wagging a finger at her father. Grow up, Luna, she tells herself. Her parents' problems are too big for her.

The lady and her thermos are gone. Luna thanks the third clerk and looks at her watch. She's run out of time to search for her father. She can't afford to miss Aiden at 4 o'clock. She gets on a return bus and when her jaw aches at the end of the ride, she realizes she's clenching her teeth.

> *A little girl*
> *Went to school*
> *The doors are locked*
> *The girl sews*

Chapter 44

Aiden pulls up to the curb, waiving two tickets for *Peter Pan*. It's just under a two-hour drive to Gananoque, a small town on the US border. Luna has to tell her mother about her father's cowboy act in person. Shake her. Then the bigger news: this whole thing has been a scam from start to finish. If that doesn't burst her mother's bubble, nothing will.

"Got to hand it to you," Aiden says as she leans over and opens the door for Luna. "You keep me on my toes."

"You gave me this necklace for good luck, but you're my real charm," Luna says as she buckles her seatbelt. Her smile is so fake she feels guilty. She focuses on her breathing.

"Mine, too. Sorry, I was late. Traffic."

"You can just say it. You couldn't tell your dad you were meeting me and he tied you up on the phone."

"That's not it."

Luna squeezes Aiden's shoulder to tell her it's fine. She's used to Doron Betel. Soon Aiden will pick up on her silence and switch the conversation in her own direction. The last thing Luna wants to discuss is herself.

"I have some hot gossip." Aiden flashes her a smile and her model white teeth are perfect against her creamy brown skin. "I'll tell you a secret, but don't tell Ian, yet. I promised."

"Secrets are like currency," Luna says. "You might owe me."

"This is big."

Luna's not sure if she has space for big. The sunroof is open but the wind doesn't cool Luna down. She rolls down her window and opens the glove compartment. Aidan always keeps something sweet in there.

"How many Moroccan women are in this whole city?"

"I don't know. One."

"Exactly. My dad's seriously going out with her, not just out, *out.*"

Luna raises her eyebrows and gives a low whistle. She's tried to tell Ian about his mother and Doron. Aiden's dropped more than a few hints, but Luna freezes after the second word. Aiden has no mother and would love one, but Ian has a father. She's afraid he won't welcome the messenger.

"So, for sure Ian doesn't know?" Luna says.

"I'm not going to be the one to tell him and you chickened out. I'm happy for my dad. He's finally a little, what's the word? Softer."

Luna can only smile at her friend's ability to read her. She needs some time to digest this news. She finds a roll of cherry Lifesavers

152

behind the sunglasses and tissues. She holds them out to Aiden, who shakes her head.

"Keep those." She pulls to the side and polishes her black sunglasses. "I shouldn't have sugar in the car."

"I'll finish them for you on the way back."

Luna unwraps the LifeSavers and pops two in her mouth at a time. Out of the corner of her eye, she looks at Aiden, her prep girl style has reached perfection. She's in beige chinos and an argyle pullover vest over a collared shirt. She might as well have dropped in from Venus. It's hard to believe they occupy the same space.

"Mind if I rest?" Luna asks.

"Wake you when we're there," Aiden says. "I'm free as a bird. My roommate's totally covering for me."

"Nice to disappear for a few hours," Luna says.

"With you," Aiden says.

Luna laughs for the first time all day and closes her eyes. She lets the rhythm of the wheels put her to sleep. Ninety minutes later, Aiden nudges Luna awake. She opens her eyes in time to read a sign: "Welcome to Gananoque, Gateway to the Thousand Islands."

"I should take Isaac here for a boat cruise to these islands," Aiden says.

"Isn't that where we're going? Thousand Islands Playhouse?"

"The directions say it's a stone's throw from the St. Lawrence River in a Canoe Club building."

"How many people live out here?" Luna says.

"Not more than 5,000. Your mom's hit the big time."

They pull up at the theater, a vintage building straddling a dock on the St. Lawrence River. Luna takes a moment to admire the large playhouse along the water. Then she hunts for her mother's Oldsmobile and finds it. Part of her believed her mother would get wind of her arrival and ditch her.

Aiden leads her into the theater and they freshen up in the bathroom. By the time they're done brushing their hair and putting on lipstick, the lights are flashing.

The show's about to begin.

The play starts with the chorus and then the narrator. The first scene involves Mary, George and John. It isn't until the second scene that Judith comes on as Peter Pan, who wants to take the three children to Never Never Land.

Luna sits on the edge of her seat each time her mother appears on stage. She feels a tingle in her body as her mother insists Never Never Land is a place where you never have to grow up. She's so convincing, Luna believes every word.

Chapter 45

"Your mom's great for her age," Aiden says.

"Do you mind?" a man's voice says behind them. Out of the corner of her eye Luna sees a guy who looks like a half jock, half geek. She expected most of the audience to be parents and children, but he's neither.

"What's that supposed to mean?" Luna whispers.

Aiden shrugs. "What I said."

"Shush," Half jock, half geek says.

Luna puts her finger to her lips when she sees Aiden's about to respond. She doesn't need to call attention to herself. She kicks the chair in front of her trying to move away from Aiden and a woman she can't make out in the dark shoots her a glance over her shoulder. Luna sinks lower in her chair.

With each passing minute her agitation increases. She can no longer follow what's happening on stage. Here's her mother, two hours from their home volunteering her time, entertaining 200 people. Her husband might be concocting a pipe bomb on a clear path to jail and what the hell is with those stolen watches?

Luna came ready for a confrontation, to stamp her foot and insist her mom face her life. But watching how engrossed her mother is in her role, Luna's deflated. Any hope she had drains out of her.

"No," she groans. "I can't back out."

"What?" Aiden asks. "Did you say something."

Now they're shushed from the front and the back.

"Sorry," Luna says. She pretends to have a coughing fit and half the row glares at her. Aiden gets up and returns with a large root beer and a bottle of water.

"Keep it low," she whispers. "No drinking in the theater."

"So, how'd you get it?"

"Flirting can get you a lot of places," Aiden says. She winks at her. Luna's envious of her lightheartedness. She finishes her root beer.

At intermission, Luna can't wait any longer. If she wants to feel freer, she must do what she came here to do.

"Be right back," she tells Aiden, who is stretching her legs in the hallway.

With each step Luna's anger increases. She storms backstage.

"Mrs. Levi?" Luna asks everyone she passes. It takes all of her energy to put on a happy smile. "I'm here to see Mrs. Levi."

"Door on the left," a woman in a mermaid costume says to her. "Judy," she calls. "Someone's looking for you."

Luna opens the door without knocking. Her mother's there with a blow-dryer in one hand and a makeup brush in the other.

"My chubby chicken," Judith says. "They said it was sold out." Judith's voice is filled with surprise, but her face is not. She pecks Luna on the cheek. "How on earth did you get here?" She looks past Luna over her shoulder.

Luna picks up her mother's sports car red lipstick and plays with it, twisting it up and down.

Judith takes two headache tablets and drinks a glass of water. She studies Luna's face.

"No, dad's not my driver, haven't seen him," Luna says. "Aiden brought me."

Judith's shoulders relax. She straightens her chair so it's fully facing the mirror. "I'm on in a few minutes." Her chair creaks as she leans back. "Guess what? We might be going over the border. You can't make it in Canada until you make it in the USA."

"Are you crazy?" Luna asks. "Mom, wake up. Show's over. I need you to come to your senses." She can see her own reflection in her mother's dressing room mirror. "You have to come home and get rid of these guys."

"They're partners and that's what they're for," Judith says. She pulls at a run in her green stockings until they're hidden under the top half of her costume. "So, I can take time off, keep up my real passion, my true calling."

Luna stares at her mother open-mouthed.

"Abba came into the restaurant," Luna says. She draws a bright red arc on her hand with the lipstick, feels its smoothness. She rubs it into her skin leaving a mark like a wound. "With a gun, mom. A real gun. He could have used it."

Luna replaces the cap on her mother's lipstick, checks to see if her mother is watching her, and puts it in her purse.

"Your father dodged bullets and bombs before his bar mitzvah. He's more than capable of taking care of himself and doesn't need his daughter to save him. You're going to love the second half," Judith says. She smacks her ultra-red lips in the mirror. "So glad you finally made it to see your mother on stage. It's about time. You brought a camera, of course."

"No, I did not bring a camera." Luna hits her forehead with her fist. She decides to play her last card. She takes a deep breath.

"Nothing's going to happen," Judith says before Luna can begin. "Men are all show-offs. They love the tough guy act. Imagine you thinking you need to shield your father from our own friends. I told you not to worry. I told you I'll find a way to take care of everything. I always tell you. You'll start listening one day."

Luna lowers her voice. "Flynn and Douglas are playing you to take over the place. Running it into the ground until you'll sign your half over for nothing." Luna folds her arms across her chest, but it does nothing to soothe the hurt inside of her.

"Who says?" Judith reaches to touch Luna's hand but she snatches it away.

"I heard them," Luna says. "Do you think I'm making this up?"

"Are you teaching me something about the world?" Judith darkens her eyebrows in the mirror with a pencil. "I told you, I've never met a man who didn't think he was a tough guy. Meanwhile, it's women with the real strength, you know, the inner kind."

Luna takes a step forward and knocks her mother's dressing table. A glass of water shatters to the floor. The door creaks open.

"Oops," Aiden says. "Should I call someone with a broom?"

"Aiden," Luna says.

"Well, welcome. More fans," Judith says. She pretends to sign her autograph in the air and Aiden laughs. "And don't worry about it." She bends down and scoops the biggest pieces of glass into a garbage bin.

"Let me help," Aiden says.

Judith and Aiden bend down to clean up the mess and look up at Luna at the same time. Luna sees them framed in her mother's dressing mirror. Aiden the model friend, her mother, the model actress. The image throws her off balance.

"Been looking for you," Aiden says to Luna.

For the first time, Luna feels a twinge of guilt. She never told Aiden why she really has to see her mom. She fed her lines about wanting to see her mother's play and Aiden didn't question her. Luna knew she wouldn't.

"Figured you'd be here with the star," Aiden continues. "They're about to turn off the lights."

"That's so thoughtful," Luna says. "One more second."

"Great show, Mrs. L," Aiden says to Judith. "You really strut your stuff."

"Why, thank you," Judith says.

Luna watches her mother scoop the rest of the glass into her palm. Her mother hasn't missed a beat since Luna got here. "I'm done. *Hazalachah rabah,* mom, good luck."

"Thanks for the blessing and don't worry so much," Judith says. "The Levis are a tough act to follow."

Luna puts her back to her mother; she doesn't want to show her more emotion on her face than she needs to see. Luna feels weak and links arms with Aiden. As she puts one foot in front of the other, she realizes it's harder than ever for her to believe that her mother co-exists with her in the same world.

Chapter 46

The following afternoon when Luna gets to work, her key no longer turns in the lock. She bangs on the door in frustration, but no one comes to her rescue. The back door produces the same unsuccessful results. She digs in her pockets and in her purse. No change for the payphone. Exhausted, she finds a shady spot under a handsome oak tree and sits with her head in her hands. The long drive with Aiden yesterday has washed her out.

Luna eyes the payphone across the street and considers calling Ian, but he's excited to see his father in Winnipeg. His flight's tonight and she hates the idea of ruining his mood. She hopes his mother will tell him the truth about her relationship with Mr. Betel soon. Keeping this from him is like having a giant rock on her back every time they speak. She can't wait to put it down.

Luna feels the warmth of the glass of the door on her skin and closes her eyes. The sun's bright today. Blinding.

"Had to change the goddammed locks," Flynn says when he arrives half an hour later.

Luna takes a deep breath and feels her muscles relax. She tells herself she needs to calm down. This lock thing has nothing to do with her father. She waits while Flynn opens and they step inside. The stale smells of yesterday's tobacco, cooking oil, and beer greet them. Flynn switches off the alarm, and flicks on the lights.

Luna strolls into the kitchen and turns on the ovens. Then she checks the open cash register to make sure there are no bills or checks leftover from the night before. Her next stop is the cigarette machine. That was cleared out last night, too. Flynn will take the cash they need out of the safe when he's ready. She opens the windows with a heave.

"Don't you want to know why the locks are changed?" Flynn asks.

Luna isn't sure what she wants and now she knows Flynn's drunk. He wouldn't be volunteering information sober. Flynn passes her a broom and a dustpan. She leans them both against a wall and goes to the bathroom to change into her uniform. Dammit. Maybe this is her punishment for not coming clean with Ian. Her cheap crimson blouse shrunk in the wash. Now it rides up. She has to squeeze into the skirt too. There's no way she can go home and get back here. And what would she change into? Her only spare uniform is in the wash. Her eyes move from her tight clothes to the state of the bathroom. Soap and toilet paper refills for the bathrooms will have to wait until she's swept the place.

"I asked you something?" Flynn says when she returns.

"Yes, what's going on?" Luna asks. She forces herself to look Flynn in the eyes. He reads her mind and he stops rifling through the cash register long enough to get her a glass of ice water.

"For you, little lady," Flynn says. She takes the glass and nods. "It's Douglas. Don't ask me to explain. He's out that's all." Flynn pops open a beer and Luna hides her surprise. He doesn't usually start drinking until they're about to close and they haven't even opened yet.

"Out where?" Luna asks. She flips the chairs that weren't flipped last night and starts to sweep old grits and cigarette butts into a pile.

Flynn loosens his tie. "As in no longer in. Plans change. We don't need him now, do we, girl?"

"I don't," Luna answers.

"That's what I want to hear," Flynn says.

Luna swallows. Shivers run up her spine whenever Flynn calls her girl. She doesn't need Flynn's explanation. So, Douglas and Flynn still disagree on taking her mother for a ride and they've split up. That means there's a very angry Douglas out there somewhere and she's been sitting in front of this locked door alone. He or one of his thugs may have been watching her the whole time. She pulls her shirt down to stop it from riding up her back when she bends to sweep the pile into the pan.

"Here," Flynn says. She opens her palm and he hands her another set of keys. "For your mom when she gets back.

Luna takes the key from Flynn, careful not to brush her fingers against his as usual. She doesn't want anything she does around him to be misinterpreted as a flirtation.

Luna shifts to the other side of the nearest table to obscure her midriff with the chairs piled on the tables, and raises her hands to her neck where she feels her hamsa necklace. There's no way she's adding the key to this place on the same chain as her good luck charm. When she's alone in the room she stuffs the key in her bra. She'll put it somewhere safe later.

Flynn whistles to himself between phone calls and Luna's taking glasses out of the mini cup-washer behind the bar. Her mind plots her next tasks. The tables need to be set, the condiments restocked and the place needs a good airing. She doesn't know why Flynn locked the doors again. The windows are still locked, too. That's his department.

"Where's your angel tonight?" Flynn asks. He has a cigarette dangling out of his mouth. The ash is so long it falls on its own onto the counter.

"Ian?" Luna asks.

"You got two angels?"

"His week off, remember?" Luna answers. She keeps her eyes on the cutlery she's wiping down before she sets. It's on the tip of her tongue to say Ian's out of town, but she's had years of training when it comes to information. She keeps it to herself. She can thank her mother for that.

Luna smiles instead of answering. It will have to be enough. She grabs a handful of matchbooks to refill along the bar. They don't even bother to pay for a name or number to put on them anymore. They're plain white.

Flynn cranks up the juke box. Men at Work's "Who Can It Be Now" is so loud the floors vibrate. Luna doesn't say anything when he pours two shots of whiskey and drinks them both one after the other. He pours another and her anxiety shoots up, but then she notices he passes it to Gears. She hadn't heard Gears come in.

Luna's not sure what else Flynn's on, but all of this alcohol before dinner is a red flag. He must be more upset about Douglas than he let on. Changing the locks from his partner of three decades is no small move. She gazes at him, trying to assess his condition. Flynn's humming to the music as he restocks the ice and wipes down the bar. He's not still enough for her to see his eyes. His pupils are permanently dilated and there are bottles of eye drops in the kitchen drawers.

"Heard you paid your mom a little visit," Flynn says.

Luna's back straightens. Are they following her? She doesn't dare ask. She takes a breath and lets it out slowly. Perhaps, he merely spoke to her mom today on the phone and she came up in conversation. Nothing more.

"Her play any good?" he continues.

"If you like fairytales," Luna answers.

"My mom was left with two kids, too," Flynn says. "Worked herself to the bone. Funny enough, my old man was in the navy, not that I ever met him."

Luna has never considered Flynn having parents or any blood relatives. She heads to the bar, swallows the last of her water and pours herself another glass, forcing it down her throat.

"You sure are jumpy today," Flynn says to Luna.

Look who's talking. "Thought I saw Ronen on the way here," Luna says. "Ridiculous I know."

It's a slow dinner hour and before long Flynn tells Luna they're closing up early.

"You sure?" Luna says. Inside, she's thrilled. If Flynn and Douglas are splitting up, she doesn't want to be anywhere near either of them.

"Not in the mood," Flynn says. "Gears, you can go, buddy. Do a once-over of the place, and lock the back door on your way out. And take a look at my car on your way, too."

"You got it," Gears says. "I'll clean up and I'm out."

Gears smiles at Luna and the snake tattoo on his neck expands. Luna takes a step back as she always does when he passes.

Flynn turns to Luna, "You can get a jump on playing catch up with your brother as soon as you wash the floors."

"Thanks," she says. "You'll lock the front?"

"After this one," Flynn answers. He raises his Labatt's. "And after Gears is out."

When the door closes behind Gears, Luna's alone with Flynn again. He's wearing a burgundy button down and a narrow black tie and long cowboy boots for the warm weather. His movements are wider than usual as he sails into space on alcohol and whatever else he's on.

Luna uses the bathroom and returns to find him staring into his beer. Flynn hasn't smiled once all night, not since he handed her the new keys to the place.

"This is bullshit," he says to no one.

She heads straight for the phone closest to the bathroom and calls Ian.

"The boss let you make a call? I can't believe it. I'm so bad at packing. SOS."

"We're closing early. Please come and get me. Like now, right now. Okay?"

"Did your dad come in?"

"No, nothing like that." Luna twists the phone cord between her fingers. She should have changed back into her regular clothes. She can't breathe in this tight skirt.

"My mom went somewhere with the car. I'm sure she'll be back soon. You want to take a cab?"

"I need a few minutes, anyway. I don't want to do anything out of the ordinary.

"I'll wait outside."

Luna makes sure everything's off in the kitchen and she's out of here. She can change at home. She hurries through the swinging kitchen doors. Flynn's still muttering to himself. She wants him to forget all about her.

Chapter 47

From the kitchen Luna hears the creaking sound of the front door opening and her toes curl in her shoes. They're supposed to be closed.

"Who the fuck is that?" Flynn asks loud enough for Luna to hear. "We're not open tonight. Sorry, folks," he says, slapping his table for emphasis.

"That's no way to serve a paying customer," Douglas says.

He uses a pretend customer voice, but Luna recognizes it. She feels a wave of dizziness. She clamps her mouth shut and leans against the kitchen door to open it a crack and peeks through. Part of her says she should disappear right now, say good night and head for the door, but she can't tear her eyes away from Flynn and Douglas.

"Just the asshole customer I wanted to see," Flynn says. He smiles like a hungry dog who has just spotted his dinner. "Sit. Right here." He gestures to a chair near his table. His cowboy hat is on the seat beside him.

Douglas doesn't move. His hands are on his hips. He's no more dressed for the warm weather than Flynn with his hip-length black leather jacket. Luna can see his baby blue tie under a wide collar of the identical color. Luna's father taught her to beware of winter jackets in summer. They're the easiest way to conceal things.

She sees Douglas scan the empty restaurant without moving his head. Only his eyes move.

Please, please, please. That Douglas is an idiot for coming in here. What was he thinking? That Flynn would buy him a beer? Please God tell me Gears forgot something and he's coming back.

Luna's palms are slippery with sweat, but she doesn't dare wipe them on her uniform, she's too petrified to move.

"I want to know what's in it for you?" Douglas asks. He's smoking a thin cigar.

"Why are you offering to lose so much dough on this place?"

"I told you the truth," Flynn answers. He wipes his mouth with the back of his hand. "We've been friends for twenty-five years. You know me." He pulls his shoulders back.

"I thought I knew you. What's your game plan?"

"I'll have to slowly clean it up," Flynn says. "Tell Judith we're revamping for a family night atmosphere. We're fifty-fifty now."

"Fifty percent of zero is zero. You're both at minus zero."

"It won't be difficult to stop serving these bum clientele and rebrand the place in this location. Once we get out of the red, I'll offer to buy her out for real. She'll be tired of the biz by then. She's got one foot out the door now. Traveling around like friggin' Peter Pan half the time. I'll get a good price on it, but it will be fair, Douglas. I don't want to steal this from her."

Flynn puts out his cigarette in an ashtray. He finishes his beer and glances to the bar for the imaginary bartender for another. Luna's lost count. He's been drinking for hours. For the first time Luna notices his hair's so blond, it's white and startling next to his red moustache.

"So, you're locking me out and cutting me out, Mr. Robin Hood?" Douglas says. "Stealing from the poor's not your game but from your partner, that's okay?" He shoves his hands in his pockets as he sticks out his chest.

"You cut yourself out." His eyes follow the direction of Douglas's hands. "I'm still in for three ways."

"Bastard!" Douglas spits. He lunges forward planting his heel under the lip of the table, thrusting it into Flynn's chest in an instant.

Flynn flies backwards in his chair and combined with the force of the table, goes tumbling down, chair and all, sending the ashtray and empty bottle shattering to the floor.

Douglas runs around the table punting his boot into Flynn's face as he's climbing from the floor. Flynn stumbles into the adjacent table sending three wooden chairs bouncing.

Douglas throws his right fist with full force to Flynn's jaw, but it just glances off Flynn as he and the falling table clatter to the ground again. But Douglas runs out of luck. His ankle gets caught between the legs of a spinning chair sending him stumbling onto his knees on all fours.

That's Flynn's chance. He jumps into the air like a wide receiver, giving him the downward force to smash his interlocked hands on the back of Douglas's head, sending Douglas face first into the floor.

"No!" Luna screams, but nothing comes out.

"Hey, man," Douglas says. He gasps between breaths. "We got better offers, faster, too. Since when did you take up babysitting and long-term planning?"

"You thought you'd come and take me out?" Flynn spits. "Is that what's left of years of friendship?"

Luna's heart pounds in her throat. She cannot bear to watch. This bar fight is different–more dangerous–there's no one to stop it.

Luna has to get out of here. Now. She grabs her bag and pulls open the back door, almost colliding with the locked security gate.

"Gears must have latched it," she says to no one. She fumbles down her shirt, inside her bra for the keys Flynn gave her. She struggles to match the new keys to the space in the padlock she can't see. There's no added streetlight out here and the sky's so dark, she can barely perceive shadows.

She's certain Flynn and Douglas will hear her keys clanging on the lock and come for her. *Come on, come on.* Just as she feels the lock open, she maneuvers the lock out of its hole, to open the gate.

A shadow covers her face and she's struck with terror. *No, no, no.* It's him.

She makes out the shadow of a gun. Douglas heard her. He's out here. He'll kill her. Her blood runs cold. She blinks a few times in the shadowy darkness. It's not Douglas or Flynn. It's her father. He's raging, about to storm past her into the restaurant via the back door with a shotgun in his hand.

"Abba no! Stop! *Halas!*" She lunges forward, grabbing his arm, and doing her best to pull him backwards.

In an instant there's the burst of a gunshot, an ear-splitting bang, and then a shattering of glass. Everything goes black. Did her father's gun fire? Her heart races. She runs her hands along her stomach, her legs, her head. She's whole. Her mind goes into overdrive.

"Abba?"

Nir grunts in response. Luna sees the gun still in his hand. She has to get it away from him, but she doesn't want to touch it. There's a second crashing sound, not as big as the first. The only thing she can think of that would make that noise is the huge crystal chandelier that hovers over the dining room plummeting to the floor.

Luna inches toward her father, not wanting to startle him. He stands motionless in terror and Luna feels his shock. His whole body trembles. With her foot closest to the gate, she yanks it enough for it to appear closed. There's no time to lock it. She's stuck in a back alley with her dad. Her brain can't process fast enough. To run for the main road or hide. Her instincts tell her to hide, just in case, Douglas and Flynn don't reach the right conclusions.

She reaches for her father's hand and pulls him behind the two steel garbage bins.

"It's me, Abba. Shshsh. Don't move. This is almost over. We're okay."

She squeezes out the image of what would have happened if she had not been here to stop her father charging in on those two. She forces her imagination to stop.

Her knees are knocking together.

"You're okay?" Nir asks.

"Yes, fine." Luna lies. There's a tremor in her voice. "We're both fine. Come."

Luna looks through the gap between the garbage bins, towards the street. In a matter of seconds, the two of them appear. Douglas and

Flynn stagger down the road like the two drunks they are. They pat each other on the back and stumble forward.

"They sensed me coming," Nir says. "I warned them."

"And they're going, Abba. Look, it worked."

"They got the message all right. What a bunch of dummies."

"You did it," Luna says. Her eyes haven't left her father's gun. They can't leave it behind here. She'll have to keep it with them.

"We can go in a minute," Luna says. "We don't want them to see us, right?"

"A born soldier."

Luna squeezes her father's hand. She watches as Douglas opens his car door after several attempts and Flynn falls into the passenger seat. They speed away and Luna wouldn't be surprised if they kept going until they drove over the US border.

The gunshot must have broken whatever spell Judith had on Flynn. Someone may have heard it and phoned the police. Luna has to get her heartrate under control and get out of here. She forces herself to count to 100. Her heart's beating so fast, she messes up the order and starts again.

At 100 she links arms with her father. Her palms are too sweaty to hold his hand.

"Come," she says.

Nir walks next to her.

There's the sound of a speeding car.

"Luna?"

"Ian," Luna calls. She'd forgotten about him. She flags for him to stop.

"Sorry it took me so long," he says. "Looks like a blackout. Is your dad okay?"

"He's more than okay," Luna says. "He's a hero."

Luna nods at Ian and he follows her eyes to the gun. Nir holds his two fingers up in a V for victory sign. Luna signs back. She's close enough to see him.

"But you don't need that anymore, Abba. They're gone." She points to the gun.

Nir smiles at her and he aims the gun at the ground.

"You're right, better to unload. What goes up must come down, so don't you worry. I'm pointing at the ground."

All at once Luna perceives every detail around her and her father. The purr of Ian's car. The way he's breathing hard from racing here to help her, the steady hum of traffic in the distance breaks the silence of the night. Her terror that the police will show up while her father's unloading a shotgun. She watches him open the breach and eject each shell with his fingers. Luna looks away before she vomits.

Finally, Nir's ready. Luna helps him into the front seat and makes sure he's buckled in. His fingers grip the gun. Her eyes beg Ian not to say anything. She collapses in the back. She crouches as low as she can and slips her jeans on under her tight skirt then stretches the skirt off over her pants.

Luna hears the tear of the seam but she doesn't care. She's never wearing that restaurant uniform again. The blouse will have to wait until she gets home, Ian's looking in his mirror too often, but at least the air isn't being squeezed out of her. She stuffs what's left of the skirt into her bag.

"Is that a police siren?" Ian asks. He's facing front. Luna's father's humming in the front seat with a satisfied expression on his face.

Luna shrugs instead of answering.

"We got those bastards, eh?" Nir says. "Crooks. Think they can take what's mine."

"We did," Luna answers. She pats her father on the shoulder.

"Piece of garbage anyway. We should get rid of it, eh Luna? What do you think? You're a smart girl. The bank wants it back. We should let them have it. Who needs these headaches? I have to stop listening to your mother. But we got them good."

Luna wishes she had put her father beside her in the back, so she could hear his heartbeat under her cheek.

"I don't want to know, do I?" Ian asks.

Luna shakes her head and motions for Ian to drive faster before the feeling of suffocation returns and with it the danger and fear.

A little girl
Went to school
The doors are locked
The girl sews

Last year in grade thirteen, Luna Levi did just enough schoolwork to keep herself from failing. She counted the months and then the weeks and then the days. A whole year has passed and nothing's changed. With a week's worth of clothes tossed in the back of Ian's car, she sped off to Ronen's place in Toronto. She didn't bother to phone her brother. Let him be rattled. From here Ian flew out to visit his father in Winnipeg and they'll return to Ottawa together.

Luna doesn't stay focused on the drive for long. Instead, Luna hears the front door open when it was supposed to be locked, Douglas grunt when Flynn nails him in the face, the explosion of the light fixture. She shuts down her mind when it ventures into the imaginary. But the question resurfaces behind her closed eyes that night: what if she had left a minute earlier and her father had charged in on those two with a shotgun? She can't return to sleep.

Luna's mind travels to the convenience store after she'd had a knife to her throat and she let her mother talk her into returning to work behind the cash. She feels as though an icy fingernail trails her neck and pulls the blanket over her head.

"Can I come in?" Ronen asks.

From under the blanket, Luna senses the sunlight and piles her pillow on top of her already covered head.

"You trying to escape something?" Ronen asks.

"Hide more like," Luna says.

"Nothing to hide from here."

Luna groans.

"You could have phoned me more."

"Maybe I had nothing to say."

"I deserve that. Come say hello to Stephanie before she heads to class."

Ronen leaves before Luna can say another word. Twenty minutes later, Luna's showered and smoothing down a dress she found at the end of her bed, a plain light blue with three buttons at the top and a scoop neck.

She gives up feathering her hair on the side. She needs a new haircut. Bangs. The first chance she gets, she's changing her hairstyle and adding copper or burgundy highlights. Maybe Stephanie took a hairdresser course at make-up school. She needs to look in the mirror and see someone new.

When Luna enters the kitchen, she takes a moment to enjoy the sight of a normal apartment with two people having coffee at a kitchen table with no broken legs and no mismatched chairs. She can't remember the last time she woke up to such an ordinary scene.

There are no envelopes or bills scattered around Stephanie and Ronen. Just three giant ceramic coffee mugs all from the same set and a jug of milk between them. The mid-morning sun streams through the window loaded with plants in macramé hangers, breathing life into the room.

"Didn't know you owned a dress," Ronen says.

"Plenty about me you don't know," Luna says.

"I deserve that," Ronen says.

"I left it out for her," Stephanie says too quickly. She hands Luna a mug of coffee. "Perfect for your coloring."

"This is what you left me for," Luna says. She accepts the coffee and sits at the table. The biscuit-colored kitchen cupboards gleam. The granite counters are lined with celestial teas, spices, and jars of rice and oats. The sharp smell of fresh coffee and warm toast fills the room and something sweet Luna can't identify until she sees the cinnamon rolls in a corner of the counter.

"I hope you're hungry," Stephanie says. When Luna doesn't answer, she inches her chair closer to hers and puts her hand on her arm. "Ronen called your mom."

"Yeah," Luna says. She stiffens but doesn't move her arm away.

"We're so sorry we weren't there."

"Actually, I'm starving," Luna says. She pats her stomach.

"Do you want to tell us about it?"

"Maybe after breakfast," Luna says. "Or lunch."

"Was it as bad as it sounds?" Ronen asks. He exchanges glances with Stephanie.

"Worse. I mean it. I don't want to go there now." Luna's voice cracks. She wishes she had something to do with her hands. She plays with her cutlery. Nobody speaks for a few minutes. "I could get really mad at this point," Luna says. "Abba nearly stormed in there with that gun and anything could have happened and where were you guys?"

"Sounds like you didn't need us, little sister. You really held it together."

"Who says I didn't need you?" Luna asks. She slams her mug on the table.

Before anyone can speak, the phone rings.

"That's my ride," Stephanie says. She gulps the last sip of her coffee and grabs her beach-bag sized purse without bothering to answer the call. "It's fashion make-up photoshoot day." Stephanie kisses Luna on the cheek. "And I do want to talk about everything when I get back. Ian tells me he's picking you up after his visit in Winnipeg. Knew it the moment I saw him." Stephanie's smile doesn't reach her eyes.

Luna adds more milk to her coffee. She clinks the teaspoon over-stirring. Some of the liquid spills over the side. She puts a napkin on the spill. There are two pairs of eyes on her. Ronen and Stephanie wait for the knot to release. The ringing of the phone begins again, but nobody moves.

"You could give me a haircut later, some streaks."

Relief echoes around the room.

"I thought you'd never ask," Stephanie says.

Luna shakes her head so the stray strands fall in front of her face.

"That urgent," Stephanie says. Her words drip with softness. She grabs a cinnamon roll from the counter and takes a bite. "I'll try to get home early."

The door closes behind Stephanie and Luna's alone with her brother for the first time since he moved away. Ronen gets up and returns with two plates of toast and scrambled eggs.

"Everything's fresh," he says. He pushes the fuller plate toward Luna. "You don't have to check any expiry dates on food at my place."

"So, what do I have to check?" Luna says. "You spoke to Mom?"

"The restaurant's over," Ronen says between bites of egg. "They used the old personal bankruptcy trick. You should be happy. I am."

"I'm sure I'll get there, too, eventually." She stares at her plate. She rubs her neck. The tick of the old-fashioned clock above the breadbox. The trill of the birds in the windowsill. The smell of dryer sheets and buttery eggs. Only now Luna hears the hum of the dryer. She concentrates on the rhythmic noise and swishes her fork around her plate.

"I heard about the chandelier shot out of the ceiling. Thank god you're all right."

The sound of the dryer turns into the ear-shattering bang of a giant chandelier splintering into a thousand pieces. Luna winces and covers her ears. Silence.

"I'm sorry. You're not ready. I'm so dumb."

Ronen rubs his fingers on the table back and forth. Luna lowers her hands, makes a sandwich out of her egg and toast, adds slices of yellow tomato and purple onion and cuts it diagonally across. She finishes her breakfast in neat, small bites, wipes her mouth with a napkin. Ronen stops rubbing the table and heats up the coffee maker, pours them both another cup of coffee. The dryer beeps, signaling that it's done.

"No more instant," Ronen says. He speaks to Luna as though she might break. "And Stephanie taught me not to make it watery. Taste how much I've improved." He takes an exaggerated sip.

One cup is enough for Luna. The room's getting hot and she opens the kitchen window. The air is still. Luna turns around and looks at her brother. His fresh coffee is still in one hand, he waves a letter in the other.

Chapter 49

There are many things in Stephanie's grandparents' apartment to look at. There's an extensive row of kosher cookbooks above the fridge, bamboo salad servers from their trips to Africa, flower trivet mats from Europe, and Armenian ceramic salt and pepper shakers from Israel.

All of these things are more compelling to Luna right now than the letter in her brother's hand. Already the air smells differently. Or maybe Luna smells her own anxiety.

Ronen leads Luna into the living room, leaves and returns with two tall glasses of orange juice, sets them on the table, digs his hand into his pocket and hands Luna the letter. He mumbles something about express delivery. The handwriting is her father's, the lettering on the white envelope written in blank ink in Hebrew. Luna thinks of the plain notes in her bedroom drawer in Ottawa. Her father's developed a ritual that suits someone who avoids the front door, telephone and mailbox ever since Luna can remember. His doctor is on to something.

Luna opens the side of the envelope with a butter knife Ronen found in the kitchen. She takes out the letter folded into thirds and reads for a few minutes, then tucks the letter into the envelope. She reopens it and repeats the action, scanning and skimming and returning.

"Well?" Ronen asks. He taps his fingers on the table. He lets out a frustrated sigh.

Luna hesitates. She's not sure where to start. If her father wanted Ronen to know he writes letters as part of his therapy, he'd tell him himself. She casts her mind back over the words. "If you read Hebrew, you could read it yourself," Luna says.

"When they make Hebrew Pac-man, I'll learn," Ronen answers.

"Abba's gone back to his old job."

"What old job? He's had dozens of jobs."

"His real old job. He's an artist, remember? With Doron Betel," Luna stops talking. She clears her throat. "Mr. Betel needs him now that he's going on his honeymoon and Isaac is off to university in September."

"Honeymoon?" Ronen leans closer to Luna. She can smell his coffee breath.

"And Abba will disappear one day, even if he doesn't snap."

Luna rubs her hamsa necklace as though it's magic. Wearing this monochrome short blue dress makes her feel two inches taller. She paces the room. She catches Ronen's eye. "We'll just have to expect less this time."

"What was that look? Are you talking about Abba or me?" Ronen asks.

"Don't do that to me, Ronen." Luna folds the sleeves of her dress up to her elbows. It's hotter in Toronto than in Ottawa. "You took off, so answer that question about expectations yourself." She almost adds: Or ask Stephanie, but she remembers the fraud, the maxed-out VISA and she's roadblocked. She sits next to Ronen instead.

Ronen turns on the fan. Luna can sense him digesting this news and the way he looks at her, as if he knows there's more.

"Now your boyfriend and your best friend will have the same last name."

"Ian has a father. I doubt that."

She thinks now of the pain Ian must be in. It's only an hour behind in Winnipeg. She glances at the phone.

"Still, they'll be step-siblings," Ronen continues. "Must be that necklace you're wearing. Maybe I should dig up the one Stephanie bought me."

"Stephanie bought you a hamsa?"

"At least four."

"She'll bring out the Yemenite in your veins."

"In my hips, you mean."

Ronen stands and performs a dance-move known as the Yemenite Step. He leans on one foot with all of his weight and then the other. Then he crosses his foot diagonally in front of him and repeats the action. Due to laws against public dancing, the steps are small and designed to move quickly on hot sand.

Luna joins him and hums the only Yemenite tune their father taught them.

"Now who is blonde?" Ronen asks.

"I take it back," Luna says.

They collapse back into their chairs.

Ronen lets out a low whistle.

"You sure there's nothing else? Someone who doesn't tell us where he is two thirds of the year sent you an express letter about his new job? That's it?"

Luna freezes, her hands in her lap. She doesn't feel comfortable in this room. She prefers the open, airy kitchen. Here there's only one small window covered in dust. The end tables and the coffee table are equally dusty and there's a stack of suitcases in the corner Luna recognizes from home. It's obvious Ronen and Stephanie live in the other rooms.

"I don't know about you, but I'm home here," Ronen says, skating over his own question. He clears his throat. "And you could be, too. There's a third bedroom.

Go back, pack and spend the whole summer with us. Tons to do in Toronto."

"You know I can't do that," Luna says. She shoves her hair out of her face.

"Is it Ian?" Ronen doesn't wait for Luna to answer. Now it's his turn to pace the room. "He might end up in Winnipeg for a while with his dad once he gets this update, maybe the whole summer, you know? Leave the new couple alone for a while. If he does spend the summer in Ottawa, he could drive up here on weekends."

"It's not Ian. I can work things out with him."

Ronen looks at Luna with such pained concern, tears come to her eyes.

"I can't just leave him, Ronen," Luna says. "I'm not like you."

"What are you saying?"

"I'm saying you have this way of ignoring stuff unless it's important to you and I'm not like that."

"Important like what?"

"Mom's leaving all of us, leaving the country," Luna reveals, her voice heavy with the weight of truth.

Ronen's immediate response is denial. "She wouldn't," he says. His voice is filled with disbelief. "That's absurd."

The room falls silent as the weight of Luna's words settles upon them. She takes a deep breath, her hands trembling slightly. "No," Luna says. "She takes the cold orange juice and drains the glass. "It's true."

"Mom's not cut out for leaving us. She always comes back. Why would this be any different?"

Ronen's hand on her shoulder offers a small comfort as Luna takes a deep breath, attempting to steady herself. She looks into Ronen's eyes, her own filled with a mixture of doubt and sadness.

"I want to believe that too, Ronen," she says without conviction. "But this feels different. It's like last chance time, you know."

Ronen sinks into his chair, his head buried in his hands. It was he who had always had faith in Judith. Luna looks at her brother in time to see tears well up in his eyes. A swipe. A tiny movement and they're gone.

Chapter 50

It's the end of August. Outside it's overcast, a dull grey as far as the eye can travel. The sky hasn't cleared for two weeks and already the days are getting shorter and the summer mugginess is almost gone.

Judith looks in her oversized mirror and slowly untangles each cranberry curler from her hair. She shakes her head, frowns at herself and switches methods. Starting from the bottom, she grabs the rollers from the roots to simultaneously brush her hair. Her features relax.

"There's no telling how long your father will last. He might snap one day. I'm sure you don't remember but he's had bad blood with that Doron Betel in the past." Her mother's words might be a warning or a justification for why she's leaving or both. Judith can give it up. Luna doesn't cringe at the words blood and Doron Betel anymore. She won't be frightened into anything.

"Aiden's dad isn't this successful for this long for nothing," Luna says. She grabs a bottle of her mother's hair mousse and squirts some into her hand. Sniffs. A wave of grape Kool-Aid engulfs her and all she can think of is a high school dance.

"I'm sure he thought it all out and covered that before he made the offer."

Her mother snorts. Luna watches as she moves on to curling her bangs with a hot iron. Luna will wait until her mother's ready to hear her. No restraint this time, no running off to bury herself in the washing machine or drown out her mother with the rumble of the vacuum.

"The cosmetic line can turn into a hair line like that." Judith snaps her fingers. "Already there are one or two agents sniffing around."

"Is this a divorce?" Luna says.

"Your father and I will never get a divorce." Judith eyes the mousse until Luna hands it to her. She squirts it into her palm and applies it to the end of her curls. "That's not something you need to worry about."

"Do you even have a contract from this producer?" Luna says.

"I have his word. He loved my performance. Left me a note on the back of the playbill."

"You mean there's nothing on paper?" Luna says. She feels a familiar pounding behind her left eyebrow.

Her mother busies herself zipping her suitcases. Her curling iron's still too hot to pack.

"It's great this producer saw your play in the States and offered you this cosmetic line, don't get me wrong, but you have no proof he offered you anything. You might be back tomorrow. You might not even find him."

"Do you ever look at the good side? I saw how he looked at me. This is it!"

Judith dances over to her curling iron and wraps it in a towel. There's no more time. She stuffs it into her suitcase along with her hot pink curlers, banana clips, and the mousse.

"I can't be late. It's you we need to talk about."

"You're leaving us because someone scribbled a compliment and an address on the back of a playbill and we'll have to deal with declaring bankruptcy." A cold sweat travels down Luna's spine. There's a bitter taste stuck in her throat, like when her father's zhug's been in the fridge too long and she dips it in her pita and then into her mouth just because she misses him.

"We did that back in June."

"There's still fallout, paperwork."

"Your father knows what to do, but it might mean some commotion." Judith opens each drawer and does an inventory for anything she's missed.

"Like moving? Maybe even on my own if Abba disappears?"

"Anything can happen," Judith says. "But you're being stubborn." She rummages through her purse. "Ronen's place is where you should be."

"It's not Ronen's. Who knows when Stephanie's grandparents will want to come home? I have Ian here. Abigal insisted Aiden move back. I want to be with my friends."

Judith strips her bed. She gathers the sheets and pillowcases into a pile. She tosses her shower towels on top.

"Your father might not last working for someone after all these years and maybe I'll want to be the main driver once this gets going, sell these products myself on the side."

"Are you kidding?"

Luna cuts off her mother before she can answer. "I'm not hanging out in case your latest plan doesn't work and another business idea comes to you overnight."

"Is that how you speak to your mother before she leaves?"

"Yes."

"Have it your way."

Luna tries to look at her mother not as a daughter and she sees what the producer saw, the face of a cosmetic line for older women. Or this guy might be a ghost by now. And if he is, would her mother come straight home or is this her first step to cutting ties for real?

"I don't have space for this."

Luna looks at the object in her mother's hand and presses her own hands together hard, she mustn't reach out too eagerly. She sucks back her smile. Her mother won't be rewarded for abandoning them, even a tiny bit.

"What would *I* do with it?"

"You can stop rummaging through it behind my back, applying the good stuff with dirty fingers, leaving wet brushes, and gunking up the bag. It's like you want me to know you were there."

The truth of her mother's words ties Luna's tongue and the silence between them confirms that, for once, it's Luna who deserves the admonishment, not the other way around.

Luna keeps her arms at her sides and lets her mother hold the makeup case for an extra beat before she takes it. Her mother's right. She has never stopped poking through the case when her mother isn't home or when she's asleep. Even her father's disapproving words have not prevented her from slipping something every day out of that bag for her own look, as though she needs a dose of her mother's eyeliner or hit of blush to complete herself.

Luna accepts the case minus a thank-you, making a show of stomaching it as a burden. Her mother has always known she wants it, but she will not be bribed, at least not outwardly. It's normal for a daughter to share her mother's makeup. Mothers are supposed to want to divide their possessions with their children. This isn't something special her mother's giving her.

"Spill in here." Luna waves her hand in front of her nose. "You've always said your stuff is for blondes."

"So I have. You're right. Toss it. *I'm* the face of a new line now."

"Your old face is for me? Why not mail me samples of new makeup in a new bag?"

"You'd think no one ever taught you how to accept a gift," Judith says.

Judith strides down the stairs and Luna shoves the makeup bag under her bed, pulls it out, moves it to her dresser, where she settles it in front of her mirror. She stands back and she shakes her head, taps her foot.

In a minute, the bag's upside down in an empty grocery bag. Luna doesn't look at the contents as they spill out; she doesn't want to know if a bottle of foundation has a leak, if a pair of nail scissors stabs through the bag, or if she's cracked a lip brush. She tosses the makeup bag itself into the bathtub where she pours hand washing powder over it and rinses it with boiling water. She hangs it on a hanger to dry, the water dripping down the drain. When it's clean and smells like her own perfume, she'll find the right place for it.

Luna follows her mother down the stairs but heads to the kitchen. She munches on a few homemade date cookies Abigal Betel sent over, but she can't keep them down and has to drink a glass of water to stop herself from throwing up. She carries the other two suitcases on lead legs and heads out to the parking lot where her mother puts on another coat of I'm-Your-Baby-Pink lipstick next to the two suitcases she dragged outside.

"Let me take those," Nir says.

Luna jumps. At sixty-two, her father still appears and reappears at will.

"Do you plan on sneaking up on us forever?" Judith asks.

"I can't give what I don't have," Nir says. "You're the one who makes the entrances."

"And you make the exits," Judith says. She pats her hair. "You left work to say goodbye?" she says.

"I left work to say good luck. Was tired of it anyway."

Luna stops herself from asking her father what he means by that. She breathes in and out instead. She doesn't hear whatever it is her mother whispers in her father's ear. It's between them, not something she can control or should. She's swayed in a parking space at four different rentals wishing her mother wouldn't leave more times than she can calculate.

This is the first time her father is with her. That must count for something. It isn't so easy for her to do anything differently than she's always done, but she will now. She won't bite her nails. She won't try to plot the next five disastrous steps ahead.

"Well," Judith says. She leans out the window and waves, revs the engine.

"You should have a good eye on you," Luna says. "Until you get back."

Nir blows a kiss in the air.

And then her mother's gone to grab a second chance at a dream that hasn't faded for half a century or to clutch onto the tail end of something that's already vanished.

Chapter 51

Luna aims the hairspray bottle at the back of her head. Squirt! She pats the sides of her mother's blonde Alice-in-Wonderland wig and attempts a smile, but it's no use. Her face is flushed with the red tinge of anxiety.

She attacks her mother's old makeup case next and doesn't care when a bottle of foundation flies out, cracks on her floor. Good. Her mother shouldn't expect there will be anything left if she wakes up one day and races back here. There won't be. With her face made up so heavily, Luna looks a lot more like her mother and less like her father. She tilts her head back and gulps the instant coffee her father made her with nondairy creamer and gags.

When will her father remember that he's making coffee for Luna and not her mother? She's not asking him next time. She gives up. She slides the mug next to the other two undrinkable coffees she hasn't had time to wash, not with her mother flustering her with instructions she can hardly decipher.

Luna prefers mood lipstick, although she knows at her age, she should be over it, but her mother is firm about her wearing red, so red it is. She can't wait for this to be over.

Today's the last Billy day. The fourth one since her mother left. Has it been eight weeks? Months of letters she burns, flushes, or shreds as soon as she reads them. She has Billy's payment ready: half a dozen bottles of model glue and an equal number of bottles of rubber cement.

The phone rings. She waits until the sixth ring before she picks up. It hurts to lie to Ian.

"Time for me today, honey?"

"Ian? I miss you so much, I wish." She misses him more than she can say. He's the best thing that's ever happened to her, but he wouldn't understand and it's too humiliating or it would be in his eyes. He wouldn't see any light in what she's doing.

"An errand's no problem. I could keep you company."

Luna counts the glue again, makes sure there are a dozen bottles. She opens the suitcase and packs them side-by-side.

"Boring. I'll be at your place in an hour."

"Are you okay? You sound distracted."

"You caught me on the way out. I wanted to surprise you."

"Is this about your mom? Please tell me it's not about her. You've been off since she left. I should be with you."

"Your family's not the only one in transition. When your parents got divorced, you followed your mother across the country, left everything behind, including your father. It's normal to be a little off."

She blots her lips with a tissue. She has no idea how to apply this red lipstick. It doesn't look anything at all on her the way it does on her mother. It's hard enough to do this without Ian on the other end of the line making her feel like she hasn't thought this through.

"Are you comparing our mothers?" Ian asks. "Are you saying you *are* doing something for your mother?"

"I'm saying, *you* followed your mother and she wasn't exactly forthright about her relationship with Aiden's dad, not until it was a done deal. There's that, too."

"I don't like what I'm hearing."

"I promise I'm there in an hour. You're making a big deal out of nothing."

"I know it's hard to be separated from a parent, any parent, but you can't let the distance from her suck you into doing things you know are wrong, we both know are wrong."

"I have to go," she says to Ian. "Honestly, an hour max and I'm at your place. Believe me, everything's fine. Love you. Love me?"

"I wouldn't be calling you if I didn't. You're going to tell me about this when you get here. Okay?"

"There's nothing to tell. See you soon." Luna kisses into the receiver and hangs up.

Inside, she shakes. She chose the wrong excuse. Ian didn't blink about the fever excuse last week, and the time before that she said she had an inspiration about her art portfolio and couldn't let it fizzle out. She should have stuck to the mundane. An alarm buzzes and Luna flies to the window. There's no time to think about Ian now. He'll have to wait.

Gustav saunters down her road, his hands deep in his pockets, a cigarette in the corner of his mouth, a fresh dragon tattoo on his neck visible even from one floor up. She breathes a sigh of relief. In a few minutes, he'll be waiting for her in his yellow Camaro at the end of the road. It's the last time. She won't do this again. From here she goes straight back to Ian. Aiden will make them a gourmet dinner and tell her all about the next track meet. Luna will suggest a dessert date, or better, she'll stop and bring doughnuts.

Luna's hand trembles as she slips on her high heeled boots, but she ignores it. With no traffic, they'll have the glue safely installed in the backroom next to the laundry room at the motel and her old boss won't know she was ever there. He might catch an image of some blonde who got lost. Her brother has always lectured her that she doesn't help the family business, that she's ashamed of her mother. Well, she's come to the party this time, while he's so far away, he might as well be on another planet. But no more, not again. She's paid her dues.

The money from the watches her mother wrote to her on the back of a serviette or it could have been a flyer. Luna flushed it down the toilet so fast, she no longer remembers. *It's our money. You need it Luna. Your father can't be trusted to stay at any job. How many times have I told you, we women have to take care of ourselves? You're lucky I remembered your stories about Billy. A godsend. The perfect hiding spot. Even he doesn't know they're there, but stock up on his reward, just in case.*

For the umpteenth time, Luna sees it all in her mind. The night she pulled her father away from the restaurant. The alarm ringing loud enough to wake up an entire city. Gustav, drunk out of his mind after generous amounts of free vodka from her mother, dragging those watches out of the restaurant in the middle of the night. Her mother directing the scene, muttering under her breath, "They think I fell off some turnip truck. He who laughs last. Anti-Semites." How she made it back to Ottawa so fast was anybody's guess. Maybe those two idiots called her once they crossed the border.

Luna wishes she could tell Ian everything, but she can't. His father's a criminal lawyer and his son has inherited his strong sense of justice. It's not worth the risk. Instead she's extra attentive around him when they're together, helping him pack and then unpack his clothes in his new house, listening to his rants about Mr. Betel, how he'll never replace his father, how he's happy for his mother, deep down, so happy, out of this world happy for her.

Luna drags the phone back into the hallway, returns to the mirror, eyes the makeup bag and shoves it off the dresser. Now the whole thing's a mess on the floor. The red lipstick rolled under her bed. She picks it up and tries again until she no longer cares. She feels as though she's walking with Gustav the last two blocks to the payphone at the end of her road. When the phone rings, she picks it up and says one word: *"Salut."* This has always been the worst part for her. The wait between spotting Gustav and his phone call.

Luna tucks her necklace into her shirt and drags her suitcase of glue down the stairs in case Billy needs a bribe to keep him quiet or to black him out. She doesn't fully understand her mother's code words.

She's careful to walk and not to run past her father, bent over his jewelry designs in the kitchen, although he's so still, he may have fallen asleep. It crosses her mind that he doesn't appear to be breathing but refuses to let that sink in. Of course, he's there for her. She can't lose both of them at the same time. She's paranoid. This whole thing is shattering her nerves.

Luna takes deep breaths as she starts Warp, her brother's condolence prize, and tries not to worry about what will happen if Gustav expects more than his ten percent payment. Surely, her mother has spelled it out, made things clear. She wouldn't dare throw her own daughter in as part of the bargain. Would she?

Luna glances at the oak trees that line the parking lot as she pulls into the road. They appear to be reaching for the last rays of sun before night hits. The wind carries streamer-shaped white clouds across the sky.

In a few minutes the sun will be beyond her grasp, but for now Luna takes the last drop of warmth as a sign that a good eye is on her, that Gustav will take his cut and disappear, that what she's done is decent, even if she can't explain herself to Ian.

Anyone would preserve a family goldmine.

Thank you to Writer's Bone for publishing my short story "Cutty Sark" that is a variation on an excerpt from this novel, December 5, 2018 and to the Bookends Review for publishing "What We Are", a variation on an excerpt from this novel, July 3, 2019.

Acknowledgements

I could not complete a novel without my critique partners and beta readers. Many of the ideas in this novel were first planted in a manuscript I sent to Pearl Luke years ago. She let me know I was telling two stories at once and that was priceless advice. Many thanks to Rivka Begun and Babette Dunkelgrün who read chapter by chapter until the end and offered insightful and valuable feedback monthly without fail. I am blessed to live in a time where I can have critique partners from Mexico to Holland to Switzerland to the USA and benefit from so many points of view. Some very early chapters were also read by Sari Friedman and Deb Lance and I also wish to thank Christi R. Suzanne for her honest and professional input on the first draft. Thank you also to Anna Olswanger for her encouragement and Madison Scalera for her valuable feedback and insights. I continue to be grateful for the Shaindy Rudoff MA in Creative Writing Program at Bar Ilan University for opening the door to English-speaking writers in Israel. Last but always first, my husband Doron Green is the most supportive partner a writer could have. Thank you to our children: Aryeh, Sivana, Gabriella, Meira and Keren Ohr for inspiring me every day.

Excerpt from the poem "Payphone" granted from
the author, Melanie Faith.